El Lobo Verde

Copyright © 2007 Donnie Daniels
All rights reserved.
ISBN: 1-4196-0203-9
ISBN-13: 978-1419602030

To order additional copies, please contact us.

Booksurge
www.booksurge.com
1-866-308-6235
orders@booksurge.com

El Lobo Verde

Donnie Daniels

2007

El Lobo Verde

This book is dedicated to all Law Enforcement Officers who have worked the southern border and especially to the memories of Gilbert Lee & Herman Railey, United States Border Patrol.

William (Bill) Eddleman, G.C. Wilson & Morley Miller, Unites States Customs Service Pilots. Thanks guys.

CHAPTER 1

The green and white sedan traveled slowly west on Hwy 83 from Rio Grande City, Texas then turned south off the highway on to a dirt road leading to the river. The driver finally parked behind a large mesquite bush and quietly opened the door. He stepped out and laid a double barrel sawed off shotgun on the hood of the vehicle. Jeff Larson softly closed the door of the Border Patrol sedan and slowly looked around. He was unaware that the events he was about to set in motion tonight would have far reaching ramifications on not only him, but also his fiancée.

Jeff was twenty-four, six foot and 175 pounds with light brown hair and brown eyes. He had been in the Border Patrol a little over two years and had been assigned to "still-watch" the river by Station Supervisor Robert Wilson. He knew that he was the only BP agent on the river for fifty miles.

Kind of like pissing into the wind Jeff thought, as he moved his holstered model 19, Smith & Wesson .357 to a more comfortable position on his lean hip. He carefully picked up his double barrel 12-gauge shotgun from the sedan's hood where he had laid it. He broke open the barrels, determined that it was loaded with double-aught buckshot and moved down the trail.

The sun was just touching the top of the mesquites to the west and he could hear the low buzz of a rattlesnake warning him to stay on the dim trail leading to the Rio Grande River. There was the soft cooing of white wing doves in the brush and he could still smell the dust in the air stirred up by the sedan. He had parked over a mile from the river that divides old Mexico from the US, so smugglers wouldn't hear the vehicle's engine.

The thick mesquite, cactus, and tall grass were almost like a jungle. Shit, thought Jeff, everything down here wants to stick you, stab you, or bite you. Jeff could almost feel his Indian heritage take over as he slipped into hiding near the edge of the river. The pungent odor of the water carried variety of smells; mud, dead fish and rotten weeds. He could hear the low buzz of mosquitoes as they swarmed around his face and neck. I sure hope the repellent works he thought.

He thought about his career in the Border Patrol and how it had almost ended before it started. Jeff was born and reared in Oklahoma and had a difficult time learning Spanish. Hell thought Jeff; as far as that goes, Okies have a hard time learning English.

Shortly after joining the BP he met the love of his life Josefina Garcia. She was the only daughter of the Comandante Napo Garcia of Camargo, Tamaulipas, Mexico. She had tutored Jeff in Spanish and they had both fallen in love. Now I sound just like a "mojado" (wetback: illegal alien; used along the Texas-Mexican border) thought Jeff.

Wilson, the BP supervisor, had introduced Jeff to the Comandante Napo Garcia. He had invited the two agents to his home for lunch that day, where Jeff met Josefina. Her sparkling hazel eyes, long brown hair, light golden skin and beautiful face, inherited from her half-Anglo mother, hit Jeff like a ton of bricks. He was in love for the first time in his life and started making all kinds of excuses to go to Camargo to see Napo.

That was several months ago and now the whole town of Camargo knew it was only a matter of time until the two young people were wed. Napo Garcia was pleased, for he thought of Jeff as the son he never had.

Napo was whipcord thin, Mexican, with a light complexion and soft brown eyes, unless he was angry, then his eyes became hard as flint. The people of Camargo dearly loved their Police Chief and his family.

Suddenly a turtle slid off a log near the edge of the water alerting him to the presence of someone on the other side. The bushes on the other side of the river rustled and from behind stepped a small man of about 40 with a sack and frog gig. All thoughts of Josefina disappeared as Jeff watched the hombre from his hiding place. He watched him, sliding in the mud as he made his way down river. Something was wrong. "Hells bells" he has passed at least four frogs and has yet to gig a single one. The SOB is a lookout for somebody thought Jeff.

About that time, Jeff's earplug walkie-talkie sounded off. "Rio Grande six, Rio Grande six this is Rio Grande one." Wilson was calling Jeff from the Border Patrol office in Rio Grande City. He quickly answered Wilson with a whispered voice. Wilson asked if he had anything going on. Jeff advised him of the man he was watching. Wilson replied that he would join Jeff as soon as possible.

It was a short time later that Wilson slipped into the brush next to him where Jeff pointed out the man who was now moving back up river. "You're right," said Wilson; "he's a lookout for somebody. Who uses this section of river for smuggling?" he asked.

"Gustavo Gonzales," replied Jeff.

"Good chance we'll get some dope then," said Wilson.

Gonzales was one of the old-time smugglers. His family had been in the business for generations. He kept his operation small by smuggling no more than 100 pounds of marijuana at any one time and had resisted efforts by the Colombians to take over his section of the river.

It was now completely dark. The half moon had not risen, so it was hard to see the man on the other side. A flash of light painted the trees as a vehicle turned off the dirt road on the Mexican side. As it went black, the two officers watched as it parked next to the riverbank.

They could barely see two men exit the car and heard them open the trunk. A splash in the water and Jeff could see one of the men pushing what appeared to be a washtub across the river. A slight breeze from the Mexican side of the river carried the acrid odor of marijuana to Jeff's nose.

"It's a load of dope," he tells Wilson.

"When he gets to the bank on this side, take him down and I'll cover you" said Wilson.

Wilson had been in the Border Patrol for eighteen years and station supervisor for three. A forty-four year old, 5'10" 200 pound, strong willed individual born and raised in Mississippi. His Spanish was spoken with a heavy southern accent.

The man pulled the tub up the bank and turning back to the Mexican side let out a low whistle to his compadre. Now's the time thinks Jeff as he leaps off the low bank where he was hid. He hit the man hard in the back of his head with his fist. He hit the ground like a sack of beans. Jeff placed his knee in the guy's back and jerked his hands behind him for the cuffs.

"Shit, he's naked," whispered Jeff to Wilson.

"Well hell bells, you not going to make love to the son-of-a-bitch, get him up here before his partner figures out what's going on," said Wilson. Jeff pushed the man in front of him grabbed the sack of marijuana. "His partner don't realize you've got him," said Wilson.

Suddenly the naked man screamed, "ayudame, ladrones, ayudame," (help me, thieves, help me) and Jeff felt the wind from a passing bullet, shortly before he heard the shot.

"Holy shit, the fat's in the fire," hollers Wilson as he fires his S&W .357 across the river as fast as he can pull the trigger while scurrying for some type of cover. Jeff dropped to the ground and grabbed his sawed off shotgun pulling back both hammers as more shots came from across the river.

Jeff was ready. The next flash from the gun was answered by both barrels of double-aught buckshot. Eighteen .32 caliber lead balls went whistling across the river. A groan came from the other side. A car door slams and with tires and engine roaring, the vehicle departs the area.

Wilson grabbed the naked man who was still hollering and gave him a good rap in the mouth. "That shut him up! Let's turn this guy over to Customs and drive over to see Napo about the other hombre, I think you put some lead in him."

"Damn, I hope so," said Jeff, "the son-of-a-bitch shot my walkie-talkie right off my belt."

"That's close partner," said Wilson.

Two hours later, after making the naked smuggler crawl through several barbwire fences, the agents turned him and seventy pounds of marijuana over to Customs Agents. Jeff and Wilson were in plain clothes in Jeff's' 51 Ford pickup heading to Camargo to see Napo.

They were still laughing about how careful the smuggler had been while going through the fences with his hands cuffed behind him.

"I'll bet you couldn't have driven a needle up his butt with a hammer," Wilson stated.

They found Napo on the edge of town in the cantina that he owned, El Perro Flaco, (the skinny dog). They related the story about gunfire from Mexico over a couple of cold cervezas. Napo seemed very concerned about Jeff and how close the bullet had come to his future son-in-law.

"If Gustavo Gonzales knows anything about it, I'll find out" said Napo "and you can be sure he'll pay."

"Please Napo, just make some inquires and let us take care of it," Jeff told him. Napo looked in Jeff's eyes and could see the pride in this young man who loved his daughter.

"Está bien" says Napo "as you wish."

"Please don't say anything to Josefina about this," Jeff requested. Napo nodded and ordered some more beers.

"Let's forget about Gonzales tonight. You go see Josefina, I'll see that Señor Wilson gets home" said Napo. Jeff finished his beer and left the cantina.

A short time later Jeff is knocking at Josefina door, which is opened by Señora Gracia. "Coma está mi hijo ? " (How are you my son) asked Señora Garcia.

"Está bien." (very good) replied Jeff. Suddenly two golden brown arms were around his neck and warm lips were on his as Josefina flew into his arms.

"Josefina," scolds Señora Garcia with a grin on her face she disappears into the kitchen.

Josefina's mother was born Carmen O'Connor. Her Irish father had settled in Mexico and married into the Mexican aristocracy. Carmen Garcia was a beautiful, forty two-year-old, slender, woman with light brown hair. She and her daughter looked more like sisters than mother and daughter.

Jeff and Josefina sat in the Garcia's living room and talked quietly about their upcoming wedding and where to honeymoon. Señora

Garcia called them into the kitchen. The odor of fresh hot tortillas and coffee made his mouth water. The table was loaded down with tortillas, re-fried beans, brown rice, chicken enchiladas and tamales with fresh jalapenos peppers on the side. Jeff had not realized how hungry he was until the smell hit him. He ate like a starving wolf.

Two days later, Jeff is once again walking to the river, this time to meet an informant. He was an hour early for the meeting as was his usual practice. He trusted the informant, Flavio, but only so far.

He had first encountered Flavio when he was smuggling illegal aliens and Jeff had apprehended him. While Jeff was patting him down Flavio jerked loose and ran for the river with Jeff in pursuit. Unable to catch him in the heavy brush, Jeff fired his .357 next to Flavio's foot. That was the last time he saw him that day.

Several days later Station Supervisor Robert Wilson, who worked many informants in Mexico approached Jeff and requested that he accompany him to Mexico to meet a new informant. Wilson told Jeff that this man wants to work, but requested a meeting with Jeff.

"He didn't know your name, but he described you to a T."

A couple of hours later they arrived at a darkened shack, where a figure comes around the corner of the house with three beers in his hand. Talking for several minutes, Flavio told Jeff he was the man that had run from him and that Jeff had scared the shit out of him when he fired next to his foot. "I 'm sorry that I ran from you," said Flavio.

It was about this time that Jeff acquired the nickname "El Lobo Verde." (The green wolf) The name resulted because of the green BP uniform he wore, and his ability to slip so quietly through the riverside brush. The Mexicans often told stories of Jeff and how he would catch them on the river. They said that, "Los Tecolotes" (owls) tell El Lobo Verde where the mojados are going to cross, and most of them were superstitious enough to believe it.

Jeff then saw Flavio cross the river in a small boat and approach the meeting place on the U.S. side. He stepped from his hiding place. After shaking hands Flavio said, "I have two gringos, who want me to cross eight ounces of heroin and carry it to Houston."

Jeff asked, "how much time do we have to set it up?"

"I told them I would meet them the day after tomorrow."

"Está bien" replied Jeff, "let me contact Customs and I will meet you at the Oso Negro (Black Bear) cantina in Miguel Aleman at 10 A.M. tomorrow."

Later that day Jeff met with two Customs Agents, Cliff Beasley, and Neil Carswell. Beasley had been with Customs for over twelve years and was a very respected Agent. Carswell was still a rookie and was hired from the Dallas Police Department. Jeff explained about the two men who wanted the heroin delivered to Houston. Cliff asked Jeff how he wanted to set it up.

"I would like to see my informant actually receive the heroin, maybe that way we can identify the two guys," said Jeff. Cliff said, "Okay, set it up and get back to me."

The next day Jeff met Flavio at the Oso Negro where the two had a few beers. He told Flavio, "we want you to set up the meet in the parking lot right here where Beasley and I can easily witness the exchange."

Flavio agreed but requested that no one else be present to see him on the Mexican side. "I trust you and Señor Beasley," stated Flavio.

"Está bien," said Jeff as he left the bar.

Jeff returned to the U.S. side to meet again with the two agents. When he laid out the plan, Carswell objected to not being at the exchange. "Why are we letting this informant tell us how to do things," he asked.

"We aren't, I am," said Jeff, "nobody sees who my informant is while he's in Mexico and that's the way it is."

When Carswell kept arguing. Cliff told him to shut up. "It's Jeff's call," he said.

"Okay," said Jeff, "Flavio will contact me with the time of the meet and I'll contact you," he told Cliff.

Wednesday the 21st, Jeff and Cliff hiding in some brush about forty yards from the Oso Negro when Jeff saw Flavio drive into the lot. "There's the informant," Jeff told Cliff.

"I'll be damn," said Cliff who recognized Flavio. "Do you know how long I tried to get that son-of-bitch to work for me, I can't believe it."

"Maybe you just didn't use the right method," said Jeff. Remembering the bullet he had fired by Flavio's foot.

They saw a new sedan pull into the lot with two gringos in it and pull next to Flavio's old truck. "There they are," said Jeff as Cliff, using a telephoto lens started taking pictures of the two and their license plate.

"Don't take any pictures of Flavio," said Jeff.

"Don't worry, I'll keep him out of focus," replied Cliff.

The two agents watched as one of the men handed over a small package to Flavio. The three talked a few minutes and the two gringos departed. When Flavio left in his truck, Cliff and Jeff followed in the old Ford pickup. Flavio turned down a dirt road and pulled off into a grove of trees.

Jeff and Cliff pulled up beside him. Cliff then took a look at the heroin and using a tester, tried a very small piece. "It's good shit," said Cliff. "Okay, here's what we'll do, I'll seal this in an evidence bag and keep it. When you cross the river Flavio, Jeff and I will pick you up and drive you to Houston. After you deliver it, we'll move in and arrest these two assholes."

Later that night Jeff and Cliff picked up Flavio and drove him to Houston. Flavio was again in possession of the heroin, which had been taken out of the evidence bag. He walked a block to Motel 6 and delivered the package. He returned to Cliff's sedan and all three departed, for home.

"Houston P.D's narcotics unit has the place staked out and will take both of these guys down when they leave. They know them well and have been after them for a long time," said Cliff. He then turned to Flavio and handed him an envelope of money, "count it and sign for it," he told Flavio.

***

Thirty miles south of Camargo at Rancho El Toro owned by Gustavo Gonzales a doctor arrives from Monterrey. The doctor removed three pieces of buckshot from his right arm and two more from his right side. As he had fired across the river he had moved to the left. It saved him from taking the full load of shot. He gave a low moan as the doctor removed the last pellet. Gustavo was 50 years old, five feet eight inches, 205 pounds with black hair and eyes.

His nephew, Carlos Saenz was angrily pacing in front of the door. "It was that damn gringo Larson who shot you, the one they call El Lobo Verde," said Carlos. "I'll take two men and bring back his huevos mi Tio."

"No," replied Gustavo, "what you will do is get word to Comandante Garcia, that I thought it was robbers who were trying to steal the mota." "You will explain to the Comandante that I did not know I was shooting at the Border Patrol." "You will inform Señor Garcia that I am very sorry for any trouble I may have caused him or Señor Larson." "I want this done today, now," stated Gustavo.

Carlos left the ranch muttering to him self that his uncle was turning into an old woman and when he "Carlos" took over, things were going to be very different. We will protect what is ours, he thought. The more Carlos thought about it. The more he believed that his uncle was not thinking clearly. I'll do what I think is right and that doesn't include begging El Comandante to forgive us. When I get through with El Lobo Verde, no one will dare to bother our smuggling operations again. We should be smuggling more mota, like the Colombians want us to, thought Carlos.

Carlos was the 21-year-old youngest son of Gustavo's sister's whose husband had been killed by the Mexican Federal Police. He had always been hot tempered. This was not the first time he had gone against his uncle's wishes.

Later, in the small town of Mier at the cantina Cuatro Vientos, (The four winds) which was owned by Gustavo, a meeting was taking place. Carlos was drinking more and telling his two henchmen how he was going to take care of the gringo agent.

"I will let my pistola talk for me and shoot me a lobo verde," stated Carlos. "That will show everybody that Carlos is the main pistolero in all of Mexico," he bragged. His two friends Manuel and Pepe Loya were buying more drinks and telling Carlos how brave he was. One of the bargirls was in his lap with her short dress hiked up, feeding him pieces of lime.

"I will kill me a lobo by tomorrow for sure," said Carlos, as the girl kissed him on the ear. "We should let the Colombians help us as I have tried to tell my uncle many times, but he won't listen."

The next day Jeff returned to Camargo, to see Josefina. Her mother told Jeff that she had gone to the grocery store. As Jeff was walking down the main street of Camargo with its unique smell, as usual there were children playing along the sidewalk with several chickens attempting to scratch up something in the street. He saw Josefina coming toward him with a bag of groceries. Her eyes shining with pleasure, when she saw Jeff.

Suddenly Josefina saw the glint of a pistol thrust from the window of a speeding sedan behind Jeff. She screamed and with her long legs flashing, pushed Jeff backward as several shots rang out. Jeff's face twisted in anguish as Josefina was hit, and fell beside him bleeding with the groceries spilling all over the street.

Jeff could hear the roar of the car and several more shots hit the sidewalk nearby as he threw his body over Josefina and pulled his model 1911, Colt .45 from under his shirt. The vehicle was sliding around the corner in a cloud of dust as he fired four shots into the trunk and back window on the old ford sedan.

He picked up Josefina's head from the sidewalk and cradled it in his lap. "Oh God, don't let her die," he pleaded as a crowd was gathered. "Get Napo, get a doctor."

A few minutes later the crowd parted and Napo bent down, "easy mi hijp, easy." I've called Señor Wilson as soon as I heard," he said.

They could hear the sound of a siren screaming down the street as a green and white Border Patrol sedan skidded to a stop in the street. Wilson had driven the Government vehicle across the border to help his friend.

"Get her in the car," shouted Wilson. Jeff picked up Josefina tenderly and gently placed her in the back seat of the BP sedan. With Napo in the front seat and Wilson driving like a mad man, the sedan made a u-turn in the street, and sped for the US border with red lights flashing and siren screaming.

Wilson was on the radio telling the operator to patch him through to the Chief Patrol Agent in McAllen. It was just minutes and Chief Johns was on the radio talking to Wilson. After being informed of the incident and who was hurt, Chief Johns stated "I'll have a chopper dispatched to Rio Grande City in minutes."

Jeff in the back seat was trying to stop the flow of blood by placing his hand and a piece of his shirt over the bullet hole under her left breast. He could see a small cut bleeding below her left eye. There was also blood on her left leg.

As they roared across the bridge into the United States, Inspectors of both Immigration and Customs were clearing a path for the speeding vehicle. It seemed as if the world had stopped for Jeff and he had no idea how much time had passed.

"I can see the chopper coming," shouted Wilson over the roar of the engine.

"Hurry, please hurry," moaned Jeff still cradling Josefina's head in his arms. Josefina opened her eyes and Jeff could see the pain there.

"Are you okay mi amor?" she asked.

"Thanks to you, now don't talk, we'll have you at a hospital in a few minutes."

A military helicopter had been flying back to McAllen when they received the emergency call. Upon seeing the flashing red lights of the BP sedan, it set down in the parking lot of a local grocery store. Jeff ran for it with Josefina in his arms. Wilson and Napo quickly followed. The helicopter lifted off and was heading for the hospital thirty miles away in McAllen even before Wilson and Napo could be belted in.

A military medic started working on Josefina, who was again unconscious. She has lost so much blood thought Jeff and she is so small. Tears streamed from his eyes unchecked, as the man the Mexicans called El Lobo Verde, watched the medic place a bandage over the wound in her chest.

"We'll be at the hospital in ten more minutes," shouted the medic, "we're landing in the parking lot and surgeons are standing by."

Touching down, the door was jerked open, Josefina was placed on a gurney, and the doctors rushed her to the operating room with Jeff close behind. Wilson and Napo were trying to keep up with the running doctors and nurses who were being urged on by a frantic Jeff.

With Josefina in the operating room and Jeff waiting outside of the door, Napo went to Wilson and said "I must get word to her mother."

"I've already dispatched two agents into Camargo to bring Señora Garcia here," said Wilson. "She should be here within the hour."

"But she has no papers to cross the border," stated Napo.

"She's with two BP agents and nobody is going to stop her from coming, my friend."

Forty-five minutes later, a green and white BP sedan with red lights flashing slid to a stop in front of the hospital. A burly BP agent jumped from the back seat before the sedan had stopped and helped Carmen Garcia from the front seat. Napo ran to his wife and held her, while he explained what had happened to their only child.

It was five hours later when one of the doctors came out to talk to Napo and his wife. He stated, "we have removed the bullet from under her heart, but she has lost a lot of blood. One bullet cut a small place under her eye and another hit her leg, neither is serious. It will be several days until we can tell if she will live."

"She will live," stated Señora Garcia, "for God will not permit this child to die." She then went to Jeff, who again had tears streaming down his face and hugged him to her.

"It's my fault," said Jeff "they were shooting at me."

"Hush mi hijo it's not your fault," said Carmen. "Josefina would have gladly given her life for you and this is not your doing."

"It's the doing of Gustavo Gonzales and he will pay," stated Napo in a cold voice.

"No, mi Jefe," said Jeff "I claim that right, but not until Josefina is out of danger."

As Napo looked into Jeff eyes it was like gazing into cold brown ice flecked with gold. He does look like a wolf thought Napo. "We'll see," said Napo, "but you are right, Josefina comes first."

For the next week Jeff refused to leave the hospital. He slept on the floor in front of intensive care where Josefina was being cared for.

The nurses, who were all taken by this young man and his love for the beautiful Señorita, brought food, little of which he ate. He used the bathroom and showers at the hospital.

Carmen Garcia came every day and sat with Jeff and brought him clean clothes. She was staying at a local motel so she too could be near her daughter. Napo returned to Camargo, but traveled to McAllen every other day to check on his daughter and wife.

Josefina finally opened her eyes and asked first for Jeff and then her mother. When Jeff and Carmen walked into the room, the sun was shining through the window on her soft brown hair. With her eyes full of pain, she was still able to smile. The room was full of the smell of flowers that had been sent by Border Patrol Agents in the sector. The doctors arrived and stated that she was now out of danger, but would require several more weeks in the hospital.

Jeff for the first time allowed Wilson to take him out to dinner where Jeff put away a steak and several bottles of beer. Wilson told him every BP agent in this sector has sent flowers. He tried not to show the tears in his eyes, "Tell them thanks,"

"I have a favor to ask, I need two weeks off for some personal business."

Wilson said "sure," and he didn't need to ask what the business was. Jeff had that cold-eyed look back. I almost feel sorry for Gonzales, thought Wilson.

Napo arrived and sat down with his two friends. "We know it was Carlos Saenz who fired the shots," he told them. "He is the sobrino, or nephew, as you say, of Gustavo Gonzales. He was ordered to report to me by Gustavo and was to tell me that Gustavo thought he was firing on robbers that night on the river."

"Gustavo has also sent word that he has ordered Carlos brought to him. So far no one knows where Carlos is hiding. Gustavo said to tell you that he is ashamed of this thing, for it is not the way of men." said Napo. "I also have people looking for him but there has been no word."

"I can find him," said Jeff. Napo and Wilson looked at this young man they both thought of as a son. The grim set of his mouth and his cold-eyed look as he remembered Josefina's blood covered body, lying in the street of Camargo sent a chill over the room. Napo and Wilson looked at each other, both wondering how they were going to keep this young man alive?

Both knew that it was Jeff's intention to find Carlos and kill him. Wilson stated "Jeff, remember you wear a badge."

Jeff looked at his boss and friend and stated. "Any time you want my damn badge, just ask for it."

"Damn it to Hell" said Wilson, "That's not what I mean and you know it."

"I'm sorry Jefe, please forgive me."

"Forget it," said Wilson.

Jeff said, "I still need that time off."

"Okay," said Wilson, but his heart was heavy.

CHAPTER 2

On Friday Jeff was once again in Camargo, talking to Napo at his cantina. They were sitting at a corner table talking in soft Spanish. Napo sensed that Jeff was still very tense. Two musicians on the patio were playing Spanish music.

Two cholos from Rio Grande City entered the Perro Flaco for a drink. They sat across from Jeff and Napo. The two knew that Jeff was with the Border Patrol and decided to have some fun. They started to make comments about the BP in general and Jeff in particular. This went on for several minutes with their voices getting louder and the comments more personal. They undoubtedly believed Jeff to be unarmed, which was a mistake on their part. Jeff was trying to control his temper, because he was in his friend's cantina.

The Comandante got up from the table, walked over to the bar, and retrieved his Colt .38 super. He put the weapon in his belt and walked over to the table.

"You two cabrones want any trouble in here, you start it with me," he said. The two men fled the bar like dogs with tin cans tied to their tails.

Napo came back to the table and sat back down with Jeff. Jeff gazed at the golden shine of the grips on the .38 super stuck in Napo's belt and stated how much he liked them. Napo went to the bar and returned with a small screwdriver.

"Let me see your pistola." Jeff pulled his Colt 45 from under his shirt and handed it over. Napo removed the wood grips from Jeff's pistol and replaced them with his.

"I can't let you do that," said Jeff when he realized what Napo was doing.

"You're my friend and soon to be mi hijo, they are yours."

Jeff could only stare at the golden grips with turquoise sets.

"They were my fathers, you can pass them down to my grandson some day."

Jeff left the cantina and went back home to Rio Grande City. As he walked into the house his telephone was ringing. It was one of the Immigration inspectors from the Roma Port of Entry, telling Jeff that some kid had been in every day for the last few days trying contact him. " He won't give his name other that El Zarco, stated the Inspector. "He should be back within the hour."

"Okay," Jeff said, "I'll be there."

As he left the house he was thinking, Zarco means the blue-eyed one in Spanish. The only blue-eyed kid he could remember was one he had caught smuggling some guys near Mier. Jeff arrived at the Port and saw a skinny kid about fourteen years old walk across the bridge and duck into the Port.

Jeff escorted him to one of the back rooms were the public couldn't see them and got two soft drinks from the machine. "Como está, El Lobo?" asked the young boy.

"Bien, bien y usted?" stated Jeff, still waiting for the youngster to come to the point.

"The man who shot your novia is not in Mier, but the man who drove the car for him is there," the boy said in soft Spanish.

"Where is he, my friend?" Jeff asked.

This was the young boy he had apprehended when the kid was guiding some men through the river. At the time, the boy was wearing a pair of shorts and the whole butt was out of them. He had begged Jeff to let him return to Mexico at that point and not make him walk across the bridge at Roma. He was at the age to be easily embarrassed. Jeff felt sorry for him and had let him swim back across the river.

"You remember where you caught me that time?" the boy asked.
" Sure," replied Jeff.

"About a hundred meters down river there is an old lighting-struck tree on the Mexican side," the boy said. " If you go about three kilometros south you will come to a small goat ranch and the driver, Manuel is hiding there. His Tio brings him food every three or four days. He is afraid El Comandante will kill him," the boy stated.

"With good reason, thanks mi amigo, here is some money to help out," said Jeff.

"Oh no Señor Lobo, this is for La Señorita, I can't take money for this."

"Okay," said Jeff as he hugged the young man, "if you ever need anything, you let me know."

"Si Señor con su permiso," (with your permission) the boy started to leave then said,

"There will be a boat hidden on this side, if needed," and left. Jeff drove slowly back home deep in thought. If I can get this asshole, I can find out where Carlos is hiding.

Later that night, a pickup drives close to the river that separates the US from Mexico and parks. A dark figure exits and moves to the edge of the riverbank. The night is still, with low scattered clouds moving from the southeast. The clouds occasionally hide the quarter moon, called a smugglers moon. There is a small bundle of one inch by eight-inch boards and canvas hidden in the brush by El Zarco. The dark figure pulls them out, pieces it together into the shape of a small boat. Drags it into the water and paddles it to the Mexican side of the river.

The splash of a fish and the soft hoot of an owl carry down river; a wolf is hunting tonight. Beneath his denim jacket and under his left arm rode a single action Colt .45. A razor sharp hunting knife holstered on his right hip. The .45 Colt automatic is at home. It has a bad habit of throwing empty brass all over and El Lobo didn't want to sign his name.

He steps out of the boat on Mexican soil; quickly his eyes scan the brush near the river. He starts south walking briskly. With his long legs, he covered the three kilometros in less than an hour. From a small hill he spots the goat shack where Manuel is supposedly staying. There is a soft misty rain now falling and it's so quiet you can hear the water dripping from the leaves on the trees. El Lobo watches the shack for over an hour and decides to move in.

Manuel awakens with a start, realizing the goats are restless, is something out there? He has not been sleeping well ever since the shooting. He knows he is a dead man if Napo Garcia finds him. He had almost been killed in Camargo, when that damn gringo fired at the car. One of the bullets had creased his skull and his head was still aching. As he was looking through a crack in the wall he sees a dark shadow moving toward the goat pen. He grabs his pistol and starts for the door.

Well hell, it's now or never, thinks El Lobo. The hunting knife slips into his right hand and he moves quietly toward the shack. He's within six feet of the door when it bursts open and Manuel runs out, firing wildly with a 9mm automatic. In a spilt second El Lobo throws the knife, it makes one rotation and buries deep in the chest of Manuel. The single action Colt followed with the hammer at full cock, almost before the knife had hit. Damn, thinks El Lobo, I wanted this cobarde (coward) alive. He feels wetness under his left arm. One of Manuel's shots had cut the skin on his arm and blood is dripping from his left hand.

The moon peeks from behind the low rain clouds and he can see the pistol near Manuel's hand. He moves to where Manuel is lying and kicks the gun away. Manuel let out a groan and looks into a pair of ice-cold brown eyes.

"I only wanted to talk," said El Lobo. He knew Manuel had only a few minutes to live.

"Where is Carlos?"

"He has gone a long way south where his uncle can't find him, but he will return to kill you and your puta." Manuel said.

"He can try. You didn't do a very good job, did you?" said El Lobo.

"You will see, when he returns he will have plenty of help," Manuel said, trying to rise, but fell back dead. El Lobo let the hammer down slowly to half cock on the single action Colt. He then rotated the cylinder until the hammer again rested on an empty chamber.

As the adrenaline wears off he feels his legs starting to shake. He sits down on a nearby rock and finally sees the blood on his left hand. He removes his jacket, holster, and shirt. He then takes his bandana and wraps it around his arm. After a few minutes he stands up, replaces his shirt, holster, and jacket. After another look around, he slides the colt back into its leather.

"Well there's one down, one to go." He pulls the knife from Manuel's chest, wipes it clean on the dead man's shirt. He takes one last look at Manuel and heads back to the river. Arriving there, he retrieves the boat and is back on the U.S. side before the sun peeks over the low brush in the east. He slowly drives back home where he doctors his arm and falls into a deep sleep for the first time in weeks.

On Saturday Jeff drives to McAllen to check on Josefina in the hospital. After visiting with her for several hours he returns to Rio Grande City where he stopped at the Border Patrol Station. Jeff walks into Wilson's office and states, "I'm ready to go back to work."

"Good, glad to have you back," said Wilson. "Take a sedan or a scout and work up around Roma tonight."

Other agents arrive at the station and are glad to see Jeff. Over coffee the stories start, with one agent trying to out do the other. "Damn that old man down river from Rio Grande is still shooting over on this side with his .22 rifle," said Jesse Douglas.

"Why is he doing that?" asked Ed Cook, a tall lanky agent from the Texas panhandle.

"Probably to see if anybody is over here before he smuggles," stated Jesse. "I sure ain't going to stay there with that crazy old bastard blazing away. Something should be done about that old fart before he kills somebody."

Jeff leaves the station and drives home, where he puts on his uniform for work. His thoughts are still on the old man down-river and his .22 rifle. I'll ease down and check this out, he thinks.

Jeff picked up an International Scout from the station and drives east of Rio Grande City, then south toward the river. Parking the scout in some heavy brush, Jeff moves quietly into a grove of trees on a bluff that is higher on the US side than Mexico. The river is running south and then makes a sharp bent back to the east. After checking for snakes he settled down under a big tree that the wind had blown over. Then using his binoculars he gazes into Mexico.

He spots the adobe house of "Old Jose" as he is called. He can also see the wooden boat that Jose uses to ferry people across the river tied up nearby, on the Mexican side. In a few minutes he observes Jose walking down the trail to the river with his rifle. Jeff hears the faint "caw, caw" of some crows flying high above.

Jose reaches the riverbank about fifty yards across from Jeff and appears to be looking around. He points his rifle toward the trees on the US side and fires off three rounds. Jeff could hear the slugs in the trees overhead and several whitewing doves depart with a flutter of wings. Jose then leans his rifle against a small tree and steps away, to answer a call of nature.

Jeff removes his .357 from his holster and sights on the rifle's stock. When he squeezed the trigger, the 158-grain bullet moved the rifle about three feet and Jose wets all over himself. Another shot moved the rifle two more feet. Jose is busy trying to run and put his business back into his pants at the same time. As he runs back up the trail, two more shots rang out and dirt flies up five feet to the right of Jose. He just picks up more speed as he makes for his shack. Jeff is dying from laughing. Damn old smuggler should try out for the Olympics.

Jeff returns to the scout and drives to the Roma Port of Entry. He had been there about fifteen minutes when his radio sounds off. "Rio Grande Six, this is Rio Grande One," Wilson is calling. Jeff answers his radio and Wilson asks him for his 10-20 (Location)

Jeff replied, "I'm at the Roma POE." Wilson relates he would contact him by telephone. When Jeff answers, Wilson tells him Old Jose was complaining that someone had shot his rifle and caused him to piss all over himself.

" I was just checking to see where you were," said Wilson.

"Must have been some disgruntled Customs Officer," replied Jeff.

"Must have been," agreed Wilson.

Jeff walked up river from the POE and settled down behind a big rock to still-watch the river. He remembered the time the whole BP station played a joke on Jesse Douglas. Jesse was a dead shot with both rifle and pistol and wasn't afraid of a living thing, except rattlesnakes.

Naturally the agents at the station were very sympathetic to his fear.

One day several of the agents made up a story about Jeff almost stepping on a rattlesnake near Roma while going to the river. They all knew Douglas used this same trail when he was doing still-watch on the river. Later Douglas approached Jeff and asked about the snake. Jeff told him that it was at least five-foot long and it got bigger each time it was told. Douglas then refused to still-watch at that location and moved up river to a place called "the barracks."

Several days later when Douglas is scheduled for still-watch duties the rest of the plan was put into action. Wilson and Jeff drove all over Starr County looking for a rattlesnake. They finally discover a dead rattler that had been run over and Jeff shot off the rattlers from the dead snake.

When they arrive at the station, Wilson takes the rattlers and tells the other agents where Douglas can hear. "Be careful up at the barracks. We were up there today and almost stepped on a snake. I took a shot at him, but only got his rattlers," which he tossed on a table. "The last time we saw him, he was crawling off into the brush."

Later Douglas follows Jeff outside and asks about the snake. Jeff backs up Wilson's story and Jesse Douglas refused to still-watch near the barracks ever again.

A few days later Jeff is in Camargo and stops to visit Napo at the Police Station.

There are two other men with him and he introduces them as State Police Officers for Tamaulipas. The two men are Sal Rivas and Victor Carrasco. Napo explained to Jeff that the officers were looking into the death of Manuel Loya.

"It seems that Loya was the driver for Carlos and has been hiding at his uncle's goat ranch near Mier," Napo said. "Si," said Carrasco, "his uncle found him dead yesterday morning. We found a 9mm pistol beside the body and a deep knife wound in his chest."

"Were there any tracks around the body?" Jeff asked.

"Only the goats, for it was raining the night he was killed. We are not looking too hard for whoever killed him, as he was one of Gonzales's narcos."

"They have also told me that Loya's brother Pepe was with them in the cantina when the plan was made to kill you," stated Napo.

"Si, that is correct," said Rivas, who had been quite until now. " We are looking for him and we believe that he is still near Mier or Miguel Aleman. We will find him."

Jeff told them he needed to get back to work and left Camargo. After the two State Police left, Napo drove over to the edge of town to talk to a gentleman named Jesus Castillo. Jose invited Napo in and made coffee.

"I need to find Pepe Loya before the State Police," Napo told him.

Jesus said, "Don Napo, I will tell you what I've heard. He is said to be staying with another cousin in Valadesas. The cousin's house is just north of the church and has a blue trim."

"I'm indebted to you," Napo told him.

"De nada," said Jesus. They talked for a few minutes then Napo left.

As Napo drove down the narrow road to the town of Valadesas his thoughts returned to his daughter and how much he loved her. He recalled her lying in the street of Camargo covered in blood and later in the hospital wrapped in bandages. Tears formed in his eyes as he remembered Josefina as a little girl. Now she is a grown woman and soon to be married. She looks so much like her mother at that age. Then his thoughts turn to Carlos and Manuel. He wonders if El Lobo had killed Manuel, I hope so, he thinks.

He finally located the house of Pepe's cousin. He walked to the back door and can see Pepe sitting at the kitchen table. Napo opened the door and walked in, Pepe sprang to his feet and tried to run. Napo slammed his .38 super against his head and Pepe falls to the floor. Napo pointed the pistol at his head. "If you try to escape I'll kill you," he said in a cold voice.

"I had nothing to do with the shooting mi Comandante," said Pepe, as he cringed on the floor.

"You tell me where Carlos is or you can die right here, right now!" said Napo.

"He's in Columbia and is hiding with Cesar Cisneros, please don't kill me," he begged as he looked at the steel-eyed Napo Garcia. "He got scared when he saw that he had hit your daughter and El Lobo almost took his head off with a bullet."

"Está bien," said Napo, "now let's go, the Policia del Estado wants to talk to you." He rolls Pepe face down and handcuffs him with his hands behind his back.

Napo returned to Camargo with his prisoner and places a call to the Tamaulipas State Police. The two State Police officers Carrasco and Rivas arrived in two hours and quickly departed for Ciudad Victoria with Pepe.

Meanwhile Jeff had returned to Rio Grande City and was again on still-watch duties. He parked his vehicle west of Rio Grande City in some brush and walked to the San Juan crossing area. This is where the San Juan River empties into the Rio Grande and is a favored place for illegal aliens to cross. Jeff hides in some brush where he can see the San Juan River and almost immediately spots five people on the Mexican side. He watches as they come to the water's edge and look into the United States.

Suddenly the five men run back into the brush and hide. What the hell happen? Jeff wondered. He then hears the high-pitched whine of an outboard motor coming up the river. He watches as the small boat driven by Robert Wilson goes speeding by. Old Wilson is out fishing and running his trotlines, he thinks to himself.

The five men slowly emerge from their hiding place and ease back to the water's edge. They suddenly jump back up and run for the brush again, as the small boat zooms back down river. That was pretty fast, thought Jeff as he waited for the men to reappear. After about ten minutes the wets again approach the water's edge and sit down. They slowly start removing their clothes in preparation for crossing the muddy "Rio Bravo" as the Mexicans refer to the Rio Grande.

While Jeff waited for the men to cross, he remembered several months back when he, Agent Joe Parker, Wilson and SPA Gene Hayden tried to catch a smuggler here. The smuggler would arrive several hours ahead of his "customers" and check out the area for the

Border Patrol. If he didn't see any, he would make the men hold on to a large truck inner tube and pull them across the river soon after sunset. The smuggler never put his foot on the US side, and stayed in water about waist deep. The agents were determined to catch this scofflaw. They had a plan.

Jeff and Joe went to the crossing about noon and were well hidden. They watched as the man arrived about 2 P.M. and eyeball the US bank. "We'll catch this cabron this time," they whispered. The men arrived just before sundown and they shed their clothes.

Wilson and Hayden were up river in a motorboat waiting for the signal from Jeff to come down river. When the smuggler reached the US side and unloaded the wets. Jeff gave the signal and the two agents charged out of their hiding place. Wilson and Hayden started down river with the boat's motor wide open and the race is on. Joe was in front of Jeff and both were running hard. Suddenly Joe's gun falls out of his holster, he stops, Jeff doesn't and runs over the top of Joe. They both go crashing into the ground.

As Jeff is spitting out dirt, he sees their smuggler running up river with his bare butt flashing. He jumps in the river behind the boat and makes it back to Mexico before Wilson and Hayden can turn around. He never used that part of the river again and they never caught him.

Suddenly Jeff's radio comes alive, "any Rio Grande unit, this is POE Rio Grande." Jeff answers with a whispered voice, "Go ahead POE this is Rio Grande Six."

"We have SPAIC Wilson here and he wants to know if you can cover the San Juan crossing. He says there are five guys waiting to cross."

"Is SPAIC Wilson where he can hear the radio?" asked Jeff.

"That's 10-4, Rio Grande Six."

"Tell him I'm at the crossing now and have been for the last two hours. As soon as some guy gets through running up and down the river in a boat scaring the mojados, I'll catch them," Jeff replied.

There is a long silence on the radio and then came a "10-4" from the Port. He can hear laughter in the background. Jeff is laughing himself as he watches the five men make their way to the US side. He waits until they have their clothes back on then steps out of hiding. "Como estañ amigos," Jeff said.

"Ay caramba," said the five guys, "El Lobo Verde has caught us."

When they reach the scout, Jeff places the five illegals in the rear and drove to the Border Patrol station. He processes the five men and continues to joke with them about how many times they had crossed the river without being caught. They all agreed that they had crossed several times, but had only been able work two or three weeks before being caught and returned to Mexico.

Finally Jeff completes the I-213, listing their names, dates of birth, mothers and fathers names. They all signed voluntarily departure forms. Which means they agree to return to Mexico, so they can try crossing again in a few hours. Jeff escorted them to the scout and drove to the Rio Grande Port of Entry. The five men all wanted to shake the hand of El Lobo Verde. Jeff gave them their possessions and they walked across the bridge to Mexico, waving to Jeff one last time—-maybe.

The next day Jeff cut for sign all day. (Which means you drive slowly down a dirt road looking for footprints.) Later that evening, Jeff is off duty drinking a cold beer when the telephone rings. It's one of Jeff's informants. He states that a load of dope will cross that night at " Midway Crossing." The informant says that the dope will be taken to a house about half way up the road and the smuggler has hired him to help carry it. Jeff instructs the informant to light a cigarette and bring it down by his side when he arrives at the house.

"With a night scope I'll be able to see it and I'll know the dope is there."

Jeff called Wilson and fills him in on the latest scoop. Wilson states, "I'll call Customs and see if they want to help on this." Jeff grabbed his Colt .45 auto remembering how he came to buy the pistol. He had been working plain clothes and was carrying a small .380 automatic when he received a call from Wilson. He had told Jeff to meet him at the Sheriff's office in town.

When Jeff arrived, Wilson motioned him into the sedan with him. As they drove off following two deputies Jeff had asked, "What's going on?"

"Well it seems that there was a bank robbery in Mexico. Two policemen caught the robbers, shot them and then they took off with the money. The Sheriff's office received a call that the two may be hiding out near the river on this side. They want a couple of Border Patrol along in case there is some shooting."

"Shit, all I have is this damn little pistol. If I shoot one of them with this thing, I'll just piss him off," Jeff said. They checked out the house, but didn't find anybody. The next day Jeff had purchased the Colt 45 from a store in Rio Grande City for a hundred dollars.

As Jeff is preparing to go, he receives another call, this time from Ed Cook. He tells Jeff, " I just received some information that there will be some smuggling near the bridge that runs to Fronton. Could you cover it? I have Ed Givens, the tick rider over for dinner and the steaks are on the fire."

"Sorry partner, I'm getting ready to go on a load myself with Customs," Jeff tells him.

"Okay, I'll just take Givens and we'll go see what the hell they are smuggling," Cook replies.

Later that night after dark, as the two Ed's hide in the brush near the bridge. They hear a pickup coming. The vehicle parks by the bridge and the driver honks his horn. They see a man run from the brush on the other side, throw a burlap bag in the pickup's bed and turns to run.

Ed Cook hollers, "Alto, Los Federales " (Stop, Federal Officers) and fires his weapon in the air. The guy just picks up speed until Ed Givens, who is armed with a long barrel Ruger .357 magnum puts a round by his ear. It must have sounded like a mad bumblebee going by.

The man fell down and began hollering, "No me mata, no me mata." (Don't kill me) Cook removes the driver while Givens handcuffs the smuggler.

"Well friend," said Cook, "let's see how much dope we have." As they both walked to the rear of the pickup with the two prisoners in tow.

As they looked into the bed Givens said, "the damn sack is moving."

"No shit," Cook said. They pull the sack over, undo the top, and find two fighting cocks looking back at them.

"These guys are chicken smugglers," said Cook.

"Oh hell," said Givens. " You know what we'll be called now? The chicken Agents."

Meanwhile Jeff and Customs Agent Neil Carswell are hidden in a field across from the house that will receive the narcotics. As he watches the house with a night scope, he sees a match flare. Then a cigarette drops to the side. The arch of fire can be clearly seen with the starlight scope. "The dope is here," he tells Neil.

A few minutes later they both watch as a car drives south down the dirt road from the highway, stop then backs into the yard. When the vehicle leaves, Jeff radios Wilson and Cliff Beasley. "The next vehicle that turns on Highway 83 is your smuggler."

Wilson and Cliff follow the sedan through Rio Grande City before pulling it over. When the trunk was opened they found eighty pounds of marijuana. When they all met at the Border Patrol Station, Wilson tells Jeff. "I just received a call from Ed Cook. He and Ed Givens caught two guys smuggling fighting roosters into the United States near Roma."

Jeff looks at Cliff and both say in harmony. "Those guys are now the Chicken Agents."

CHAPTER 3

Carlos is in Columbia at the hacienda of the drug lord, Cesar Cisneros "La Vibora" (The snake) Carlos is telling Cesar how he would run the smuggling operations if he were in charge. Cesar says, "You're right, I have tried reasoning with your Uncle and give him help, but he refuses."

"He is an old woman, he is frightened of the Border Patrol," said Carlos. They talked for several hours and Cesar thought of a plan.

"You are my guest, enjoy yourself. There are plenty of liqueur and women here. Let me think on this problem of ours."

Cesar walks outside and tells his teniente. (Lieutenant) Felipe Salinas to call Alejandro in Argentina. "Tell him we'll have work for him shortly. If Gustavo wants to live with the Americans he can die with them," said Cesar. "I want to talk this over with Alejandro, have him come here."

"Si mi Jefe," Felipe replied.

"Say nothing of this to Carlos. See that he's well supplied with women and cocaine," Cesar continued.

Alejandro Crocefiso Weggener is a thirty-six year old, blue-eyed man born to an Italian mother and German father. It is rumored that his father was one of Hitler's staff officers who escaped to Argentina after World War II. His father was smuggled out of Germany by the "Odessa" Alejandro joined the Argentinean Army where he received training in "Special Operations." This launched his career as an assassin after military service. He has been a paid assassin for twelve years. He is a master of disguise and a crack shot with a rifle. He has performed many jobs for Cesar in the past.

When the call came in from Felipe, Alejandro was elated, as he was bored. He told Felipe that he would meet him at the Hotel De la Paz in Quito, Ecuador. He instructed Felipe to park on a side street at the hotel in three days. Alejandro packed a small bag and left for Buenos Aires, where he purchased a ticket to Quito, Ecuador using a false passport.

After arriving in Quito, he spent two days obtaining another false passport. On the third day he walked into the lobby and out a side door where he found Felipe as planned. Felipe drove to a small local airport, where they boarded a Cessna 210 for the flight to another of Cesar's ranches in Columbia.

The next day Felipe drove Alejandro to the coast where a small boat was waiting. They took this boat to the yacht 'Orta Vez', which was anchored about two miles off shore. Cesar and Alejandro sat down to lunch on the aft-deck. After the two men finished the meal and several more drinks, they were left alone.

" How can I help you?" asked Alejandro.

"There is a man in Camargo, Mexico I want taken out. I want it done in a way that will let the Americans know where the hit was ordered from without being too direct." Cesar continued. "I have tried to increase this man's income and he wants nothing to do with it. He wants to remain a small operation. I have his nephew here and after this pollo (chicken; derogatory term) is out of the way, he will do exactly what I say," said Cesar as he slammed his fist into his open hand.

Alejandro smiling maliciously asked Cesar, "Can you get me an M1 Garland from the Columbia military?"

Cesar was puzzled by the request, but replied, "I can get anything I want from the military. I have General De la Fuente on my payroll."

"Good, very good, I will need the rifle and several hundred rounds of ammunition," Alejandro said.

"You will have whatever you need. When you are ready, I'll have one of my dope planes fly you into Mexico. I will also arrange a guide for you in Camargo." Cesar called Felipe and told him, "Go into town and call the General. Tell him I need a M1 Garland in good condition. Tell him I need to shoot a pig for dinner."

In less than two hours a small military patrol boat approached the yacht and Cesar could see one of the General's staff officers in the boat. Alejandro slipped out of sight while the Captain came on board. He handed over a long paper wrapped package and a sealed tin of ammunition. "With the General's compliments," he told Cesar and departed the yacht.

Alejandro returned to the deck, tore off the wrapping, and examined the rifle. "It's perfect," he said. "It's a model D, a sniper rifle with a M84 scope."

"Will that do the job for you?" asked Cesar.

"Its perfect," replied Alejandro. "Now I need a place where I can shoot and devise my plan without being disturbed."

"As you wish mi comparde," said Cesar. "The ranch where you are has a five hundred-meter range behind the barn. You will have everything you need."

The next day Alejandro had one of the servants load several pumpkins into the bed of the pickup he was using. He then drove behind the barn where he found a bench set up for shooting and a five hundred-meter range. He tacked up a bulls-eye target at one hundred meters and positioned the rifle on a sandbag. A light breeze was blowing on his back. He opened the ammo tin and examined the ammo, noticing that it had black tips. Perfect its armor piercing he thought.

He then loaded an eight-round clip into the MI being careful not to catch his thumb. He wrapped the sling around his left arm and looked through the scope. He was breathing easily, and then held his breath as he squeezed the trigger. The gas operated rifle kicked back against his shoulder. He fired twice more then walked down to look at the target. The three round group was low and right.

Back at the bench he made an adjustment to the scope and fired three more rounds. Again he checked the target and found all three rounds in the bull. He made one more adjustment to the scope so that the rifle would shoot an inch high at one hundred meters.

He fired the last two rounds and the rifle locked open. This time he drove the pickup to the target and removed it. He then drove to the three hundred-meter post and placed five pumpkins on the ground in a line.

Back at the bench he loaded another eight-round clip into the MI and again wrapped the sling around his left arm and took a rest on the sandbag. As he looked through the scope, the pumpkins appeared as tiny dots. He sighted the rifle on the far right pumpkin and when he squeezed the trigger, the pumpkin exploded!

Alejandro aimed at another one and watched it explode. He walked forward one hundred meters and firing off-hand, shot the remaining three pumpkins. He walked back to the pickup and unloaded the remaining rounds.

When he returned to the house he called Cesar and told him he was ready. "Good, very good," Cesar said. "I will have one of my pilots pick you up in the morning and fly you to Mexico."

Early the next day one of Cesar's pilots showed up and they drove out to a dirt airstrip that had been carved out of the jungle. He loaded the cased rifle, ammo, and his bag into the twin engine Cessna. He noticed the rear seats were out and a bladder tank had been installed. Bags of marijuana were stacked in the rear and on top of the bladder tank. The pilot motioned to Alejandro to fasten his seat belt and started the engines. They taxed to the end of the runway, as the pilot went over his checklist. The pilot turned into the wind and red-lined both engines while holding the brakes. When he released them, the aircraft surged down the runway and struggled into the air.

The pilot turned to Alejandro, "We'll refuel in Honduras and then fly into China, Nuevo Leon. There is a small dirt strip fifteen kilometers south of town, sleep, if you can." It was late in the evening when they finally reached the strip and the sun had already set. Alejandro could see a house, barn, and several pickups. The pilot made a smooth landing and taxied over to the barn where several men armed with automatic weapons met them. One of the men carried Alejandro's bag to a black Ford pickup and handed him the keys.

"There is a map on the seat and your contact will meet you at the hotel in China tomorrow," he said. Alejandro carefully placed the cased rifle in the pickup and drove off. Arriving in China he checked into the hotel San Carlos and had dinner.

The next day he went shopping for clothes in China. He wanted to be able to pass as a local. After making his purchases he returned to his room, had a light meal, and studied the map he had been given. About two in the afternoon, there was a tap on his door. Alejandro, holding his luger behind his back, opened it.

"Good evening Señor," said the small man. He had a large scar on his left jaw, and appeared to be about sixty-five years old. "I am Pedro. Don Cesar has instructed me to help you in any way you wish. I will take you to a house about twenty kilometers from here."

In less than an hour Alejandro and Pedro arrived at a ranch house northwest of China.

"This will be perfect," said Alejandro.

"My wife will have something fixed to eat very soon," said Pedro.

The next day Pedro and Alejandro drove to Camargo where they scouted various roads and trails leading to the river. They soon drove to the concrete bridge that separates the United States from Mexico. They could see the American flags flying from the Port of Entry on the US side.

Alejandro recalled a saying that he had heard. " Poor Mexico! So far from God and so close to the United States." (General Porfirio Diaz, President of Mexico 1877-1911) From studies in history, Alejandro recalled that Camargo had been occupied by United States troops during the war with Mexico in 1846. There had been over 12,000 troops stationed southwest of town along the banks of the San Juan River. Over 1,500 of these troops had died of diseases while waiting to attack Monterrey.

"I have a plan," said Alejandro. "It would help to know what Gustavo is doing and what his plans are."

"No problem, said Pedro, I have a nephew who works for him."

"Good, I want to check some of the roads down river from here."

"As you wish Señor," replied Pedro. They drove back toward Camargo, turning east on a dirt road leading to the muddy Rio Grande. When they arrived at the river, Alejandro walked to the bank and looked upriver. He could see the bridge and cars crossing both ways.

"That's enough for today, let's have some lunch," he told Pedro.

"There is a good place in Camargo or we can drive to China," Pedro replied.

"We'll go to China, I don't want to be seen in Camargo." The two drove through Camargo and took the dirt road leading to China.

The day finally came when Josefina was released from the hospital in McAllen. Napo and Jeff planned to rent a Cadillac from a local car dealer to take her home. When the owner discovered what the Cadillac was for, he refused payment. He also stated that one of his men would drive Jeff's pickup to Camargo and return the Cadillac so Jeff could remain with Josefina.

Carmen was waiting for her at home and had her room ready, as she was still very weak. The wound under her eye had healed but left a small pencil thin scar. Jeff thought the small blemish made her even more beautiful. The wound on her left leg had healed nicely.

When Josefina was placed in her bed, her mother pushed Jeff and Napo out saying, "She needs her rest." The two men sat in the living room drinking coffee.

Napo told Jeff, "Gustavo wants to make amends. He wants to meet with me and then with you. He says Carlos is no longer here and that he has disowned him."

"Okay," said Jeff. "I'll meet with Gustavo and perhaps we can put this all behind us."

"Está bien," said Napo. "I'll get word to Gustavo and let you know."

"Well I'd better get back or Wilson will have my hide," Jeff said. He walked into Josefina's bedroom and kissed her on the cheek. "I'll see you tomorrow."

Later that day, Napo met one of Gustavo's men named Arturo on the street and told him that Jeff was willing to meet. "Have him meet with me tomorrow here first," Napo told Arturo. Neither one of them noticed the small man with a scar on his jaw sitting on the sidewalk, as they parted.

Napo went to the Police Station in Camargo where one of his men told him about a telephone call from Victor Carrasco in Ciudad

Victoria. He said that Victor told him that Pepe had tried to escape en route to Cd. Victoria and had been shot. The family had been notified to come for the body. "Too bad," Napo said.

The next day Gustavo came to the police station to talk with Napo. "How can I make things right between us?" he asked Napo.

"That's easy," said Napo. "Tell me where Carlos is hiding and stop smuggling."

"I don't know for sure," Gustavo replied. "But I believe he is in Colombia. I have disowned him and he has no place to live here. As for the smuggling, you are right I will stop. I will stay on my ranch and raise cattle."

The two men walked outside, where Napo told Gustavo. "I'll get word to Señor Larson that you can meet him tomorrow."

"I'll gladly go to the US side to meet with him if he wants." Gustavo replied.

"Okay, check with me tomorrow about eleven in the morning," Napo told him.

Neither of them noticed the little old man selling fried fish from a small cart on the street. Napo went back into his office, as Gustavo got in his car and left. The old man hurriedly pushed his cart down a side street. He placed his cart next to the wall of the police station and was standing next to the open window. Napo placed a call to Jeff and told him what Gustavo had said.

Jeff replied, "have him meet me at noon tomorrow at the Port of Entry at Rio Grande City. Perhaps we can straighten things out."

"Tomorrow at noon at the Port of Rio Grande then," said Napo as he put down the telephone.

The old man quickly pushed his cart down the street where he left it with its owner. Two hours later the old man met Alejandro and relayed the information. Alejandro with a menacing laugh said, "Here's what I want you to do," as he whispered in the old man's ear. The old man's under lip twitches as he listens to the plan.

"As you wish," he says and left for Camargo.

The following day Jeff is in civilian clothes at the Port of Entry. In Camargo, Gustavo parked his car across the street from the police station and went inside to talk to Napo. No one notices the little old man. He bends down near the right front of Gustavo's sedan. The soft sound of escaping air can't be heard from a foot away.

Gustavo returns to his car after being told that Jeff is waiting for him at the Port of Entry. He starts his car and heads for the bridge across the Rio Grande River about two miles away. As Gustavo drives on the bridge he feels the car pulling to the right and stops just over on the US side. He gets out and checks his tires. What bad luck he thinks as he sees the flat tire on the right front. He goes to the rear of the vehicle, opens the trunk, and gets out the jack. He places it under the front and begins jacking up the sedan.

Jeff sees Gustavo is having trouble and walks out on the bridge toward the car. Gustavo is sitting on the lip of the bridge removing the lug nuts when Jeff walks up. "Que paso?"" asked Jeff.

"Just a flat," says Gustavo and stands up to shake Jeff's hand. Suddenly Gustavo's head explodes and blood and brains hit Jeff as Gustavo falls to road. Jeff drops to the pavement behind the lip of the bridge as bits of concrete hit his leg. He hears three more shots and they seem to be coming from down river.

Jeff takes a quick peek over the lip and sees movement near a small bush on the riverbank about 270 yards down-river. Another shot hits the bridge and showers him with bits of concrete. Enough of this shit, he thinks. He aims his Colt 1911 down river and fires all eight rounds holding high. The bush moves as some of the 230-grain slugs skip off the river and others hit in and around the bush. He catches a quick glimpse of a figure running back into the heavy brush that lines the riverbank.

Several of the Inspectors heard the shooting and called Wilson. Jeff can hear the sirens as he looks where Gustavo is laying in a pool of blood his head all out of shape. Just then Wilson skids a green and white sedan to a stop beside Jeff.

"You hurt?" he asks.

"No, just scared, I may have to change my pants," Jeff said.

"I told the Inspectors to call the Mexican Aduana, the Sheriff's Department and to send an ambulance," Wilson continued.

EL LOBO VERDE

"I think it's too late for Gustavo," Jeff said. They both knelt by Gustavo and Wilson feels for a pulse.

"He's dead," said Wilson. "Are you sure you're all right? You have blood on you."

"It's not mine, its Gustavo's. I was talking to him when the bullet hit. Look at his head or rather what's left of it."

One of the deputies arrived and took some pictures of the body. When he was through, the ambulance driver loads Gustavo's body and heads back to Rio Grande City. "I'd better call the Chief and the FBI and let they know what's going on," Wilson said. Just then the Mexican Customs arrives and Jeff points to the bush where he believes the shots came from. The officers and Jeff walk down river on the Mexican side. When they reached the bush, Jeff points to a scoped rifle lying nearby.

One of the Mexican Customs picks up the rifle and Jeff can see several spots of blood on the stock. He cuts for sign and finds the imprints of running boots and a few more drops of blood. Jeff points these out to the officers as one of them unloads the rifle. There were still two rounds of black tipped cartridges in the rifle. "It is pure luck if I hit him with my pistol," he tells them.

Jeff returns to the Rio Grande City Border Patrol Station where Wilson is talking to Chief Johns in McAllen. The Chief said he would call the FBI for whatever good it will do. "You know what they say, "FBI, "Famous but Incompetent," said Wilson. "Somebody wanted Gustavo dead and obviously didn't care if they hit a Federal Agent or not."

"Get back to me if you find out anything else," said Chief Johns. "Try keeping a leash on Larson, you know how he is," he continued.

"I'll do my best, but it ain't going to be easy. The Mexicans don't call him El Lobo Verde for nothing," Wilson said.

Napo arrived at the BP office and asked Jeff if he's okay. "Sure," Jeff replied. "Just a few scratches from flying concrete."

"Is it true that Gustavo is dead?" he asked.

" I'm afraid so, he took a rifle slug through the head. The Mexican Aduana recovered a MI Garland on your side and I believe I may have hit him. There were a few drops of blood near the hiding place and on the rifle," Jeff told him.

***

Alejandro returned to the house and changed clothes as his were covered with blood. One of the .45 slugs hit the outer edge of his right ear and a small piece is missing. Pedro's wife bandages the ear while he drank tequila and cursed. Now it's personal, I will kill that damn gringo agent. He remembers the bullets coming into the brush like mad bees. Who would think a damn gringo could hit anything with a pistol at that range.

Pedro arrives a few hours later. One look at Alejandro told him that he had better be careful around this pissed off hombre. "What did you hear?" he asked Pedro.

"They know you were wounded," said Pedro. "It's all over town that Gustavo is dead. What do you want me to do?" he asked.

"Nothing for now. I'm leaving for Tampico and I'll get word to Cesar. Keep you ears open until I contact you." Alejandro then picked up his packed bag and drove off.

After arriving in Tampico and checking into a hotel, he called Cesar and reported the death of Gustavo. He then began drinking heavily. The wound on his ear was not that painful, but he was very vain about his looks. He sat in his room overlooking the Gulf of Mexico and brooded. He was unable to throw off his anger and deal with it, as a professional hit man should.

I will kill that damn migra (Immigration Agent) if it's the last thing I do. Usually after a job he celebrated with a few drinks and a woman. Now with a small bandage on his ear, all he can think of is revenge. He will wait until the time is right. So they call him El Lobo Verde, do they? Well, I'll kill me a wolf and skin him.

CHAPTER 4

On Friday two FBI agents arrive at the Border Patrol Station to talk with Wilson. Agent Karl Brady is 37 years old and has been a federal law enforcement officer for fourteen years. He had been a Border Patrol agent where he received his law degree and shortly after joined the FBI. The other agent was Cecil Allison who had joined the FBI fresh out of college and had only been an agent for three years. Brady knew Wilson and liked the crusty supervisor.

"Robert," he said. "Meet Agent Cecil Allison."

"How are you?" asked Wilson as he shook the two agent's hands. " What can I do for you?"

"We're here to find out what happened on the bridge. The local Sheriff's Department doesn't seem too interested," said Brady.

"I'm not surprised, replied Wilson, you know how they are." "Well to make a long story short, Gustavo was coming to talk to Jeff and somebody blew his head off. Mexican Customs have the rifle that was used and I'm sure Jeff can get you in to talk with them."

"We don't need a Border Patrol Agent," piped up Allison. "This is our jurisdiction," pointing at his badge, which he still had in his hand. "We'll meet with the Mexican Officials. I would like to know if Larson is trying to start a war and what authority he has to meet with Gonzales."

Wilson's temper flared and with his Mississippi drawl said, "Let me tell you what you can do. You can take your jurisdiction, wrap it around your badge, and stick it up your ass you pompous prick. As for the Mexicans, let's see what good your little badge does you on the other side of the river. Hell, they don't know what badges are and could give a rat's ass whether you're FBI or Donald Duck!"

"Allison wait outside, now!" commanded Brady. "Please accept my apology, he's new at this." Both watched Allison traipse out of the office.

"With that type of attitude he may have a damn short career, some "BP Agent" will kick his ass," said Wilson.

"I know," said Brady. "What I'll do is send him over by himself and let him learn the hard way. After the Federales get through with him, maybe he'll find out how important he is or in this case isn't."

"That sounds like a good plan," Wilson replied.

"Let me get him on his way and I'll buy you some lunch," Brady said.

Brady walked outside and over to where Allison was standing by their sedan. "That was real chicken shit Cecil," he said. "You can be a real dumb shit at times."

"Well, he pissed me off," replied Allison. "Why does the BP think they're such hot shit? We don't need them."

"Because they are hot shit around here and that man in there has been in places you wouldn't go in a tank. As for Larson, he's engaged to Camargo's Chief of Police, Napo Garcia's daughter. It was Gonzales's nephew who was shooting at Larson when he hit the girl and almost killed her. Now how about you going on over and check on that rifle."

"Okay, okay," said Allison as he slammed the door and drives off toward the Port of Entry. Just then Wilson came out and approaches Brady.

"Let's go have some lunch while that young man gets a new chapter in his education," he tells Wilson.

Some three hours later Allison returns. " How did it go?" asked Brady.

"Shit, nobody over there speaks English," Allison replied. "I had to hire an interpreter."

Wilson and Brady smile at each other, as they both know most of Mexican Customs speak fluent English. "Well, they said the Comandante of the Aduana is not there and no one knows the location of the rifle. I spent over two hours trying to find out who I could talk to about the shooting and they finally tell me in half-ass English that only the Comandante can release any information."

"Do you want some help from the Border Patrol now?" asked Brady. Allison looked like he had been kicked and with a stricken look on his face, turned to Wilson.

"Yes, I'm sorry about what I said earlier," he told Wilson.

Wilson picked up the telephone and called Jeff at home. "There are two FBI Agents here who want some information on the shooting and the rifle. Can you come and go over to Mexico with them?" Wilson listened for a minute and hangs up. "Jeff will be here in about fifteen minutes," he said.

When Jeff arrived, he greeted Brady and was introduced to Allison who was still smarting from his treatment by Mexican Customs. Jeff, Brady, and Allison climb into the FBI sedan with Allison in the back seat. They drive across the bridge into Mexico and Camargo. Jeff stops by the Police Station and checks with Napo. He introduces the two agents and then asks if the Comandante of Customs was in his office in Miguel Aleman.

"Yes," replied Napo. "I just got off the phone with him. He was very impressed with your shooting. He said there was a puddle of blood where the assassin parked his vehicle."

"Let's drive to Miguel Aleman and see Comandante Jacinto Morales," said Jeff. Allison was still tight jawed and red faced as he realizes he hadn't even known that the Comandante didn't have an office in Camargo.

When the three arrived in Miguel Aleman, they entered the offices of Mexican Customs. Jeff asks one of the officers if he could meet with the Comandante. "Of course," replies the officer. He walks to the Comandante's door. "Señor Larson está aqui mi Jefe." (Mr. Larson is here, Boss) Comandante Morales came out of his office and embraced Jeff in the Mexican abrazo.

"How are you my friend?" he asked. "Just fine," Jeff replied.

"That was some damn good shooting for a gringo," he said in a joking manner. "It was over 250 meters and there was blood on the rifle and where the cabrone parked."

" Just pure luck," said Jeff.

"Sure, right," smiled Morales.

Jeff introduces the two FBI Agents to Morales. Brady told him that he was ready to help in any manner. Morales then had the rifle brought out and shown to the three agents.

"If your lab could check for any prints it would help us," stated the Comandante. "As you can see we have been very careful." The rifle had a piece of wire; one end tied in the trigger guard and the other around the barrel. The five-digit serial number was visible on the rifle and the clip with the loose ammo was next to the rifle. The Comandante asked one of his office staff to type a receipt, turning the rifle over to the FBI.

"We believe the Colombians hired someone to kill Gonzales so his nephew can take over," said Morales. He then turned to a hard eyed Jeff and said, "You be very careful my friend, they may try for you again."

"Have you heard if Carlos is around?" Jeff asked in a cold hard voice.

"No, my friend, if any of my men see him they are to arrest him immediately." The typed receipt was handed to the Comandante and he handed it to Brady. " Please sign for the rifle."

Morales walked the three agents to the door, where he told Jeff, "If anyone fools with you, shoot them first and then call me." He shook hands with the three agents as they left.

As the three drove back to Camargo, Brady turned to Jeff and asked, "When am I going to meet your intended?"

"How about right now," Jeff replied.

"Fine with me, how about you Cecil?" Brady asked.

"Sure, okay," said Allison who still could not get over how he had been given the run around by the Mexican Customs. Jeff directed Brady to the home of Napo Garcia.

Carmen Garcia opened the door at Jeff's knock and gave him a hug as he introduced the two FBI Agents. She escorted them into the living room just as Josefina appeared in the doorway using a cane. Jeff quickly helped her to a chair as he kissed her cheek.

"Josefina I would for you to meet a friend of mine. This is FBI Agent Karl Brady and his fellow agent Cecil Allison." Josefina held out her hand and as Brady held it he said in fluent Spanish, "you are even more beautiful that Jeff told me."

Josefina smiled and it seemed to light up the room. "You are too kind," she replied in English.

Cecil was in shock; he thought Mrs. Garcia was beautiful until he met Josefina. He stammered out a greeting and just stood there. " Close your mouth Cecil before something flies in," Brady told him.

Carmen came back from the kitchen with coffee and fresh baked cookies. She could see that Allison was ill at ease and fussed over him with a smile. Allison was openly taken by the two beautiful women and could not keep from staring. He noticed the small white scar under Josefina's left eye and wondered what had caused it.

Napo came into the room from his office and welcomed the agents to his home. He walked over to where Jeff was sitting on the floor next to Josefina and handed him a letter. Brady, still standing next to Josefina noted that it was a letter signed by the Mayor of Camargo. It authorized Jeff to legally carry a firearm in Camargo, Mexico.

Jeff looked up at Napo and said, "Gracias amigo."

"De nada," Napo replied.

Brady spoke up, "we need to get back to San Antonio with the rifle. Do you need a ride back over to Rio Grande Jeff?"

"Yes, I'll get my own vehicle and come back over if I'm not a "bother" to Josefina." She tried to hit him with her cane, but Jeff was too quick. Still laughing, he kissed her and said, "I'll be right back."

After clearing Customs and Immigration, Brady drove to the Border Patrol Station. He turned to Jeff and thanked him for all of his help. "I'll let you know what we find. If the Comandante is correct and the Colombians are behind this, we'll discover that the rifle was in a shipment to their military."

Brady turned to Cecil as they drove off, "did you learn anything today?"

"Yes," Cecil replied. "I was just a little full of myself. The Mexicans did a real number on me."

"Yes they did, but you deserved it. For your info the Border Patrol has a good reputation here and let me tell you when someone shoots at them, they will return fire. No matter where the bullet comes from. Did you hear what Comandante Morales told Jeff in Miguel Aleman?" asked Brady.

"You mean about shooting anyone who messes with him?"

"Yes, he meant what he said, he just gave El Lobo Verde a license to kill in Mexico."

"Why do they call Larson, El Lobo Verde?"

"The Mexicans give nicknames to everybody. They call Wilson "El Pescador" because he fishes the Rio Grande River. El Lobo Verde means the Green Wolf. They say that Larson talks to animals and that the owls or as they call them "Los Tecolotes," tell him where the aliens are going to cross. I have worked with him in the brush and he does move like a wolf. You never see a wolf unless he wants you too. Some of them even believe that Jeff can shift change into a wolf when he wants too," said Brady.

"That's pure bullshit," Cecil said. " I don't believe it."

"Believe it or not, the Mexicans do. Most of them really like Larson, even the ones he apprehends. Larson has made some serious dents in the smuggling of aliens and narcotics along the border. He uses many informants because he gets along well with people. You could take a few lessons on that," Brady said.

"I guess so, replied Cecil. I'll quit shooting off my mouth."

"That would be a damn good start," laughed Brady.

***

Meanwhile, Cesar and Felipe are having a meeting with Carlos. "Gustavo is dead," He tells Carlos. Carlos pales visibly and with a shaking hand picks up his drink.

"How, when?" he asks.

"How and when doesn't matter anymore. What matters now is that you are to return to Mexico and prepare everything for larger shipments of Mota (marijuana) to the U.S. he tells Carlos. Carlos can only agree, he knows in his heart that Cesar had his Uncle killed and he also knows that it was his fault.

"Be ready in about four weeks to cross about 800 kilos," he tells Carlos. " I will let you know when and will make the arrangements for it to be picked up on the U.S. side."

Carols nods and leaves the room, sick at heart about the death of his Uncle. He slowly packs his bag. One of Cesar's men drives him to the dirt airstrip. He recalls the times his Uncle Gustavo helped him and how good he had been to the family when his Father was killed. He decides that he will have to go along for now, but when the time is right. He would kill Cesar, if he had anything to do with Gustavo's death.

The driver tells him that the plane will be ready in a few minutes. Carlos walks to the plane, which is being loaded with bags of marijuana and climbs into the right seat. The pilot gets into the left seat and starts both engines. As the plane warms up he turns to Carlos and asks, " Are you ready to go?"

"Yes," replied Carlos, "I am."

The plane takes off into the wind and turns northwest toward Mexico. The pilot not knowing about Gustavo started talking about flying a man with a rifle to China, Tamaulipas. Carlos knew at once that it was the man who had killed his Uncle. Suddenly it dawns on Carlos if he doesn't play along with Cesar he too will be dead. I will have to act like I hated my uncle and wished him dead, he thinks to himself.

He talks to the pilot trying to find out everything he can about the killer. The pilot was eager to talk and tells Carlos all about the man. He knew that a man from China was his contact. By the time they landed at the ranch south of China, Carlos had a good description of the killer and his contact.

After landing near China, Carlos drives to his Uncle's ranch to visit his Aunt and form a plan of sorts. His Aunt tells him of the death of Manuel and Pepe. "The people believe that El Lobo killed Manuel and the State Police shot Pepe when he tried to escape," she told Carlos.

"He didn't try to escape," he told her. "They just killed him. I'll take care of El Lobo when the time is right."

Carlos sent for two of his most trusted henchmen to plan for the upcoming load of narcotics. As Carlos meets with Chico and Eduardo he tells them, "be very careful of who you deal with. I believe we may have a snitch working with us. I want everybody in the organization checked. I want the person who killed my Uncle. An old man helped him from China who has a scar on his jaw. I want his name," Carlos stated.

"Si mi Jefe," both Chico and Eduardo said. "We'll have everything ready to move the load across the river." They both left the ranch to carry out Carlos's orders.

Two days later in the Cuarto Vientos Cantina in Mier, Carlos is sitting alone at a corner table when Chico and Eduardo walks in. "Mi Jefe, We have learned that the old man is Pedro and he is the Uncle of Emilio Santos. He was seen with another man who had blue eyes, near the river at Camargo."

"So it would seem that Emilio has been talking," replied Carlos.

"Do you want me to kill him?" Chico asked.

"No, not now, we must not let on that we know about the assassin or the old man," Carlos replied, motioning for the bartender for more drinks. "I received a call from Cesar and the load of "Mota" will be here in three days. We will cross it down river from here." Neither of the three noticed a small shoeshine boy with blue eyes at the next table shining the shoes of another one of Carlos's men. They continued making their plans on where and when the dope load would cross.

The small boy finished the shoes and quickly left the bar. Nobody paid any attention, as there are always shoeshine boys about the bar. The youngster hurried to a small adobe house where he left his shine box and started down the road to Miguel Aleman trying to hitch a ride.

A short time later the boy crossed the bridge into the Port of Entry at Roma and asked one of the Inspectors to please call Jeff Larson. The Inspector escorted the boy to a room in the back and told him to wait. He then called the Border Patrol Station in Rio Grande City, where he told Wilson that a young boy was at the POE and wanted to talk to Larson. Wilson told the Inspector that Jeff was sign cutting near Roma and he would contact him by radio. In a few minutes a green and white scout drives into the parking lot and out steps Jeff. He hurries into the port and is directed to the boy.

"Como está, Señor Lobo," said El Zarco.

"I'm fine and you?" asked Jeff in Spanish.

"Bien, bien," stated El Zarco. " I have something important to tell you," the boy said. "Carlos has returned to Mier and is planning to cross a large load of marijuana in about three days," the boy stated.

"Where?" Jeff asked.

"I don't know yet, but I'll try to find out. I do know they plan to cross it down river from Mier," the boy continued.

"You're worth your weight in gold," stated Jeff. " This time you 'will' take some money." He removed his billfold and handed what money he had, about twenty dollars to the boy.

The boy said, " Thank you, I accept only because we have no food in the house and my mother is unable to work."

"Where is your father?" asked Jeff.

"He is in jail in Reynosa. He was caught trying to smuggle a gas stove into Mexico by the Aduana."

"Let me see what I can do about it, what's your fathers name?" Jeff asked.

"He is called Alberto Rivera," replied El Zarco.

"Okay," said Jeff, "and you are?"

"My name is Antonio," the boy said.

"Okay Antonio, you had better get home before someone sees you here. I will meet you the day after tomorrow at noon where I caught you that time."

"Si Señor Lobo, the boy replied and left the port.

Jeff drove to the BP Station where he brought Wilson up to date on Carlos and the load of dope. Wilson said, " I'll call Cliff Beasley at Customs and bring him up to speed. I also received a call from the FBI. They said that they traced the rifle to a shipment sent to the military in Colombia. You know what that means, somebody has a lot of pull down there."

"Yea you're right about that. I'm going over to Camargo to talk to Napo about this."

"Napo my butt, you just want to see Josefina," Wilson replied.

"That too," laughed Jeff. " But I need to help my informant out on a little matter."

"Okay, better get into some civilian clothes before you go over. No use being a walking target more that you are already," Wilson said, "and be careful, you hear?"

"Sure boss," replied Jeff, "You know me."

"Yes I do, that's what worries me," Wilson replied.

After changing clothes, Jeff drove across the bridge and cleared Mexican Customs. He drove into Camargo where he met with Napo. " How are you mi hijo?" he asked Jeff.

"I'm fine mi Jefe," Jeff replied. " But I do need some help."

"Whatever you need. You know that," Napo said.

"There is a man in the Reynosa jail named Alberto Rivera, see if it's possible to get him out. He was caught smuggling a stove into Mexico," Jeff stated. "I don't want anyone to know my interest in this hombre."

"That shouldn't be a problem," stated Napo. " I'll get right on it."

"Thanks amigo, it's important," said Jeff. "By the way, for your information Carlos is back, but please keep it to yourself for now."

"As you wish," Napo replied as Jeff departs.

He drives over to Josefina's home and is greeted at the door by Carmen Garcia. " How are you mi hijo?" she asks.

"I'm just fine, thanks, where's Josefina?"

"I'll get her," Carmen said.

Jeff walked into the living room and is joined shortly by Josefina, who still has a slight limp. He hugs her to himself as her arms go around him. "How are you mi amor?" she asks.

"I'm fine now, as long as you hold me," he replied.

"You're spoiled rotten," Josefina said.

"I hope so," Jeff replied as the two lovers break their embrace and sat on the couch.

Carmen came in with a plate of sweet bread and coffee for Jeff. "I sure could get used to this attention," he stated.

"Just you wait until we're married, I'll have you washing dishes every night."

"For you, I'll do anything," Jeff stated and leaned over and kissed her lips.

Carmen left the room so that the two young people could be alone. Jeff told Josefina, "I'm going to be very busy the next few days and may not be able to come over as often as I want." Josefina knew not to ask questions about where he would be or what he would be doing.

"Just be very careful, please for me," she pleaded.

"You know I will," he replied.

Napo Garcia arrived at home and told Jeff, "I made a few calls and Señor Rivera will be released from jail tomorrow."

"That's good news, thanks amigo," Jeff said.

"Por nada," replied Napo. " Now what's for dinner?" he asked Josefina.

"Mother baked a chicken, I'll help her set the table," Josefina said as she started to rise.

"No, you stay where you are, I'll help her," said Napo as he left the room.

Josefina looked at Jeff, "that's the first time I have ever seen my father help in the kitchen," she stated. "You're a good influence."

"I think Napo is a better influence on me. I believe I'm a better person for knowing your father and having him as a friend."

"He already thinks of you as his son," replied Josefina. Jeff kissed her again on her soft red lips.

After supper Jeff kissed Josefina goodbye and returned home as he was scheduled to work with Wilson at 4 pm.

That night Jeff and Wilson were scouting out some of the roads west of Roma. He observed a man come from the direction of the river and questioned him as to his citizenship. The man denied that he was an illegal, but didn't have any identification on him. Jeff and Wilson were convinced that he was from Mexico. The man insisted that he was a US citizen but refused to say where he lived. Jeff drove slowly down to one of the fields that border the river and turned off the engine.

The night was deadly quiet. It was if they were a hundred miles from town. Wilson turned to Jeff and asked in Spanish, " Is the shovel still in the trunk?"

Before Jeff could reply, the man in the back seat of the sedan stated that he was indeed from Mexico. He said his father was from Mexico and so was his Grandfather. He stated that none of his relatives had ever lived in the United States nor did they want too. The two agents, both trying to keep from laughing drove back to Roma and allowed him to return to Mexico

CHAPTER 5

The next day, Jeff drove to the pre-determined meeting place down river from Mier. He walked the last mile after hiding the unmarked Border Patrol sedan. As he approached the river he carefully watched for any sign of people. He knew if Carlos suspected that Antonio was giving information he would have the boy killed. He slipped into some heavy brush as he saw Antonio cross the river in his small canvas boat.

He gave a low dove call and the boy slipped into the brush beside him. "My father is home," he told Jeff.

"How about that," Jeff said.

"My father says somebody called the aduana and the charges were dropped. I know you had something to do with this," said Antonio.

Jeff changed the subject. "What do you hear about the drugs?"

Antonio replied, "Carlos is planning to cross the load Friday night between 11 o'clock and midnight down river from here by the big rocks. I don't know what kind of vehicle they will use on this side. He is going to send about ten mojados to cross down-river from Roma and will make sure the Migra knows they are coming."

"That sly bastard," replied Jeff. "While the BP is dealing with a load of immigrants, he's going to run his load. Here are two phone numbers, the first is for my house and the other is the Border Patrol Station in Rio Grande. I want you to memorize both numbers and call collect if you get more info. Use the name El Zarco when you call."

"Okay," said Antonio. "I can call from the pay phone on the square. I better get back home we're having a celebration at my house tonight."

"Good," Jeff said, " you take care of yourself." He watched until the young boy was safely on the other side of the river before returning to the sedan.

As soon as Jeff was back in the vehicle, he radioed the BP station. He advised Wilson to have Customs and the other BP supervisor meet at the station as soon as possible.

When Jeff arrived at the station both Customs Agents along with SPA Hayden were in Wilson's office. "Well, what's going on," he asked Jeff.

Jeff pulled up a chair. "It seems Carlos is going into smuggling in a big way. He plans to cross narcotics down-river from Mier, Friday night. He is also going to send a bunch of aliens across the river between Rio Grande and Roma in an attempt to keep the BP busy."

"How do you want to handle this?" Wilson asked Jeff.

"What we need is someone to apprehend the aliens while the rest of us lay in on the crossing point. I don't know what kind of vehicle will be involved on this side for the load." Jeff replied.

"Okay, here's the plan, Gene you take Parker and Kitchens with you to grab the wets," Wilson said. "Jeff and I with Douglas, Cook and Customs will lay in on the crossing point. How does that sound Cliff?"

Customs Agent Cliff Beasley spoke up, "We're going to need someone to relay radio traffic. The walkie-talkies won't reach the tower from that part of the river. I'll put Neil in a vehicle up on the other side of the highway where he can hide and still have radio contact with us."

"It'll be a long walk in," said Jeff. "They'll have lookouts on most, if not all of the roads."

"You're sure right about that," Wilson replied. "I suggest that we be dropped off about 5 PM on Friday down river from the crossing point and that will give us plenty of time to set up."

Beasley said, "let's try to get the load vehicle along with any of Carlos's people. I suggest that we all met here about 3 PM for any last minute updates. Is your informant going to contact you prior to the load crossing?"

"Only if he hears of any changes. When this is over I'd like to see about getting him paid," Jeff said.

EL LOBO VERDE

"You bet," Beasley said. "If what he says is true, it means the Colombians are increasing the amount of narcotics in this area."

Jeff turned to Wilson, " I gave him this phone number and told him to call collect using the name "El Zarco."

"Not a problem," Wilson replied. " Anybody have any questions." No one did and the two Customs Agents left the Border Patrol station.

SPA Hayden then spoke up, "I sure hate to miss all of the fun."

"I know," Wilson replied. "But we need someone with brains down on this end. When you have the wets arrested, bring them to the station. I'll arrange to have a couple of inspectors to do the processing and you guys can then move to Roma. You'll be available for the seizure."

"That's a lot better," Hayden said. "I don't want Jeff to have all of the fun."

Jeff laughed, "Why does everybody think this is fun. Do you know most people would consider us crazy?"

"How's that," Hayden asked.

"Most sensible people hide from gunfire, we drive like hell to get there to be shot at."

Jeff arrived on Friday about 2:30 to find everybody involved already there. Damn, he thought, I must be late. He hurried into the station to find the two Customs Agents talking to Wilson. Cliff said, "Hey Jeff, you're just in time. We have obtained a pickup and it will drop us near the river. Neil is going to drive and the rest of us can hide in the bed."

Wilson spoke up, "When we get in position, I'll click the walkie-talkie twice. If Neal is receiving, he'll answer with two clicks. If he doesn't hear from us in two hours, he'll have to move closer until he can receive. Once we have the communications established, if Neil sees any vehicle going into the river, he'll click once and I'll answer with one click. Hayden I want you to generate a lot of radio traffic in reference to the wet load. Right up until you place them in custody. After that I want radio silence until you guys are in Roma, then click your radio three times and I'll answer the same. When the load goes down I'll be on the radio with voice commands. Everybody clear on this?" he asked.

All of the agents nodded and were eager to get moving. Wilson said, "We'll go in two sedans to Falcon Dam where Cliff has the pickup hidden. If there aren't any questions, let's roll."

Arriving at Falcon Dam Wilson, Beasley, Cook, and Douglas hid in the bed of the pickup. Jeff hunched down in front with Neil to direct him to the drop off point. When he reached it, he pulled over to the side of the road and the agents quickly got out. Neil made a U-turn and left the area.

They headed to the river with Jeff leading the way. " Try to be quiet in the brush with your size 13 shoes," he told Cook.

"Are you kidding? I walk so quiet, you can hear a gnat fart," Cook replied. Jeff laughed softly which apparently help relieve the tension for all of them.

The group of agents made their way up-river with Jeff in the lead. He does move through the brush like a wolf thought Wilson, as he watched from his position at the rear. When Jeff reached the rocks where the load was to cross he signaled to the other officers and they slipped into hiding places along the bank.

All of the agents were equipped with walkie-talkies with earplugs and heard Wilson's two clicks for Neil. It was answered by two clicks. They had radio contact. Jeff signaled to Wilson that he was going to scout up river toward Mier and Wilson nodded in agreement. The other officers settled into their places of concealment.

Jeff moved quietly up-river about a mile and hid behind a log. He was in place about an hour when he first observed two men on the Mexican side watching the US side. He watched as they moved slowly down river toward the rocks where the other agents were hidden. He let them pass his location then easily slipped past them on his side and arrived first. He moved into the brush where Wilson was hiding and in a whisper told him of the two men. Wilson told Jeff to advise the others. He wanted to maintain radio silence.

One by one each was told of the two men scouting the river and to remain quite and hidden. Shortly the two were seen on the Mexican side. The hidden agents watched as they slipped into a small bush near the riverbank. The sun was sinking rapidly in the west.

Jeff's thought returned to Josefina and the Garcias. I'll be glad when this is over and I can deal with Carlos before he tries anything else in Camargo. Jeff was worried about Napo. If the Colombians tried to offer the plata o plomo to him they would get the lead, a bullet. (Plata o Plomo; means take the bribe, silver or the lead, a bullet)

About 10 at night, the agents heard radio traffic as Hayden and his crew moved toward the river to apprehend the mojados sent to draw off the Border Patrol. Shortly after 11 PM each heard one click on the radio. This meant that Neil had spotted a vehicle driving into the area. Wilson answered with a single click.

Shortly they heard the engine noise and a pickup stopped about thirty yards from the riverbank. The driver got out and whistled. The two men on the other side came out of hiding and whistled back. The agents then saw several men with bags come from behind them and start toward the river. As the men and bags of marijuana were crossed Jeff whispered, "I don't see Carlos."

"Me neither," replied Wilson. "Well hell, we'll take what we can get."

The river near the rocks was only about two feet deep and the bags were quickly crossed and placed in the bed of the pickup. As the driver prepared to get back into the truck, Wilson stood up and shouted, " Manos arriba, Los Federales." (Hands up Federal Officers)

The driver made a dive for the truck, only to be stopped by Ed Cook who was hiding two feet away. The others tried to run to the river only to find Jeff, Wilson, Douglas and Beasley in their way. One made it to the river but fell down in the water. Jeff waded in grabbed him by the hair and pulled him back onto the bank.

The men were handcuffed along with the driver. Jeff looked into the bed of the pickup. "This must have been a trial run, there's only about 250 pounds here," he said.

"Do you recognize any of these guys?" Beasley asked.

"No, I don't," replied Jeff.

"The driver is from Zapata," stated Cook, who was holding the driver's ID.

Wilson radioed Hayden that everything was under control and additional help was not needed. He then contacted Neil and told him to come on in to the crossing point and assist with the transportation of the captives. "It's still a good night's work," he said, "and a few more pounds that won't make it to the street or to some school."

Jeff walked over to Beasley and said, " I'll like to pay my informant about Three hundred dollars if that's okay with you."

"That's a bargain," replied Beasley. "I'll get the money and a receipt for him to sign."

Just then Neil arrived and loaded the arrested people into the bed of his truck. Cook crawled in with them with his weapon drawn. Beasley got into the cab with Neil. Jeff drove the seized pickup with the marijuana with Wilson and Douglas crowded into the cab.

When they arrived at the Border Patrol Station the prisoners were fingerprinted and photographed. Their personal data was taken and the marijuana marked and weighed. It came to two hundred eighty six pounds. "That's a damn good haul," Wilson told the officers.

Beasley walked over to where Jeff was filling out forms. "When do you want the money for your informant?" he asked.

"I'll try to get up to your office sometime in the next few days. I'll call first to see if you're in." Jeff stated.

"Okay, whenever you're ready it'll be there," Beasley replied.

Monday found Jeff and several other agents tracking two men who had crossed illegally into the US north of Rio Grande City. Jeff had been on the tracks for over three miles while the others were sign cutting on trails north of him, looking for the wets. A Border Patrol Super Cub " which is a slow flying plane" flew over Jeff to get a line on the tracks as he followed in the heavy brush.

Jeff was following the tracks up a small sendaro (a trail through the brush) running parallel to a fence line. He saw a local rancher working on a cross fence about fifty yards off to one side of the trail. Jeff knew that the plane had not seen the rancher or he would have said so.

Jeff walked over and asked him if he had seen two men. "Yes I did, they came by about twenty minutes ago asking for work. I didn't have any for them and they continued on north. One is wearing a blue shirt and a black cap. The other has on a red shirt and a straw hat." Jeff thanked him and returned to the trail.

After returning to the tracks, Jeff decided to have some fun. He called the other units and the plane on his radio. He then advised them, "These tracks are really smoking. They are only about twenty minutes ahead." He then told them he had found blue thread about chest high and a black thread head high on a mesquite bush. He went on to tell them about some red thread and a piece of straw on the other side of the bush. "One of them must be wearing blue shirt with a black cap and the other has a red shirt with a straw hat."

There was dead silence for about thirty seconds and then the radio came alive with hoots of laughter. "Who do you think you are, Daniel Boone?" said Parker. "Get him out of the sun, he's gone bonkers on us."

About fifteen minutes later the plane radioed. "I think I have them spotted hiding in some brush below me. I can see a spot of red. The pilot then got on his loud speaker, telling the men to come out and directing Parker into the location. When the two crawled out, one was wearing a blue shirt with a black cap. The other one had on a red shirt with a straw hat. Parker was very quite when he picked Jeff up and Jeff never told him about talking to the local rancher.

Later that night when Jeff was asleep, the telephone rang. He picked it up and the operator said, "I have a collect call from a Mr. Zarco, will you accept the charges?"

"I sure will," he replied as he tried to get the sleep out of his eyes.

"Señor Lobo," said a small voice and Jeff recognized Antonio. " Yes, go ahead, but don't use any names."

"Si Señor, your friend who returned from a trip down south is planning another delivery."

"When and where?" Jeff asked. "They should be crossing soon at Midway. I couldn't get to a telephone until now." " Don't worry about it and thanks, Jeff said. " I'll contact you later," and broke the connection.

Jeff dialed Wilson's number and when he answered the telephone said, " Carlos is moving a load right now at Midway crossing."

"Okay," Wilson said. "It's just you and me, the others are tied up with a smuggling load of Cubans."

Jeff said, "I'm going to drive across the field where I can see the crossing."

"I'll be there as soon as I get dressed. I'll hide near the highway and give you two clicks when I'm in place," Wilson told him.

Jeff said, "When I see something I'll click three times."

He dressed quickly and grabbed his Colt 45 auto sticking it in his pants on the left side with the butt of the pistol forward. He had one of the unmarked BP sedans at his house and started it without any headlights. It's blacker that a whore's heart he thought as he drove out of his yard. He eased the sedan down the dirt road leading to the highway. He then drove into a field that was north of midway crossing. Parking behind a small bush where he could see the river crossing he shut off the engine. He then rolled down the window so he could hear any sounds.

A few minutes later he heard two clicks on the radio. Okay, Wilson is now in position. Damn it's cold in here, but I don't want to run the engine thought Jeff. He put on his BP jacket and clipped on his badge to the front. Two fully loaded magazines of 45's went in the lower left pocket. Another was placed in the flap pocket of the jacket opposite the badge.

About thirty minutes later he saw a flash of light like someone with a flashlight near the crossing. He then saw the running lights of a truck coming up the slight rise from the river. He gave three clicks on the radio. Three answered it.

Jeff watched as the truck drove slowly up the road then saw another set of headlights suddenly appear. He could see a pickup in front of the truck perhaps scouting the road. He broke radio silence and told Wilson what he was watching.

Wilson said, "I'll try to block the road, see if you can cut the truck off."

"I'll try if I can get out of this field," Jeff said as he drove the Plymouth sedan across the plowed ground. Before Jeff could reach the road the lead pickup was approaching the highway. Wilson drove his marked sedan across the road in front and blocked it. The driver threw it reverse, backing down the dirt road in a cloud of dust.

Jeff saw the big truck make a u-turn on the narrow dirt road and slid his vehicle in behind it. As the truck drove south Jeff turned on the red lights in the grill and hit the siren. It appeared to be a water truck of the type used in road construction in the thick dust, as the driver slowly came to a halt. Jeff could see the driver looking for him in the big mirrors on the side.

He shouted to the driver, "Come out with your hands up, US Border Patrol," while standing beside his sedan.

The driver's door came open and flame stabbed out at Jeff. Shit, he's trying to kill me, he thought. He fired twice at the driver. One bullet hit the door, while the other one angrily ricocheted off into the still night air.

The lead pickup suddenly appeared without lights and rammed Jeff's sedan. The roof hit Jeff in the head and he was knocked to one side, which probably saved his life. As several more shots came from the water truck and hit the sedan.

The dust was so thick you could cut it with a knife. As Jeff got to his knees, he could feel wetness on his head and was having trouble focusing his eyes. He looked up to see the driver of the truck walking toward him with a pistol in his hand. Jeff raised his weapon and shot him twice in the chest. The 230-grain slugs knocked the man off his feet. Jeff staggered to his feet trying to see what had hit his sedan as the dust drifted slowly away. Several shots were fired from the pickup, two hit him, and he went down hard.

Wilson arrived just in time to see Jeff hit and collapse. He opened fire with his sawed off chrome-plated shotgun. "You sons-of-bitches," he screamed as he fired both barrels. He pulled his .357 revolver and put all six rounds into the cab of the pickup. Suddenly it was very quite and all you could hear was the heat sounds from the vehicles. He reloaded his revolver and radioed sector to send backup and an ambulance to his location.

Wilson slowly approached the pickup. He could see one person slumped over in the cab and reached in, felt for a pulse. There was none. He could see red lights coming as other BP units rushed to assist. It may be too late for Jeff, he thought. He walked over where Jeff was lying in the dirt and saw blood on his head. He knelt down and raised Jeff's head into his lap.

"Don't you go die on me now," he said.

Jeff was unconscious and Wilson could see more blood on his right side, but his pulse was strong. A Border Patrol sedan rolled up and Hayden jumped out with his weapon drawn.

"Look around the pickup," Wilson told him. "There is a dead one in the cab, but there may be some more nearby." Another BP unit arrived with Cook and Douglas in it. Both jumped out with drawn weapons. Wilson shouted at Cook to bring a first aid kit, as he still had Jeff's head in his lap.

Wilson ripped Jeff's shirt open and could see blood oozing from a wound on his right side. He also saw a large red bruise higher up on the same side. "What the hell caused this?" he asked Cook as he knelt down with the first aid kit. As Cook was placing a bandage on the wound, Wilson reached into Jeff's jacket pocket and removed the magazine. "Look," he told Cook. The magazine had been hit by a bullet and was still imbedded in the metal.

As Cook and Wilson were trying desperately to stop Jeff from losing more blood, Douglas was checking the man Jeff had shot. " This guy is bien dead," he told them, as Hayden returned from the field.

"Somebody put some lead in at least one of them. There is a blood trail with two sets of footprints going toward the river," he told Wilson.

The ambulance arrived and the unconscious Jeff was loaded into it. Wilson reached down and picked up Jeff's 45 that had been lying beside him. "Take him to McAllen and this damn thing had better not get under 90 going down there!" Wilson said. " Ed, you go with him and see that it don't."

As the ambulance left with lights and siren blasting Wilson walked over to the truck. "Let's see what we have here that they were ready to kill for," he said. He crawled on the back and peered into the tank. "Gene contact Customs that we must have over a half a ton of marijuana here. I want you to take charge, as I'll go to Camargo and pick up Josefina. Something I wish I didn't have to do."

Hayden asked, "You want me to go get her?"

"No, I'll go. I just hate to face her with nothing to tell her about Jeff."

"Hey Boss," called Douglas. "Cook just called from the ambulance and said Jeff is now conscious and talking. He wanted to know if you were all right."

"Shit," said Wilson and turned away so no one could see the wetness in his eyes.

Hayden spoke up, "take off and pick up that girl, we'll take care of everything here."

Wilson drove to the station for his personal vehicle and drove to Camargo. When he arrived at the Garcia home, the sun was just peeking over the mesquites in the East. Wilson knocked on the door and Napo opened it. When Napo saw his face, he went pale. "What is wrong my friend?" he asked.

"Jeff is wounded, but talking," Wilson told him. He quickly briefed him on what had happened.

Josefina entered the room in a robe and seeing her father's face asked, "what's wrong?" Napo quickly informed her about Jeff in rapid Spanish. She left the room running, but returned in a few minutes fully dressed, along with her mother.

"Please Mr. Wilson, will you take me to him?" she asked.

"That's what I'm here for, honey," he told the young girl.

"I'm going too," Napo stated.

"Call as soon as you know something, I'll go pray at the church for him," said Carmen.

When they arrived at the hospital, Cook met them at the emergency room. "Jeff is okay," he told them. With tears flowing down her face, Josefina ran to the room where Jeff was being treated.

"Are you alright mi vida?" she asked.

"I'm fine mi querida," Jeff replied. As soon as the nurse finished wrapping a bandage around his head, Josefina hugged him.

Wilson and Napo entered the room and the nurse turned to Wilson. "The doctor says he should stay overnight, but Mr. Hardhead here doesn't want to," she said, as the doctor entered the room.

"How is he Doc?" Wilson asked.

"Very lucky," replied the doctor. "If the bullet had not hit a rib and glanced off, it would probably have hit his heart. As it is, he has a cracked rib, which will be painful, and a slight concussion. He also has a very bad bruise on his right side. I don't know what caused it."

Wilson reached into his pocket and removed the damaged magazine. He showed it to the doctor. "This was in his jacket pocket," he told them. Josefina's face went pale as she saw it and hugged Jeff even tighter.

He's not in bad shape," continued the doctor. "What he mostly needs is plenty of bed rest for the next few days."

Wilson told Jeff, "You need to stay here."

"No, I don't," stated Jeff. "If I stay here, I'll really get sick."

Wilson asked the doctor, "What do you think Doc?"

"If he stays in bed and doesn't move around much, he should be alright. If he starts to run a high fever, get him back down here at once."

"You can count on that and I'll see that he stays in bed," Josefina stated.

Wilson reached under his shirt and handed Jeff his .45 Colt. "I thought you might want this."

"Thanks Boss, I don't feel so naked now," he said and slipped the pistol next to his leg. The nurse returned with a wheelchair and a scrub shirt for Jeff as his was covered with blood.

"Thanks for the shirt, but I don't need that," he said pointing to the wheelchair.

"You'll get in the chair or I'll tie you to the bed," the nurse replied with fire in her eyes.

"Get in the chair Jeff," said Josefina in a tone of voice that Jeff had never heard before.

"Ha," said Wilson. "That's telling him Josefina, now do what the ladies tell you."

"Okay, okay," said Jeff. "I know when it's time to quit."

"There's always a first time," laughed Wilson as Jeff meekly got in the wheelchair.

With the nurse pushing and Josefina walking beside him, holding his hand, Jeff was wheeled to the hospital door. Wilson retrieved his car and helped Josefina put Jeff in the back seat. Cook and Napo crowded into the front seat with Wilson.

When they arrived at Jeff's home and had him settled in bed, Josefina went to her father. " Please have mother send me some clothes."

"Si mi hija," replied Napo. "I'll ask your cousin Elena to come help."

"Thanks Papa," she said and kissed him on the cheek. "I'll make some coffee for us."

While they were drinking the coffee, SPA Hayden arrived and came in. As Josefina poured him some coffee, Wilson asked. "What's going on with the seizure?"

"You guys caught over sixteen hundred pounds of marijuana in the truck. The driver was identified as Rafael Acosta. He was wanted for murder in Laredo, and has connections with the Colombians. The dead guy in the pickup has not been identified. He had a .38 S&W break top with four rounds gone. We found a Browning Hi-Power 9mm by the body of the truck driver and another one in the cab. We also picked up some .38 Super brass near the pickup, those guys were loaded for bear," Hayden stated.

"The .38 S&W must have been what hit Jeff in the ribs and his magazine. A .38 Super would have gone through him," said Wilson. "Good work Gene, let's clear out and give Jeff some rest."

Later Napo returned with Josefina's cousin Elena along with her clothes and some food. Jeff was still in bed but was sitting up being fussed over by Josefina. "The story is out in Camargo that you were wounded but that you shot two of them," he told Jeff.

"I think Wilson shot the one in the pickup," Jeff told him. "It's still kind of fuzzy."

"I'll try to find out where Carlos is, but my jurisdiction is only in Camargo," said Napo. "Call if you need anything else," he said as he kissed his daughter and left.

The next morning there was a knock on the door. When Josefina opened it the man standing there introduced himself as Agent Sidney Seaborn of Immigration Internal Affairs.

"I need to speak with Patrol Agent Larson," he stated.

"Please come in," replied Josefina. "Can I get you some coffee?"

"No thanks, I'll only be a few minutes," he said. Josefina escorted him into the living room where Jeff and Elena were sitting.

Jeff started to rise, but was stopped by Elena. " No you don't, you sit still," she told him.

"I'm Investigator Seaborn of Immigration Internal Affairs. I need to ask you some questions if we could have a few minutes alone," he told Jeff.

"Whatever you want to ask, you can ask in front of my friends," Jeff told him.

"Very well," said Seaborn. "I wish to advise you that you don't have to talk without your attorney present. You may stop at any time until you speak to an attorney if you desire," he continued in a take-over officious manner.

"Let's cut the crap, what is it you want?" Jeff asked who was getting very pissed off.

"To begin with, I need the weapon that was used in the murder of Acosta," Seaborn stated.

Jeff's eyes grew hard. "What murder? The son-of-a-bitch was trying to kill me," he stated.

"That's still under investigation," replied Seaborn. "However, I need to get all of the facts, I'm here to help," assuming a posture of superiority.

Jeff pulled his .45 from its position in the couch and removed the magazine. He locked back the slide and removed the round from the barrel. "I'll need a receipt for this, with a notation of the type of grips that are on it," he said as he handed it to Seaborn.

"We don't steal things," Seaborn replied as he wrote out the receipt for the weapon in a very perturbed manner.

"Yea, well don't piss down my back and tell me it's raining," replied Jeff. "Josefina please show the fellow to the door. If you want anything else, check the reports. Because I ain't talking to you anymore."

"This way Señor," said Josefina as Elena tried to stare holes in Seaborn.

"Very well, if you don't wish to cooperate that will be in my report," stated Seaborn.

"You can also put in your report that I think you're a pompous asshole and that you have to take off your hat to pee," Jeff replied as Elena tried to keep from laughing. By this time Josefina had Seaborn by the arm and was escorting him to the door.

When Seaborn reached the door he turned to Josefina and said, "that man has a bad attitude."

"Jeff has put his life on the line several times trying to stop the dope from coming into this country. What have you ever done "Mister Seaborn?" Josefina asked.

Seaborn dropped his head and quickly entered his vehicle. He was gone in a cloud of dust. Josefina returned to the living room talking to herself in Spanish.

"What does all this mean Jeff?" she asked.

"Darn if I know, Jeff replied. I'll just have to wait and see. I know it was a good shoot. The guy had a gun in his hand and had already fired at me, when I shot the bastard."

"I just don't understand any of this," Josefina replied.

"I don't either, but I'm going to find out. Hand me that phone," he requested.

He dialed the BP office and when Wilson answered told him what had happened.

"Are you shitting me," Wilson asked.

"Not at all boss," replied Jeff. "Josefina and Elena were both witness. What a load of crap. That guy was shooting at me. It's a damn wonder he didn't hit me."

"Well, don't worry about it. I'll call the chief and let him take care of this crap. You just get well my friend."

"Thanks boss. Stop by for coffee when ever you want," Jeff said.

CHAPTER 6

Carlos was at his Uncle's ranch trying to put his organization back together. He had a wound on his left shoulder where a bullet had creased it. Eduardo had a bullet wound in his right shoulder. "They must have killed Chico and Rafael," said Eduardo.

"Yes, Chico wasn't moving when we jumped from the pickup. Why did you crash into the sedan?" asked Carlos.

"I didn't see it. The dust was too thick," replied Eduardo.

Carlos turned to another of his men Luis, "drive to Camargo and see what you can find out. I'll call Cesar and tell him we've lost two loads."

"Si, he's going to be very angry," Eduardo said.

"Then he can send his hired killer back if he wants too. "Let him" take care of El Lobo. For now, we got to find out who is snitching us to the Migra on where we are crossing the mota." (Mota; slang for marijuana)

"Wait, instead of going to Camargo, you and Roberto take Emilio out somewhere, and find out what he knows about Cesar's hired killer. If he talked about Gustavo to his Uncle he may be also talking to the migra. When you are through with him, I don't want to see him again. I don't want anyone else to see him. Do you understand me?" asked Carlos.

"Si mi Jefe," replied Luis. He walked outside where he found Roberto and told him what they had been ordered to do. "Get some rope from the barn and I'll find Emilio." Luis walked to the bunkhouse where Emilio was working on one of the vehicles used to haul dope. "Let's go Emilio," he said. "Carlos has a job for us."

They both walked to Luis's pickup just as Roberto threw some rope into the bed. Luis motioned Emilio into the cab and Roberto got in beside him. As they drove off Roberto reached over and removed Emilio's pistol.

"What's going on, what are you doing?" he asked with his voice quavering.

"It seems you have been talking," replied Luis. "We want to know who you have been talking to."

"I haven't told anybody anything," Emilio said.

Roberto hit Emilio in the face with his own gun. "You're lying Emilio," he said.

They rode in silence for twenty minutes until they reached a place where the road was under construction. All of the workers had left, but several pieces of equipment were parked nearby. They removed Emilio from the truck and walked him over to where the road had been graded. Making Emilio lie down and using the rope with wooden stakes, they tied him spread eagle on the road. Emilio seemed to be in a daze as they finished.

"Last chance," Luis told him.

"I only told my uncle that Gustavo was meeting El Lobo after Carlos shot his novia, I swear. Please turn me loose," pleaded Emilio.

Luis turned to Roberto, "start the grader and bring it here." As Roberto walked to the road grader, Emilio started to tug at his ropes and beg.

"Please Luis, I'm telling the truth."

"Have you been telling the migra about our loads and where they were crossing?"

"No, I swear, I only told my Uncle that Gustavo was going to meet with El Lobo, please don't kill me Luis," begged Emilio.

As the road-grader approached, Emilio looked between his legs and saw the huge tires of the grader. He began to scream and beg, " Madre de Dios, (Mother of God) Luis, please don't. I'm telling the truth." His screams became even louder. The tire rolled over his groin and he is crushed almost flat.

Roberto parked the grader back where he found it and walked back to the crushed body.

"Damn, I could hear him screaming over the engine, what'll we do with him?"

Luis pointed down the road. "I noticed a place where they are going to pour concrete tomorrow. We'll put him under where they will pour, he'll have a bridge for a tombstone."

After placing Emilio's body in a shallow hole and covering it up, they spread dirt where he had been killed. "I don't think he was telling anybody about the loads. He was scared out of his wits. If he had been talking, he would have admitted it. He would have turned in his own mother to stop that grader. He admitted that he'd told his uncle about Gustavo meeting with El Lobo," Luis said.

Later that night when they returned to the ranch, Luis told Carlos that Emilio had been killed in a head-on wreck. He told him what Emilio had said before he died. "Do you think he was telling the truth?" Carlos asked.

"Yes, I do, I believe he told his uncle about the meeting between Gustavo and el Lobo, but that's all," replied Luis

"Well, may so, maybe no, if he was talking about our business sooner or later he would've turned us in. You guys did a good job. I'll call Cesar and tell him what's going on and we'll see what he wants to do," Carlos stated.

When Cesar received the call, he became so angry, he threw a full bottle of brandy against the wall. He ranted and raved for twenty minutes then became deadly quiet. Felipe knew someone was going to die. "Where is Alejandro?" he asked.

"He is still in Mexico Jefe," Felipe told him.

"Send him word that I want that damn green-shirted bastard dead. Do you hear me? Dead now, right now," he shouted.

"I'll take care of it at once," Felipe replied hurriedly leaving the room. He placed a call to the hotel where Alejandro was staying. When he answered told him that Cesar was having trouble with wolves. " They are killing cattle and need to be killed."

Alejandro grinned into the telephone and said, "tell him not to worry, I'll take care of it soon." He sat down at the window and started to plan. He thought to himself, this is getting too personal. I need to control myself. He felt his ear that had been shot and became angry all over again. He tried to reason with himself, to no avail. He called one of his contacts and said, " I need to meet with you."

The voice on the other end said, "Come to my shop tomorrow at noon."

The next day, Alejandro left the hotel and walked down several side streets to make sure he was not followed. No one is looking for me, he thought, but old habits die-hard. Reaching the leather shop of his contact, he entered the store and requested a pair of boots.

The old man locked the front door and said, "Follow me." They went down a set of stairs and into a room hidden behind a false wall. There were rows of weapons alone the opposite wall and stacks of boxes in another corner. "What are you looking for?" the little old man asked Alejandro.

Alejandro walked over to a row and looked at several pump shotguns. He then took down a hammerless, double barrel, 12 gauge with fourteen-inch barrels. The stock had been cut-off behind the pistol grip. "This is what I want, along with a box of double-aught buck shot," he said. So El Lobo likes shotguns, does he, we'll see if he likes this one, he thought to himself.

"Do you want to take it with you?" asked the old man. Alejandro nodded.

The old man produced a violin case. Placed the weapon and ammo inside and closed the lid. "That will be six hundred American dollars," he told Alejandro. Who counted out the money and left the store.

He returned to his room took apart the shotgun and cleaned it. The next morning he packed his bags and checked out. He placed the cased shotgun behind the seat of the pickup and drove toward China. When he arrived at Pedro's, he told him to send his wife off somewhere.

"We have work to do."

"Si Señor," Pedro replied. He drove his wife to her cousin's house about three miles distance. When he returned Alejandro was sitting at the kitchen table with a large map showing both sides of the border.

"Do you know where this Larson lives?" he asked.

"Si Mi Jefe, he lives just west of Rio Grande City near the Midway Crossing about a quarter of a mile north of Hwy 83. It's a little place called Los Villarreales.

"Show me on the map," commanded Alejandro.

Pedro looked at the map, and then placed a small cross near the highway. " Right here," he stated. "His house is on a dirt road just off the highway."

"Does he live alone?" Alejandro asked.

"Si Señor, he is engaged to the Comandante Garcia's daughter. I understand she and her cousin are staying at his house now, while he is recuperating from his wounds."

"Good, tomorrow we will scout some of the roads near Midway. Right now I need a place to try out a shotgun. I want to see how this buck shot spreads."

"You can use the old shed behind the barn," Pedro suggested.

Alejandro removed the sawed-off shotgun from its case and loaded it. He put several more shells in his pocket and he and Pedro walked out to the shed. He stopped about sixteen meters from the wall of the shed and fired one barrel into the shed's wall. He and Pedro walked over and examined the pattern. The nine pellets had covered an area of about four feet by four feet. He backed up until he was about two meters and fired the other barrel. This time the nine pellets tore a gaping hole in the wood.

"That should take care of a wolf, right Pedro?"

"Si Señor" Pedro replied.

"I want to give him one barrel from about fifteen meters and then give him the other right in his face while he is looking at me," Alejandro stated.

At the Border Patrol station SPAIC Wilson was on the telephone with Chief Johns. "He accused Jeff of murdering the driver of the tank truck," said Wilson. The Chief advised Wilson that he would look into the allegations and get back to him. Wilson also requested that Jeff's .45 be returned as soon as possible.

"Why didn't the son-of-a-bitch want my gun?" he asked Chief Johns.

"Well, he just came over from Inspections. The FBI has already reported that it was a good shooting. You tell Jeff not to worry about it," Johns stated. "When someone shoots at an agent, I expect him to return fire and he better hit something. You guys get plenty of ammo to practice with, use it," Johns continued.

"I guess I need to do more practice myself. I missed two of the assholes in the pickup," stated Wilson.

"That's not what I heard," said Johns. "I heard they were both bleeding when they crossed the river. Too damn bad we don't have Piranhas in the Rio Grande," said Chief Johns.

"Hell no, I fish that river," Wilson replied.

"That's what I mean," laughed Johns as they disconnected.

Several days later Jeff walked into the Border Patrol station after taking Josefina and Elena home to Camargo.

"How's it going?" Wilson asked.

"I'm doing okay, guess I'll have to start eating my own cooking again. Josefina sure is a good cook." Jeff replied.

"When you get married, I'll bet you get fat. Then we'll call you, El Lobo Gordo," (fat wolf) said Wilson. "The Chief just called. He said to tell you that Seaborn was a little mixed up," Wilson continued. "What he was supposed to do was check to see if you had qualified with your .45, just in case there was any flap about the shooting. He took it on himself to do an investigation. He'll be lucky if he's not transferred to Louisiana. The Chief said your weapon would be back sometime this week. What are you carrying now?"

Jeff lifted his jacked. He had his Colt .45 single action resting in a 'Skeleton pattern shoulder holster.'

"Damn, that old thing belongs in a museum somewhere," Wilson stated. "Why do you carry that old gun, why don't you carry your issued .357?"

"Because this old thing, as you call it, shoots where I point it. If you are hit with a 255-grain slug, you're going down. As for the Smith, maybe one of these days the BP will issue semi-autos to carry," Jeff said.

"Don't hold your breath, said Wilson. You and I will be long gone before that happens."

"The doctor says it'll be about two more weeks before I can come back to work," Jeff told him.

"No hurry, it's been fairly quiet lately, Wilson said. By the way, the guys are having a little party at the catfish Inn Friday night. See if you can make it. It's just going to be us men and maybe the Chief."

"Okay, I'll see you there," said Jeff as he left to go home.

***

Alejandro and Pedro had placed fishing poles in the bed of the pickup so they were visible over the tailgate. They scouted out the roads leading to the Midway crossing. From one place they could see traffic on highway 83 and Pedro pointed out the location of Jeff's house.

"The man I was talking to in Camargo this morning told me that the Migra are having a party in Rio Grande Friday night. Most of them will be there, including El Lobo," Pedro told Alejandro.

"Very good Pedro, he stated. That may very well be his last party."

Just after sundown Friday night, a dark pickup driving without lights came to the river's edge. Two men were in the truck, but only the passenger got out. "You wait for me," he told the driver. He opened a fiddle case and removed the weapon inside, placing the case in the cab. He walked to the water's edge where a small boat was hidden. The boat made from two automobile hoods welded together rocked as he stepped in. He carefully poled the boat to the American side of the river and hid it under a large tree. He started walking north away from the river, moving slowly.

The party at the Catfish Inn was in full swing. Border Patrol Agents from McAllen were working in Rio Grande City so the local agents could have their party. They had just finished eating when Chief Johns rapped his glass for attention.

They quieted down to hear what he had to say. "Men, I want to take this opportunity to thank all of you for a job well done. This station has led the sector in apprehensions. You have caught more illegal aliens per man than any other station along the border. You have also seized more narcotics." Chief Johns then pulled a plaque from his briefcase and said. "Robert, you and Gene stand up."

"I want to present you both with this plaque in recognition of this station's outstanding achievement under your leadership. The men in the sector have named you guys, "The magnificent Seven," after the western movie."

Wilson and Hayden both thanked the Chief and sat back down. "I have another award to present," said the Chief. "Jeff, will you please come up here." Jeff stood and made his way slowly to the Chief. "Jeff, it gives me great pleasure to award you this plaque along with a check in the amount of five hundred dollars. This is for your outstanding work along the International Border. You have put in many long hard hours, including off-duty time, gathering information on alien and narcotics smuggling."

Chief Johns then read the inscription on the ten-inch by twelve-inch plaque. "Presented to Patrol Agent Jeff Larson, Rio Grande City, Texas, McAllen Sector. For your outstanding performance along the International Border and the apprehension of smugglers of illegal aliens and narcotics." The Chief then hands Jeff the plaque along with the check and shook his hand.

The agents all stood clapping their hands as Jeff made his way back to his chair. Two agents nearby slapped him on the back, which embarrassed him. He laid the plaque on the table near his plate. "Let me see that," said Ed Cook quickly grabbing it. The plaque was made of heavy wood with a bronze plate bolted to the wood. "Very nice," Cook stated. "You deserve it too."

All Jeff could stammer out was, "Thanks."

After another hour, Jeff made his way over to where the Chief and Wilson were sitting. "I hate to leave a good party, but I need my sleep," he told them.

"Glad you could make it," Wilson told him. "I know you have not fully recovered yet." Jeff shook both their hands and turned to leave.

"Hey Jeff," Cook said. "Don't forget this, someone might steal it. Jeff took the plaque and placed it in the small of his back under his jacket.

Jeff walked outside to his pickup and started home. His thoughts were of Josefina and how much he loved her. Maybe we should move the wedding date up, he thought as he pulled into his driveway. He turned off the engine and sat for a few minutes before opening the door. As he stepped out, he felt the plaque that was under his belt in back.

Damn, that thing is going to give me a backache, he thought as he shut the pickup door. He heard some gravel crunch behind him and alarm bells went off in his head. He moved to his left while turning, spinning on his left foot and drawing his weapon from under his jacket. He heard a load blast and felt a heavy blow to his back, and a deep burning pain in his chest. He was knocked against the truck as he completed his turn.

He could see a man standing several yards away in the faint light holding some kind of weapon. He slipped the hammer on his Colt single action twice before total darkness closed in and he slumped slowly to the ground.

※※※

While the party had been going on, Alejandro had been waiting at Jeff house. He began recalling the events leading up to this time and became angry again. He was becoming very impatient when he suddenly saw a flash of lights as a vehicle turned off the highway. He was hiding behind an above ground water cistern about twenty meters from the house. He watched as the pickup drove into the yard. The driver didn't get out, but sat still for a few minutes. This made him more impatient, but finally the driver opened the door.

Alejandro started toward the pickup. He had taken only two steps when his left foot slipped on some gravel making a noise. He saw the figure start to turn and fired the right barrel. He saw the man fall against the truck while still turning.

Flame stabbed at him and he felt a blow to his stomach, which doubled him over. He felt a tug on his jacket and a burning in his left arm. He managed to straighten up and fire the other barrel. The next thing he knew he was on the ground with grass in his mouth. He slowly regained his feet, but was unable to find the shotgun.

I've been hit, he thought. I have to get out of here. He could see the man lying near the truck in the faint light from the house. Alejandro stumbled out of the yard and started back to the river. He trotted about two hundred meters and fell again. He could feel wetness above his belt and using his handkerchief tried to plug the hole. I must get to the river, he kept repeating to himself.

He staggered across Hwy 83 almost getting hit by a pickup traveling west. He fell again in the plowed field north of the river and passed out. He came too and stumbled on toward the river.

※※※

The party was still going strong at the Catfish Inn, when the owner hurried over to Wilson and said, " Señor Wilson, the Port just called and said one of Señor Larson's neighbors reported gunfire at his house."

Wilson turned to the Chief, "Shit, let's go." As they both jumped to their feet, Wilson shouted. "Jeff's in trouble." The entire group of agents headed for the door, following the two running supervisors.

The two jumped into the Chief's unmarked Plymouth, leaving in a cloud of burning rubber. With red lights and siren going the car was doing over 120 MPH before they reached the city limits. As they approached the turnoff to Jeff's house Wilson said, "the guys are right behind." Chief Johns slid the big sedan through the turn and onto the dirt road with the engine screaming.

As they roared into the yard, they could see a figure slumped beside the pickup. "Oh damn, damn, damn," said Wilson as they skidded to a stop. Both men jumped out with guns drawn. The Chief kept the yard covered as Wilson knelt down by Jeff.

Suddenly the yard was full of vehicles as the rest of the BP Agents arrived. Wilson saw blood on Jeff's head and his jacket. "Get him in the car," the Chief said. "We can't wait for an ambulance."

"Hayden, secure the area," Wilson shouted as he picked up Jeff placing him in the back seat and crawled in beside him.

The high-powered Plymouth left the yard in a cloud of dust headed for the hospital thirty-five miles away in McAllen. Chief

Johns was on the radio to sector requesting that the hospital stand by for a gunshot victim.

Wilson was working on Jeff in the backseat. He tried to remove the pistol that was still clutched in Jeff's hand. He finally pried his fingers loose and pushed the weapon under the front seat. Pulling up Jeff's shirt he placed a bandaged on his chest. Chief Johns had the big sedan up to 140 MPH, as he blasted down the highway toward McAllen with red lights and siren.

Two hours later Hayden came into the hospital accompanied by Napo Garcia and Josefina. Wilson went to the crying, distraught girl and hugged her.

"He's still alive sweetheart, and they're working on him. I know he's going to make it," he told her.

"What did you find?" he asked Gene.

"It appears one person was waiting with a shotgun. We found it near the cistern with both barrels fired. We also found blood nearby and a set of tracks leading to the river. Whoever it is, he was losing blood. We found where he fell several times before he reached the river. I notified Comandante Morales, and Napo has his men looking too," Hayden stated.

Napo said, "If he's still in the area, we'll find him. Was Jeff able to talk?" he asked Wilson.

"No, he never regained consciousness on the way down here. He was having trouble breathing, but his pulse was strong. That reminds me, I'll be right back," Wilson replied as he left the room.

He returned in a few minutes with Jeff's old .45, the hammer on halfcock. "Take a look," he said. "Jeff got off two shots with this old thing."

"Damn," said Hayden as he took the old Colt. "We counted eleven holes in Jeff's truck." Just then one of the doctors came out and walked over to the Chief.

"How is he?" he asked the doctor.

"He's still critical, but I believe he'll pull through. We removed a lead pellet from his chest, which had collapsed one lung. Another from his shoulder and one cut a path along side his head. We also found this under his belt in the back." stated the doctor, as he handed over the plaque Jeff had received. It had three pellets imbedded in the wood.

"Would you look at that," said Wilson. "That's the first time one of these plaques came in handy. I saw Jeff stuff it under his jacket when he left the party.

Josefina asked the doctor, "Can I see him?"

"He's in intensive care, but you can go in. He's still out and there is a nurse with him," the doctor replied.

Josefina quickly left toward the intensive care unit.

"How in hell could he get off two shots and hit that bastard after he was shot?" Hayden asked.

"Pure adrenaline, nothing but pure adrenaline," said Wilson. "He told me the other day that this old gun shot where he pointed it, I guess he was right. I had to pry his fingers loose from it."

The Chief spoke up, "I'm calling region in the morning. We're going to seal this damn border off until this bastard is found."

Napo spoke up, "I'll assist on our side. I'll call the Governor of Tamaulipas tomorrow and see if we can get the military here. I'll also check with all of my informants."

"Good," replied the Chief. "Maybe that will flush him out."

CHAPTER 7

Alejandro had fallen several times on the way to the river. Once he fainted for a minute, but came to and continued on his way. I must get to the river he kept repeating to himself. He knew the Border Patrol would soon be on his trail, and if they found him they would shoot first and ask questions later. At least, I killed that damn migra, he thought.

He finally made it to the river and fell into the boat. After pushing away from the bank he was able to give a weak shout, which alerted Pedro. He was unable to pole and the current took the boat down stream. Pedro ran to the bank and jumped in the water. He quickly swam to the boat, grabbed the rope, and pulled it to the Mexican shore. He walked back upstream tugging the boat against the current until he was near the pickup.

He pulled the boat up on the bank and helped Alejandro out. He half carried him to the truck and eased him in the cab. Pedro removed an axe from the bed and walked back to the boat. He chopped a hole in the bottom and pushed it back into the current. He hurried back to the truck and departed the area.

***

Three of the BP agents were hot on Alejandro's trail. While one followed the tracks, another would run ahead fifty yards and cut for sign. When he found it, he would begin following the tracks, while one of the others would run ahead. The third one kept them covered, with a drawn weapon as they leap frog the trail to the river.

They were able to move the tracks to the river in less than twenty minutes. They found where the man had fallen and a blood spot on the ground where he had laid. They arrived shortly after Pedro had left, dust from the pickup could still be seen on the Mexican side.

Pedro drove as fast as he dared, as he didn't want to be stopped by any law enforcement. When he arrived at his house he helped Alejandro inside and put him to bed. Alejandro passed out again. His wife was still gone and he was alone with a wounded man who needed help. I must get word to Señor Cisneros at once, he thought.

There was a small camera on the dresser that had been left by one of Pedro's nieces. He picked it up and took several pictures of the unconscious Alejandro. I may have to prove he was alive when I brought him home, thought Pedro. He left the house and drove almost to China where he located a telephone and called one of Cesar's men.

He had just arrived back home when speeding suburban came into the yard. Three men jumped out, ran into the house, and placed Alejandro on a stretcher. They carried him out, placed him in the back of the vehicle, and departed in a cloud of dust.

Pedro began straightening up the room and while removing the bloodstained sheets heard a clunk on the floor. Looking down he saw Alejandro's pistol and picked it up. He placed it on the dresser behind the camera. He carried the sheets outside to be washed and made himself some coffee. He sat at the table wondering what would happen now as he drank the coffee.

It was the next day before Jeff finally opened his eyes. The first thing he saw was Josefina. He gave her a small smile and squeezed her hand. His eyes closed and his head dropped to one side. "Doctor," Josefina shouted.

The doctor came running into the room and checked Jeff's pulse. "Its okay, he's just sleeping, that's what he needs now. I believe he will be fine. You need to get some rest yourself."

Josefina shook her head, "I can't leave."

The doctor walked down the hall and motioned for one of the orderlies. "Go to my office and bring that big easy chair down here. I want that little lady to be as comfortable as possible."

US Federal Agents moved into the area and shut down all highways leading north. The various Ports of Entry received directives to perform full inspections on every vehicle coming into the country.

Napo had traveled to Miguel Aleman for a conference with Comandante Morales. They both placed calls, first to the Governor and then to Mexico City, trying to obtain more assistance from the military.

After Napo returned home, Carmen could see that he was still angry. It was obvious by the set of his mouth and jaw. He sat in the kitchen drinking coffee for several hours. It grew dark outside. He kissed Carmen, walked to his truck, and drove away.

Driving a short way out of town, he made his way to the home of Jesus Castillo. He parked and walked to the door. Jesus answered his knock and bid the policeman to enter.

"Don Napoleon, you honor my humble home. I have heard the news, where will it end my friend?"

"That is the reason I'm here," replied Napo. The two men drank coffee silently for several minutes, and then Napo said. " My friend, I need your help. I believe there is a stranger here, have you heard anything?"

Jesus thought for several minutes and replied. "There was someone here with Pedro Santos. He had blue-eyes and blond hair. Of course Pedro is from China, Nuevo Leon and many of the people from there are blond and blue-eyed. The two were together fishing when I saw them."

"What does Pedro look like?" asked Napo.

"He's about 60 or so years old with a large scar on his left jaw," Jesus replied.

"Thank you my friend, I am in your debt as always," Napo told him.

"Not at all," replied Jesus. "I pray that Señor Larson will recover soon and you will have many grandchildren."

Napo drove back into town and stopped at his cantina. He picked up one of the wooden chairs and placed it in the bed of his truck. He walked back inside and over to the cooler, where he removed several bottles of soda.

He slowly drove downtown and parked where he could observe two other cantinas. Both were where the rougher group of people hung out. Sitting there for over an hour, he saw Javier Gamboa, one of Carlos's henchmen, come out of the Cantina and walk down the street.

Napo drove up beside Javier and opened the passenger door of his truck. Javier looked up and turned pale. He saw Napo motion him into the truck with his Colt .38 super.

"What's wrong El Comandante?" he asked as he got into the front seat.

"Shut up," Napo replied. He drove several miles out of town until he found a small clearing next to a creek and parked. He had Javier get out and removed the chair from the bed of the truck. He made him sit down in the chair and bound his arms to the side with duct tape. He then taped both feet to the legs of the chair.

He tilted the chair against the tailgate of the pickup and tied it there with a small rope. When he was through Javier could struggle, but was unable to move. "I have some questions for you," he told Javier.

"I don't know anything," Javier cried.

"You don't know what I'm going to ask," Napo said. "I want to know who is the assassin that shot Gustavo and who is helping him? Where does he live?"

"I'm telling you, I don't know anything," Javier replied.

"We'll see," said Napo. He picked up one of the sodas, removed the cap, and placing his thumb over the top of the bottle shook it up. He grabbed Javier by his hair and tilted his head back, letting the soda squirt up his nose. Javier tried to breathe, but only succeeded in pulling more liquid down his throat.

When he was finally able to catch his breath, he coughed and puked at the side of the chair. "Who is he?" Napo asked again.

"Please Jefe," said Javier. "I don't know, I don't know." Again, Napo shook the bottle and squirted soda up Javier's nose. This time he let the bottle run out before releasing Javier's hair.

"I've heard of men drowning this way," he said.

When Javier was finally able to breathe, he watched with horror as Napo grabbed another bottle of soda. " Madre de Dios, Jefe, Please no, I'll tell you everything," he said.

"Okay, that's better, let's hear it," Napo told him.

"It was Pedro Santos, the uncle of Emilio Santos, who has been helping."

"Who is the assassin?" asked Napo.

"I don't know, I swear Jefe. It's somebody that Cesar Cisneros sent here."

"Who is Cisneros?" Napo asked him.

"He's the main man with the mota. The big supplier," Javier replied.

"Where does Pedro Santos live?" Napo asked Javier

"You take the dirt road south from Camargo that goes to Los Aldamas. When you reach Los Aldamas, take the dirt road to China. About ten kilometers before you get to China, there's a big wooden windmill on the right side of the road. The next road to the right goes to Santo's house. He lives just over the hill from the windmill," Javier stated.

Napo stood next to the bound man and thought about the information for several minutes. He looked down at the terrified Javier who was still breathing hard.

"You better be telling the truth," he said.

"I swear on my Mother's grave," replied Javier.

"You had better be worrying about your grave," said Napo, as he untied Javier. "Get in the truck," he told him. Javier was still coughing as they drove back into town. Napo stopped the truck at a street corner and let Javier out.

"I better not see you in Camargo ever again. You tell Carlos, if I see him or any of his people in my town, I will shoot them on sight. Do you understand me?"

"Si Comandante, I will tell him of your orders," Javier stated.

Napo pulled away from the corner and drove slowly out of town toward Los Aldamas. As he drove down the dirt road several jackrabbits ran along in his headlights. They twisted and dodged until they finally ran into the ditch, leaving little puffs of dust.

When Napo arrived at the wooden windmill the sun was just peaking over the brush to the east. He parked, removed a pair of binoculars, and started walking to the top of the low hill. When he was at the top he could see the house about three hundred meters to the west. There was smoke coming from the chimney and a black ford pickup was parked in the yard. He watched the house for over an hour and observed a man come out to feed his chickens.

When he went back inside, Napo left his hiding place and approached the house, keeping one of the sheds between them. He entered the house slowly with his weapon ready. He eased into the kitchen and saw a man with a scar on his jaw standing at the stove.

Pedro heard a slight noise and turned around. He saw Napo standing in the door with his pistol pointing at him. He turned pale, "what do you want?" he asked.

"I know you, I've seen you in Camargo and you know what I want. Where is he?"

"Where is who," Pedro asked.

With two steps Napo was in Pedro's face. He slammed his pistol against his head and Pedro fell to the floor groaning.

Napo pulled him back to his feet and again asked, "Where is he?"

"He's not here, they came for him Saturday," Pedro replied.

"That's better, now tell me his name," Napo commanded.

"I don't know, he never told me his name. I first met him in China and he did stay here, but I don't know who he is, but I do have a picture of him," Pedro replied.

"How did you get that?" asked Napo.

"I was afraid he was going to die and they would blame me. So I took several pictures of him while he was unconscious. He was shot in the stomach and he lost a lot of blood. I have the camera in the bedroom," Pedro continued.

"Let's see it, but don't try anything," Napo commanded.

Pedro walked into the bedroom followed by Napo. "It's here on the dresser," he told him. Napo could see the small camera sitting on the dresser, but didn't see the Luger 9mm behind it. Pedro reached for the camera with his left hand, while his right hidden from view, picked up the Luger. If I kill this policeman Cesar will pay well, he thought to himself.

Pedro turned and held out the camera to Napo. He quickly brought the Luger up, pushed down on the safety lever, and squeezed the trigger. The weapon did not fire! Pedro looked down at the weapon and pushed on the lever again. When he looked back up the last thing he saw was flame from Napo's weapon.

Napo had been taken by surprise by Pedro's actions, saw he was having trouble with the weapon and quickly fired twice. Both bullets hit Pedro in the chest, punching on through him and the thin wood boards of the wall. Blood covered his chest as he slid down the wall to the floor.

Napo checked Pedro's pulse, nothing. He picked up the Luger and saw what had saved him. Pedro had been trying to push the safety lever down and it was already down. If he had known more about Lugers he would have moved the lever up so it could be fired.

Napo placed the weapon under his belt, and picked up the two-fired hulls from his pistol, placing them in his pocket. He picked up the camera where Pedro had dropped it. Rolled back the exposed film, removed it, and replaced the camera on the dresser. He left the house and looked into the parked pickup. He could see blood on the seat. He returned to his parked vehicle and headed for home.

In the days following the shooting, Jeff continued to improve. He started to bitch about the agents assigned to guard him. "I can take care of myself, if you would return my pistol," he told Wilson.

"I wondered how long it would be before you got around to that," Wilson replied. He reached under his shirt, removed Jeff's Model 1911, and handed it over along with an extra magazine.

Josefina had finally allowed Wilson to register her at a local motel. It had been difficult to get her to leave Jeff. It had taken both Wilson and her Father to convince the young girl that she needed more rest. Wilson discreetly assigned an armed agent to watch over her when she was not at the hospital.

"What's been happening at the station?" Jeff asked Robert.

"It's been very quiet around Rio Grande, of course we have over a hundred agents patrolling the river. Napo's call to the Mexican Government resulted in a flood of military on all the roads leading to the border."

Napo who had been standing on the other side of Jeff spoke up. "No one has seen Carlos or any of his men." He had not told anyone about shooting Pedro Santos. "I do have some information on the man who shot you and Gustavo." Both Jeff and Wilson perked up. "It seems he was hired by a Cesar Cisneros who is a large supplier of narcotics. It looks like you hit him very hard and Cisneros sent someone to pick him up. Its not known if he is still alive. However, I may have a picture of him soon."

Neither Robert nor Jeff would ask Napo how he was going to obtain a picture of the man or where he got his information. There are some things you just don't want to know.

Napo looked at Jeff and asked, "What do you remember about that night?"

"Not a lot," Jeff said. "I remember getting out of my truck when I heard something behind me. Before I could turn something hit me in the back, and that's all I recall.

"You don't remember firing your old peacemaker?" Robert asked him.

"No, I sure don't. The next thing I remember is waking up in the hospital," Jeff replied.

"You got off two shots with that damned old antique, which I have locked up at the office. The guys found a sawed-off shotgun with blood on it near your cistern. You put some lead into him before you went down. That plaque you received stopped three double-aught buck shot from going into your back," Robert continued.

"I guess I was lucky," Jeff said.

"Yes, you were," Robert replied.

Just then Josefina entered the room and asked Jeff, "How are you feeling today?" Kissing him on the cheek.

"Like I want to go home and have you as my nurse," Jeff stated.

"When the doctors say its okay, I'll be your nurse," she replied as she carefully hugged him. Wilson and Napo could clearly see the love these two had for each other. Wilson turned away, so no one could see that his eyes were wet.

"When do I get out of here?" Jeff asked with his arm around Josefina.

"The Doctor told me that you could go home in a few more days. I've arranged for a lady from Rio Grande City to give Josefina a hand, mostly keeping you in bed," Wilson told him.

"Well, I'm ready to go right now," stated Jeff.

"You better take it easy. The doctors removed a buck shot pellet from your chest, and another one from your shoulder. It was touch and go there for awhile amigo," said Wilson.

"Where do you think Carlos is hiding?" Jeff asked Napo.

"I've heard that he has gone to the state of Guerrero, but no one knows for sure. None of his people have been seen in Camargo," Napo replied. He didn't tell Jeff or Robert that he had issued a shoot-on-sight order for Carlos or any of his men.

As the days passed, Jeff continued to improve. After fifteen days in the hospital he was allowed to go home with orders to limit his activities. The first thing he wanted to do was go outside. Josefina, backed up by Mrs. Alvarez, flatly refused to permit it. Wilson had returned his old Colt and Josefina finally allowed him to clean the old single action revolver.

He sat in his big easy chair with his cleaning kit on a small table. Josefina stayed nearby watching him take the old gun apart. "How old is that gun?" she finally asked.

"It was made in 1897," Jeff replied as he ran a cloth patch through the barrel. "It's a natural pointer, it shoots right where you point it. My Grandfather Jeremiah Larson purchased it new and carried it for years as a Texas Ranger." He put the Colt back together, checked the cylinder once again, and handed it to Josefina.

She took the large nickel-plated revolver in her small hand and asked, "Must you pull the hammer back each time you fire it?"

"That's right," Jeff answered. "That's why it's called a single action. With double action revolvers you just pull the trigger."

Josefina handed the Colt back to Jeff. He opened the loading gate and with the hammer on half cock, loaded five cartridges. He slowly let the hammer down on an empty chamber and placed it on the end table.

Josefina moved to his chair, and sitting on the arm, reached over and kissed him. "When will it all end?" she asked.

"Probably when Carlos is dead," Jeff replied as he held the girl in his arms and moved her into his lap.

"You be careful, if you tear out those stitches, I'll beat you," she told him.

"It'll be worth it and I'd like to move up our marriage date," he told her.

Josefina looked at Jeff and replied, "That's okay with me, I realize each time I'm with you may be our last. We can't change things that are in God's hand. We must trust in him, but be careful in our daily lives."

"How did you get so smart and so pretty?" Jeff asked.

"I'm not smart. I wouldn't be in love with a man that could die at any time, if I were very smart. I've watched my Mother suffer with the knowledge that my Father could be killed every time he leaves the house. But that didn't stop her from loving him."

"I know it's hard on you and believe me, I don't want to kill anybody," Jeff said. "But people like Carlos feed on the misery of others and they must be stopped. I try to be careful and I'll be more so now."

"Okay, enough," said Josefina as Jeff's hand reached up and cupped her breast.

"You're not strong enough for that."

"It would do wonders for my recovery," stated Jeff.

"It would put you back in the hospital," she replied as she stood up and straightened her clothes. "I'll fix you some soup, maybe that'll take your mind off some things. As for moving up our wedding date, I'm more than ready, just as soon as you can walk."

***

Alejandro had been rushed to a hospital in Monterrey where doctors were able to save him. When he was well enough to be moved, he was transported to one of Cesar's ranches. He had a team of nurse's around the clock and a doctor who came every third day. When he was finally out of danger, Cesar called him.

"How are you feeling?" he asked Alejandro.

"Like a damn fool for letting than damn gringo shoot me. At least he's dead."

"No, he's alive or so I'm told," Cesar replied. "He had some type of plaque under his jacket that stopped some of the pellets. He was in very serious condition for several days, but I'm told he'll recover."

"It's my fault, I should have shot the son-of-a-bitch from a couple of hundred meters like I did Gustavo."

"You'll get another chance," Cesar stated. "Right now you need to rest. The doctors gave you several transfusions as you lost a lot of blood. The bullet went in just over your belt buckle and out your back. It just missed the big artery. If it had been hit, you would have bled to death in a matter of minutes."

"The Americans have shut down the border near Camargo. I've moved some of my operations west to the Arizona area. Carlos is hiding like a rat and so are his people. The Comandante in Camargo issued a shoot-on-sight order. He needs to be taken care of too, but that can wait," Cesar stated.

"As soon as I'm well, I'll take care of him. What else has been going on?"

"Well, Pedro was found dead in his house near China. He had been shot twice, but nothing else is known. If you need anything, let the doctor know," Cesar told him.

"Thanks Jefe, I owe you my life," Alejandro replied.

***

Carlos had moved to the town of Tlapa in the state of Guerrero. He was staying at the house of one of his men, while he planned how to put his organization back together.

"If that damn Comandante thinks he can keep me out of Camargo, I'll show him who's the boss," he told Fernando. "Get two more people, we're returning to Camargo and I'm going to take Garcia out."

Two days later they arrived at Gustavo's old ranch. Carlos told his aunt to go visit her daughter for a few days. He had Fernando drive her there. When he returned with a bottle of liquor, they began to plan.

"We need someone the Comandante doesn't know," Carlos stated.

"We could use my little brother Ruben. He's about eighteen and is not known in Camargo," Fernando said.

"Okay, have him hang around Camargo like he's looking for work. He needs to see what Garcia drives and if he has a pattern of travel," Carlos told them. "Tell him to be careful and give him some money."

Several days later, Ruben returned to the ranch. "What did you find out?" Carlos asked.

"The Comandante leaves his house at different times and never goes the same way. But I did see him go to the police station every morning between 9:30 and 10. Sometimes he comes from the north and sometimes from the south, but he always parks in front of the office. When he comes from the south he parks against the traffic," Ruben told them.

"Good work," said Carlos. "Tomorrow we'll go to Camargo. We'll park down the street in one of the alleys and when Ruben sees Garcia drive up to the office, he'll give us a signal. We'll just drive around front and blast him to hell."

The next day Carlos was in the front seat with Fernando driving. He had Roberto and Luis in the back seat, all armed with semi-automatic pistols. They parked a block south of the police station in an alley. Ruben was standing at the entrance where he could see the office. He saw the Comandante drive past him toward the station and signaled Carlos.

"Let's go," Carlos commanded. Roberto and Luis both drew their weapons as the sedan turned out of the alley and toward the Police station.

Napo had just parked his pickup in front of the station, against traffic. When he stepped onto the sidewalk, he almost stepped on a discarded beer bottle. As he reached down to pick it up, Robert and Luis opened fire.

Napo heard the gunfire and the bullets striking his truck. He dropped behind the truck and rolled into the gutter, drawing his weapon. Under the truck he could see a stopped vehicle in the street, with empty brass falling around it. He saw the back door open and watched as a pair of feet approaching him.

He raised his Colt, and shot the man in the foot. The man fell, regained his footing, and lurched back toward the car. He fired twice more when he saw the wounded man trying to get back inside. One bullet hit the man in the leg.

One of Napo's officers was inside the station when the gunfire started. He ran out in time to see the man trying to get back into the vehicle. He could see Napo laying in the gutter firing his weapon. Pulling his sidearm, he too opened fire as more shots rang out from the sedan.

As both officers opened fire, Fernando stomped the gas pedal and tried to drive clear with the rear tires burning rubber. Roberto, who Napo had shot in the foot and leg, was not all the way inside as it sped down the street. Unable to hang on, he fell, rolling over several times then struggled to his feet. He watched as the sedan slid around a corner and then turned to face the two officers with his pistol in his hand.

Napo had walked into the street after reloading his weapon and shouted at Roberto to drop his weapon. He fired twice when Roberto raised his gun. Both rounds hit Roberto in the chest and he fell in the street. Napo slowly walked over to him and kicked the gun away.

His officer approached, "are you all right Jefe?" he asked.

"I'm fine, call the Federal Police, this one is dead," Napo told him. A crowd started to gather, but Napo told them to keep back.

CHAPTER 8

After Jeff was released from the hospital, he had one of his friends take his pickup to Miguel Aleman. The body shop patched the bullet holes, repainted the truck a dark green, and put in new upholstery. When it was returned, it looked like a new truck.

A few days after the shooting in Camargo, Napo came to visit Jeff. Mrs. Alvarez who had been helping Josefina with Jeff decided to go home for a few hours. Jeff could see that Napo wanted to talk so he asked Josefina to take his pickup into town for some groceries. She got the keys from the kitchen and drove off.

As soon as she was gone, Jeff asked Napo, "What's cooking?"

"I guess you heard about the shooting in Camargo," Napo replied.

"Yes, I heard they tried to shoot you at the police station."

"That's right. There is also some news from Miguel Aleman," Napo said. "It seems that Fernando met two of Comandante Morales's men in Mier. He made the mistake of going for his weapon. They shot him nine times before he could get it out from under his shirt. Carlos has disappeared again, along with Luis."

"How are you doing?" asked Jeff, who was very concerned about his friend and future father-in-law.

"I'm doing okay," Napo replied. "I have something you need to see." He reached into his jacket and removed several pictures. "This is the man who killed Gustavo and shot you," he stated as he handed them to Jeff. The pictures showed a man lying in a bed with closed eyes. Jeff studied the man's face, committing it to memory. He didn't ask where Napo had obtained the pictures.

"I talked to one of Carlos's men who told me about Pedro Santos. Pedro lived near China and he helped this man when he came here to kill Gustavo," Napo continued.

"Where does Pedro live?" not catching the past tense used by Napo.

"You take the road from Camargo that goes to Los Aldamas. Then from Aldamas take the dirt road to China. Just before you get to China there is a big wooden windmill on the right side of the road. Pedro's house is just over the hill and you take the next road to the right. This assassin was driving a black Ford pickup when he and Pedro scouted out the roads near Camargo."

"Maybe we should have a talk with Pedro," Jeff replied.

"That would not be possible," Napo said. Jeff didn't ask why, as he had a pretty good idea now that Pedro was no longer among the living.

"Do you think this guy will return?" Jeff asked.

"He may not be alive, Pedro said he was hit very hard, that's why he had the pictures."

"You need to be very careful Jefe, they may try for you again," Jeff stated.

"I'm not worried about Carlos, he never could do anything right. This man does worry me," Napo said as he held up the picture of Alejandro.

"Let me keep one of the pictures and I'll see if I can get him identified," Jeff said.

"I'd better get back to Camargo, I still have a lot of work to do. When you are well enough to travel, you and Josefina come to dinner."

"I believe I can travel a short distance now, how about this Sunday? I know Josefina would like to see her Mother, she misses you both," Jeff asked.

"Until Sunday then," Napo stated as he left the house and drove back to Camargo.

Jeff stretched out on the couch and fell asleep while waiting for Josefina's return. She drove into the yard, parked and seeing Jeff was sleeping put the groceries away. Later she walked into the living room where Jeff was still sleeping and sat watching him for a while. She was thinking of how much she loved this man as she stood up and removed her clothes.

She moved over to the couch and reaching inside Jeff's pajamas placed her hand on him. Jeff thought he was dreaming, as he became aware of her soft body. Josefina slowly lowered herself on top of him and he felt himself explode inside her. She kissed him, with her long brown hair covering his face.

Jeff and Josefina were sitting in the kitchen table drinking coffee when Mrs. Alvarez returned. She had them move into the living room while she fixed supper. Jeff had a very satisfied look and Josefina was glowing as they sat on the couch.

"Well, I guess we had better move up the wedding, if its okay with you," Jeff said.

"That would probably be very wise as I don't believe my Father would like for us to live together. I don't intend to be apart from you very much longer," Josefina replied.

"Okay, instead of a June wedding, what date would you like? Jeff asked her.

"Well, let's see," said Josefina as she picked up the calendar. "How would you feel about February 9th? It's on a Sunday."

"If I can wait that long," laughed Jeff as he reached for her. "Keep your hands to yourself," she stated and went into the kitchen to help Mrs. Alvarez.

On Sunday morning, in Jeff's pickup, Josefina drove across the international bridge with Jeff sitting beside her. When they pulled into the Mexican Customs all of the Officers wanted to talk to Jeff, naturally this took awhile. They finally were able to leave and drive on to Josefina's home where Carmen met them at the door.

"You look so thin, we need to feed you more," she told Jeff as she embraced him. "Dinner is ready, come sit down."

"He's starting to eat like a horse again Mother," Josefina stated.

Jeff slowly walked into the dinning room where Napo was waiting. The table was loaded down with food and Napo seated Carmen at the table. He saw Jeff pull out a chair for Josefina and noticed that she had a glow about her.

After finishing dinner, while lingering over coffee and fresh baked peach pie, Jeff turned to Napo and Carmen. "With your permission, Josefina and I want to be married on February 9th here in Camargo."

Carmen hugged her daughter, "I'm so happy for you mi Hija." Napo stood up, "this calls for something a little stronger than coffee. Is it okay for you to have a drink?"

Before Jeff could say anything, Josefina spoke up, "a small one Papa."

"I guess the boss has spoken," Jeff told Napo.

Napo removed a bottle of ten-year-old brandy. He poured it into four glasses, with Jeff getting the smaller portion. "May you both be as happy as Carmen and I, and may your lives be long and full of love."

Later, as Josefina and Jeff were driving back to Rio Grande, Jeff said, "I think you had better return home soon and let Mrs. Alvarez do the housework."

"You are tired of me so soon?" asked Josefina with a twinkle in her eye.

"You know that's not so. I just don't think I can keep my hands off you. A little taste of heaven and I want it all," Jeff replied.

"I know, said Josefina, I too have desires."

"Okay, I'll ask Wilson to drive you home tomorrow."

Later that night, the door to Jeff's bedroom slowly opened and Jeff could see Josefina in the soft moonlight. She was wearing a sheer white night gown as she walked in. She pulled the bed covers back, and slid in next to Jeff.

"Be quiet, Mrs. Alvarez is asleep," she whispered. I wanted one more night with you until the wedding," she told him. Jeff put his arm around her and pulled her close. Early in the morning hours, Josefina slipped quietly from the bed and returned to her room.

The next morning, Jeff called Wilson and asked if he would drive Josefina home to Camargo. "Of course, I'll be there about four."

True to his word, Wilson arrived and loaded Josefina along with her luggage into his pickup. Jeff kissed her goodbye and sadly watched Wilson's truck until it was out of sight.

After she was gone, Jeff moped around the house at loose ends. "Go for a short walk," Mrs. Alvarez told him. "It will do you good."

As Jeff pulled on some tennis shoes, he could hear her talking to herself in Spanish about two young people who thought they had put something over on her.

***

Three weeks had passed since Josefina had returned home and Jeff was walking a mile every day. He was returning from his walk when Wilson drove into the yard. "How are you feeling?" he asked Jeff.

"I'm doing fine," Jeff replied. "I'd like to get back to work, but the doctors won't release me. They say it's too soon."

"Come go with me, there are five illegals crossing just down the road. You can help me catch them," Wilson told him.

"Okay," said Jeff, "I'll be right back," as he went into the house. He came back out with his .45 single action in the waistband of his pants. Wilson just looked at the old gun and shook his head.

"I'm not going to say a damn thing," he stated.

They drove down Hwy 83 about a mile west of Jeff's house and parked by the side of the highway. "The trail they'll use crosses the highway about fifty yards west of here," Wilson said. Both officers crawled through the barbwire fence and walked west along it to the trail.

Jeff checked for tracks and said, "They haven't been by here. They may not have made it this far, or they're just waiting for dark to cross the road."

"You're right, lead the way, your eyesight is better than mine," Wilson replied. With Jeff in the lead the two officers walked south on the trail. After going about a half-mile, they suddenly entered a small clearing where the five men were sitting. The men jumped to their feet and started to run.

Jeff pulled his Colt from his pants, thumbed back the hammer, and fired a round into the air. "Parase ay." (stop right there) he hollered. Three of the men stopped like frozen statues. The other two continued running south along the bank of an arroyo. Jeff fired another round over their heads and the bullet cut a small limb off one of the trees. As it fluttered to the ground, one of the men shouted and fell into the arroyo.

Oh shit, thought Jeff, I hope that bullet didn't ricochet and hit him. He walked to the top of the bank and saw him getting to his feet. "What happened?" Jeff asked in Spanish.

"I thought you shot me," the man replied.

"Get your butt up here," Jeff commanded.

The alien climbed to the top of the arroyo as Wilson approached. Jeff asked, "what's your friends name?"

"He is Javier," the man replied.

"You call to Javier and tell him to come back." Jeff looked at Wilson and winked.

The man turned and yelled, "Javier, come back."

"Shit," said Jeff. "He couldn't hear you ten feet away." Jeff put the .45 Colt under the man's chin and said, "If he doesn't come back, I'm going to kill you."

"Javier! Javier! Come back," the man screamed at the top of his voice.

They heard Javier answer, it sounded like he was about two hundred yards away. In a few minutes Javier came walking back through the brush. "Okay, let's go," said Wilson, leading the way to the sedan. Jeff brought up the rear with his pistol still in his hand.

As they loaded the Mexicans into the sedan, Jeff was having a hard time trying to keep from laughing. He said, "That guy really thought I was going to kill him."

"You forget, they deal with the Mexican Federal Police, who "do" shoot when they run," Wilson replied.

"You are right, "La Ley de Fuga" (law of flight) said Jeff feeling guilty. " Let's stop before we get to the office and I'll buy some hamburgers." Jeff turned to the five in the back seat and asked in Spanish, "would you guys like something to eat?"

"Si Señor," they all replied. Wilson stopped at the Catfish Inn and Jeff went in for hamburgers and cokes. They drove on to the office where two agents were just coming on duty. They agreed to write up the aliens and transport them to the bridge.

In the following weeks Jeff continued to improve and extended his walks to two miles a day. Just before Christmas, he drove to McAllen and bought Josefina a beautiful necklace and a .38 Colt Detective Special. On Christmas day he drove to Camargo for dinner, where he gave Josefina her presents. Napo's house was full of friends who had been invited for dinner.

***

Alejandro was also recovering from his wounds. He had moved to a villa owned by Cesar near the town of Tuxpan just down the coast from Tampico. The doctors had removed several feet of his lower intestine. He walked hunched over like an old man, and his disposition had not improved.

Cesar called him and told him to return to Argentina when he was well enough. Cesar had admitted he made a mistake when he challenged the United States Federal Officers.

"Let's cut our losses and move on, Carlos is on his own. He will cross no more of my mota. I'm moving my operation west near El Paso," Cesar told him. Alejandro wanted to argue with Cesar, but was told to drop it. "Let someone else kill that damn gringo," Cesar told him.

Alejandro sat day after day brooding about the shooting. In his long career, he had never been wounded. Now this hijo de la puta (son-of-a-bitch) has shot me, not once but twice. I will kill this gallo (rooster, meaning someone who struts around) if it's the last thing I do. He called his contact in Tampico and ordered a bolt-action rifle with a telescope.

***

In late January, Jeff was at home when the telephone rang. He answered it and could hear someone breathing heavily. He kept saying, "hello, hello." He was almost ready to hang up when a weak voice said, "Jeff, I need help." He recognized Wilson's voice.

"What's wrong Jefe, where are you?" he asked. "Come and get me in Mier, I'll be on the square."

"I'll be right there." He ran outside, jumped into his pickup, and drove to Roma, where he crossed into Mexico. When he arrived in

Mier, he circled the town square several times, before finally spotting a figure laying on one of the benches. He ran over to it and found a badly beaten Wilson lying in his own blood. Wilson was barely able to walk to the truck with Jeff's help.

Jeff drove back to the States, crossing the border at the dam on Falcon Lake. Wilson had pulled his hat down and the Inspectors thought he was asleep or drunk. They knew Jeff, so just waved them through. After clearing the Port, Robert said, "take me to your house."

"I'm taking you to the hospital," Jeff said.

"No, do what I say, I'll explain later," Wilson stated.

When they arrived, Jeff almost had to carry Wilson inside. He helped him remove his shirt and got a pan of warm water. He gently started to remove the blood from Wilson's face. "What happened Robert?" he asked.

"It was that damn Carlos, I was in one of the bars and I thought I saw him outside the door. Like a damn fool I had left my gun in the car and was going out to get it. As soon as I stepped out the door two men jumped me. They beat the shit out of me and the whole time I could see Carlos standing by the wall laughing."

"You need to see a doctor, you may have some broken ribs."

"Just bandage me up and get the blood off me and I'll be all right," Wilson said.

After Jeff wrapped Robert's chest and cleaned off the blood, he drove him home. "Let me have your keys and I'll go get your vehicle."

"Okay, don't tell anybody about this," Wilson said as he handed Jeff his keys.

By daylight Jeff was back in Mier with a friend. They located Wilson's sedan parked on a side street and Jeff found Robert's pistol under the seat. Jeff drove the sedan while his friend followed him in the pickup. They parked the sedan at Wilson's house and Jeff carried the keys and pistol inside. He found Wilson sitting on the couch, looking a lot better.

Jeff handed Robert his pistol and keys. "What do you want me to do about this, should I call Morales?" he asked Wilson.

"No, let's just drop it for now. I should have been armed, I know better. Carlos will get his sooner or later, his kind always does," Wilson stated.

"Okay, you're the boss," Jeff replied. Jeff returned home after dropping off his friend. He made a pot of coffee and sat drinking it while thinking about Carlos and the yet unidentified assassin. I should go over to Mier and nose around for some information, but I need to get ready for the wedding.

***

About a week later, late one night a pickup drove down a dim trail to the riverbank, slightly upriver from Mier. There is a faint moon. As a dark figure emerges from the truck, the moonlight is reflected from an object carried by the person. He quickly removed his clothes, placed them over his head, and waded into the water. A startled owl on a nearby tree began its flight down-river with a soft hoot. The person wades from the river on the Mexico side, quickly dressed, and began walking briskly south.

He soon arrives near a small adobe house half hidden in a grove of trees about two miles from the river. The mysterious figure finds a hiding place and removes a small pair of binoculars. He studies the house and surrounding sheds in the early morning light. Just as the sun peeks over the mesquite, he observes a man leaving the house.

With the binoculars he was able to identify the individual as Luis, One of Carlos's henchmen. He watched Luis get into a vehicle and drive off. Turning the glasses back to the house, he can see smoke is rising from the chimney. He carefully studies the house for a few more minutes then wrapped a burlap bag around each foot. He ties them in place, gets to his feet, and walks toward the house. A shiny object is carried along side one leg.

He approached the house on the side where there are no windows. He walked softly to the rear door where he listens. He can hear someone moving around in the kitchen. He slowly opens the door and sees Carlos standing at the stove putting wood into it. Carlos heard a small noise and looked over his left shoulder to see the figure standing in the door. He can see the glare off the object carried by the person, but fails to understand what it is.

He freezes as his face goes white. "You!" he cried.

"Yes, me," said the figure. "You do remember me don't you?"

Carlos grabbed for the pistol in his pants. A tremendous blast knocked him over the stove, as he took both barrels of the shiny sawed-off shotgun carried by the figure at the door.

Gun smoke and dust swirl around the room as the figure breaks open the weapon. He removes the two empties and replaced them with two live rounds of double-aught buckshot. He slowly walked over to where Carlos lay crumpled, with the pistol still in his hand. The shotgun had almost blown him in half.

"Tell the devil I said hello, you dope dealing son-of-a-bitch," the figure said.

He took a last look at Carlos, left the house, and hurried back to the river. He quickly waded to the US side where he placed the shotgun behind the seat of his pickup got in and drove away.

Two days later in Camargo, Jeff stopped by the Police Station to visit Napo. Napo is just finishing a telephone call as Jeff walks into his office. "Como Está mi Jefe."

"I'm fine mi hijo, sit down," Napo replied. "That was Comandante Morales, he just told me that Luis came in and gave himself up."

"You're kidding, Jeff said.

"No, Luis told Morales that he and Carlos had been hiding out west of Mier. It seems that Carlos sent Luis into town to buy some groceries. When he returned, he found Carlos dead in the kitchen. Morales said it looked like Carlos had gone for his gun and had been shot at close range, by a shotgun. What is even more peculiar, Morales said they couldn't find any tracks. They found where Luis walked into the house and where he came running back out. Luis is scared almost out of his mind. He wouldn't get out of the vehicle, he just sit in it, shaking."

Both men sat in silence for a few minutes. Jeff finally asked, "What is Morales going to do about the shooting?"

"Not a lot, he believes someone just made things a lot easier for him. He said it could have been the same man that shot you, nothing has been heard about him."

"Well, I had better get my butt over to your house," Jeff replied. "Josefina wants to go over the wedding plans."

"I know, that is all she and her mother talk about," Napo said.

Jeff left the station and drove over to the Garcia's home. He walked up to the front door and gently rapped on it. Not waiting for it to open, he walked into the house. Josefina and Carmen were standing in the living room. Josefina had her wedding dress over her head with both arms in it. She was in frilly white panties and no bra, when Jeff walked in. Her golden skin contrasted with the white briefs and her melon-breasts stood out.

Josefina gave a squeal and bolted from the room. Carmen burst out laughing and Jeff turned a bright red. Carmen said, "at least you didn't see her in the wedding dress, that's bad luck."

When Josefina came back dressed, Jeff could only stammer and tried to apologize. She walked over and hit him on the arm. " Did you get an eye full?" she asked.

"I'm sorry, next time I'll wait at the door," he replied.

"Oh no, you won't," said Carmen. "This is your home now and I'm glad you're here. The Padre will be here in a little while and he wants to talk with both of you about the wedding. I'll make some coffee," she stated and went into the kitchen.

Jeff took Josefina in his arms, "you grow more beautiful each time I see you," he said.

"You're so full of it," said Josefina, but still gave him a kiss. Carmen returned with the coffee just as the Padre arrived. They talked for over two hours about the wedding, music, and other items that needed to be discussed.

When they were finally alone, he told her, "Your father just advised me that Carlos is dead. We won't have to worry about him anymore."

"I wish I could say I'm sorry, but I can't," Josefina replied. "I'll not be a hypocrite. All he's ever done is deal in misery and he caused his Uncle's death."

"You're right, let's forget him and remember you'll soon be Mrs.

Larson." Josefina moved closer and sat in Jeff's lap giving him a long kiss.

The next day when Jeff came to work, he noticed that Wilson seemed very quite. Jeff finished his paper work just as several of the other agents came into the office.

Ed Cook said, "Well look who's here, the Okie. I'll bet you rode a wagon to school," he teased.

"No I didn't, but my brother Jerry did ride his horse to school."

"I knew there would be horses involved in Oklahoma," Ed replied.

"One time my brother's friend, who was sweet on this girl, talked my brother into helping him," said Jeff. The agents all gathered around to hear the story.

"This friend wanted to get into the girl's room after she had gone to bed and she lived out in the country. Well, they rode their horses near the house and my brother was to stay with them about three hundred yards away. My bud tried to talk his friend out of doing this." He told him, "You're going to scare the shit out of her."

"No," his friend said, "When she sees it's me, she'll let me stay."

"Well, my brother is holding both horses and he can see when his friend slipped through the window, by the moonlight. Suddenly, there was this piercing scream from the house. The girl woke up, saw this figure in her room, and started screaming. Instead of going back out the window, he ran for the front door. My brother said he still would have been all right if he had kept his mouth shut. He said, every few feet he would holler, " Bring the horses."

"The girl's father came out the front door and let him have a load of birdshot right in the ass. My bud said he had to pick out the shot, which was just under the skin with his pocketknife. He then used whiskey to clean the wounds, as they didn't dare go see a doctor."

The agents were still laughing as Jeff left to go still watch.

CHAPTER 9

On February 8th Jeff is having a pachunga (an all-male party) at his house for all of his friends. Wilson was frying catfish and hush puppies. One of Napo's men was cooking a cow's head (meat is cut from the head and then cooked in a Dutch oven) over a mesquite fire. A tub of iced beer was at one side of the fire, and bottles of tequila, rum, and brandy were nearby on a long wooden board.

The yard was full of pickups, sedans, and even two horses ridden by two of the tick riders. (Tick Riders' are State of Texas employees hired to ride the river and turn back Mexican cattle) Napo had arranged for three musicians and their music could barley be heard over the talking and laughter.

The party was still going strong at midnight, when Jeff decided to call it a night. "One more drink," said Cook, who was feeling no pain.

"Come on guys. I have to be fresh in the morning. You don't want me to knock over the padre with my breath, do you?"

"You meant you don't want to knock over that beautiful gal," said Cook. "What she sees in you, I'll never know."

"My charm, good looks, and suave ways," Jeff replied.

"Yea right," replied Cook.

Jeff had one more drink and said, "You guys stay as long as you want, as I'm hitting the hay."

The next morning, Jeff was up by 7 o'clock, nervous as a whore in church. He endlessly paced the floor. Wilson arrived and said, "come on, I'm taking you to breakfast. That was one hell of a party last night," he continued. "Wish I could remember it all."

Over coffee, Wilson asked, "where did y'all decide to go for the honeymoon?"

"We're planning on driving down the coast to Vera Cruz and spend several days there," said Jeff. "I guess I'd better go home and get dressed. If I'm not at the Church two hours early, Josefina will think I've changed my mind."

"That little gal is the best thing that ever happened to you," Wilson replied.

By noon, a crowd had begun to form at the church. No one noticed a black ford pickup turning down one of the side streets. It pulled behind a flat roofed building under construction a block south of the church. There was a ladder against the back wall. The driver climbed the ladder with a long wrapped object. He disappeared behind a wall that was about eighteen inches above the flat roof.

He found a place on the roof, where he could see the entire front of the church. He then unwrapped the object to reveal a scoped rifle. There was a chimney nearby, where he could remain hidden, and still see the church. He loaded the rifle with five rounds, four in the magazine, one in the chamber.

Jeff arrived at the church dressed in a dark western cut suit with a black string tie. Everybody there greeted him and it was some time before he was able to enter the church. Napo was standing just inside the door dressed in a gray suit and looking very distinguished. He placed his arm around the nervous Jeff.

"Well, mi hijo, soon you will be my son."

"I'm so scared, I think I'm going to be sick," Jeff told him.

"You El Lobo Verde, scared?" asked Napo.

"Those aren't bells ringing, it's my knees knocking," said Jeff. Napo laughed aloud then turned when Carmen arrived. She hugged Jeff and smiled at Napo.

"Our daughter is so beautiful," she said.

"How could she be otherwise with you as her mother," replied Napo.

The music began and Napo left to escort Josefina. Jeff escorted Carmen down front and seated her with her father Cory O'Connor, who had arrived, from his ranch for the wedding. Jeff then took his place at the front and turned to watch for Josefina.

Napo and Josefina made their way down the aisle to the front of the church. She was dressed in a white lace-wedding gown. Her hair was piled on top of her head and held there with a silver comb that had been her grandmothers. A lace mantilla covered her head. She was so lovely that it took Jeff's breath away. How did I get so lucky, he thought as Josefina took her place beside him.

"Who gives this woman in marriage?" asked the priest.

"Her mother and I," replied Napo, and then took his seat next to Carmen and his father-in-law in the front row.

After the ceremony, Jeff and Josefina made their way slowly up the aisle, through the massive wooden doors and out to the front. The streets were full of people who couldn't get inside but still wanted to see the bride and groom. Someone had brought Jeff's pickup around to the front and parked it near the church.

As they headed toward the truck, the crowd surged forward. Napo stepped in front of Jeff and Josefina to clear a path to the pickup. A shot rang out and the bullet meant for Jeff hit Napo in the chest. He was knocked against Jeff, and all three fell to the sidewalk.

Even shot through the heart, Napo had managed to pull his Colt Combat Commander. He still had it in his hand, when another shot rang out hitting one of the people in the crowd.

Jeff had thrown his body over Josefina. He reached and grabbed the .38 Colt from Napo's dead hand. He caught a glimpse of a rifle barrel on top of a building with a head behind it. He jumped up to draw gunfire away from Josefina and fired twice at the figure down the street. Two of Napo's policemen saw what Jeff was firing at, and they too began shooting.

Jeff could hear Josefina screaming, as she cradled her father's body. Carmen was kneeling along side Napo crying. Jeff broke into a run toward the building. As he turned the corner into the alley, he saw a man jump into a black truck still carrying a rifle. As the man gunned the motor, Jeff raised Napo's pistol and started firing. He saw the rounds hit the top of the cab and realized he was shooting high.

He remembered that the .38 super shot flatter than his .45, and put the last round into the back of the cab directly behind the driver.

He watched as the truck slid around a corner then walked slowly back to the church. Napo's body had been carried inside where the priest was giving him last rites. Jeff went inside where Josefina and her mother were kneeling beside the body.

Josefina looked up and gave a loud cry, "Jeff, you're hurt!"

He looked down and saw the blood on his shirt. "It's not mine, it's your father's." He took both women in his arms, as tears rolled down his cheeks.

"Who could do such a thing?" asked Carmen.

"I think I know. He was shooting at me," Jeff replied. He remembered his conversation with Napo several weeks ago after Napo had given him the picture of the assassin. He could hear the words again as he looked at the cold body of his father-in-law. ("The assassin and Pedro were driving a black ford pickup.") He also remembered that Napo had told him where Pedro had lived.

Wilson, along with several Border Patrol Agents and the two Camargo Policemen entered the church. "Jeff, you and Mr. O'Connor take the ladies home, we'll see to Napo."

When he had Josefina and Carmen in the house with Cory and several of the neighbors helping, he told Josefina, "I have to go."

"Oh no, please Jeffie, don't leave me now," she begged.

"I'm sorry sweetheart, there is something very urgent I must do."

Jeff went into Napo's home office and found another magazine for the .38 Colt along with a box of cartridges. He entered his pickup and retrieved his .45 from under the seat. As he drove south out of town, he thought of all the good times he had spent with Napo fishing, telling stories, and drinking beer. Tears ran down his face and his anger grew with each passing mile. The window was down and the air was ruffling his hair. He picked up a ball cap and placed it on his head.

In less that an hour Jeff had found the wooden windmill. He parked his pickup next to it and stepped out. He placed the Colt .45, in his waistband. He had reloaded Napo's Colt, which he stuck it on the left side with the butt forward. He began walking around the low hill, until he could see Pedro's house.

***

Alejandro had placed the crosshairs of the scope on Jeff as he came out of the church. His view was restricted, as he had closed his left eye to aim. He did not see Napo suddenly step in front of Jeff as he squeezed the trigger. He looked up as they all fell and at first thought he had hit Jeff, but decided to put another bullet into his body. The crowd was milling around in a panic and his second shot hit a bystander.

He again looked over the scope and saw Jeff grab Napo's pistol as he worked the bolt to eject the fired case. A bullet went by his head like an angry bee and chips of the chimney peppered him in the face. He saw two of Camargo's Policemen firing at him from the sidewalk.

Shit, It's time to leave, he thought and scrambled down the ladder to the pickup. As he sped down the alley he heard bullets hitting the top of the cab and ducked down as low as he could. With his foot all the way to the floor and motor screaming, he was starting to make a turn out of the alley when he felt a burning on his right shoulder. He looked back and was in the clear, but blood was running down his arm. He placed his handkerchief under his shirt and on top of the wound.

When he arrived at Pedro's house, he ran in and grabbed his bag. He removed a clean shirt and threw the rest of his crap into the bag. He slowly removed the bloody shirt, and heated water to wash the shallow wound. He then used a first aid kit and bandaged it as best he could, then changed into the clean shirt.

While he was heating more water for coffee he carried his bag to the pickup and placed it inside. He kept the rifle in his hand until he got back inside then placed it near the front door.

His 9mm Browning Hi-power was in his waistband. He carefully looked around the house to make sure he was not leaving anything that could identify him. He poured himself a cup of the hot coffee and glanced at his watch. He had been here a little over thirty minutes, its time to leave.

Jeff could see the house from the side of the low hill and the black pickup parked in the yard. It was too far away to see any bullet holes, but it looked like the same one. There was an arroyo that ran from the hill to the back of one of the sheds. Jeff crawled into it and started toward the house. When he emerged from the arroyo, he walked softly to the wall of the house and listened. He drew his Colt, removed the safety, and slowly moved to the front of the house.

Just as he eased around the corner, Alejandro stepped out. Not seeing Jeff he started for his pickup with the rifle in his right hand. He was within a couple of feet of the vehicle when he heard Jeff's voice.

"Hold it right there, you son-of-a-bitch," Jeff commanded.

Alejandro froze in his tracks and slowly turned, he saw Jeff standing near the corner of the house about twenty feet away.

"Drop that rifle," Jeff told him.

Alejandro stood still for a few seconds then threw the rifle toward the front of the pickup. When he pitched it, he knew Jeff's eyes would be drawn to the weapon briefly. "Hijo de la Puta," he screamed as he drew his 9mm. He was bringing it up, when he was knocked hard against the truck. He fired and saw dirt kick up in front of Jeff. Another blow hit his left side. He grabbed the truck to steady himself and began firing at the hated gringo.

As Alejandro threw the rifle Jeff's eyes had watched it hit the ground. However his peripheral vision caught Alejandro going for his pistol and he squeezed the trigger on the .45. He thought no draw could beat one already in the hand you bastard. As he shot into Alejandro, he saw him fire, and shot him again.

He saw the assassin knocked back against the truck. Saw him steady himself and fire again. Jeff felt a blow on his left leg and fell to the ground. He rolled as more bullets hit, where he had just been. He drew the .38 Colt with his left hand and from a prone position with both pistols extended, began firing.

He saw the bullets hitting Alejandro and screamed, "This is for Napo you cock sucker." He continued to fire until both autos were empty and the slides locked open. He watched as Alejandro slowly slid down the side of the truck covered with blood. The 9mm fell from his hand into the dirt.

Jeff lay his head down in the dirt for a minute, then rolled over and slowly got to his feet. He slammed a fresh magazine in the .45, released the slide, and returned it to his waistband. He also reloaded the .38. With Napo's pistol in his left hand, he hobbled over to Alejandro and kicked his weapon away. He could see Alejandro still twitching beside the truck. He pulled his cap off his head, using it for a shield from the blood; he shot Alejandro in the head.

"Let's see you recover from that, asshole."

Jeff looked down at his left leg and could see blood where one of the bullets had gone through. He tied his handkerchief around his leg to stop the bleeding and headed back to his pickup.

He drove back to Camargo and stopped at a house located at the edge of town. He knocked on the door and Dr. Kesler appeared. "Hello Jeff," he said, then saw the blood on his leg. "You're hurt, come in to the office." He quickly escorted Jeff to his small office and began cleaning the wound. The bullet had penetrated the muscle in the upper thigh, but didn't hit the bone.

"It looks pretty fair," the Doctor said, as he bandaged it. "But we'll have to watch for infection. Tell me if you can, is the man who murdered Napo dead?"

"Yes Doctor, he is now," Jeff replied.

"Bien, bien, do you have any clean clothes?"

"Yes Sir, in my pickup," Jeff stated.

"I'll get them and you can wash up in here," replied Dr. Kesler.

Jeff removed the dirt as best as he could, and put on clean clothes from his bag. Dr. Kesler placed his bloody trousers in a paper bag. "I'll dispose of these in my burn barrel," he stated.

"Thanks Doc, how much do I owe you?"

"If I had done anything, you would owe me money, but since this was just a visit to talk about Napo's death, you owe me nothing," the Doctor stated.

"Thanks Doc, I'll always be in your debt," Jeff replied.

When he arrived back at the Garcia's, Josefina her eyes red from crying, threw herself into his arms. "Jeff, where have you been? I've been worried sick," she told him.

"I'm very sorry mi querida, but this was necessary," he told her. He held his beautiful new bride of only a few hours in his arms. She began crying again as Carmen came in from the kitchen. She went to Jeff who pulled her to him and all three broke down again.

Carmen regaining her composure wiped her eyes. " Jeff, where have you been? They have moved Napo to the funeral home in Miguel Aleman."

Jeff looked at his Mother-in-law and said, "The bastard that killed Napo is dead." Both Josefina and Carmen could see the horrendous pain and torment in Jeff's eyes.

"Are you okay?" asked Carmen.

"I will be, but I need to call Commandante Morales in Miguel Aleman."

"Use Napo's office," Carmen told him.

"I also need to return this," said Jeff as he handed the Colt .38 to Carmen. She took the weapon, looked at it, and with tears in her eyes handed it back to Jeff.

"No, Napo would have wanted you to have it. You were like a son to him, he loved you so very much."

Jeff looked at the satin nickel Colt, with the Mexican eagle and snake carved into the ivory grips. "Thanks Carmen," was all he could say to her. He released Josefina and walked into Napo's Office. He dialed the Customs office in Miguel Aleman and asked to speak to Morales.

When the Comandante came on he asked, "How are you my friend? I've heard the news about Napo and have dispatched several men to Camargo to help with the search."

"There is no need for a search. You'll find the man near China at the house of Pedro Santos."

"Is the cabron dead?" asked Morales.

"He is now. I'll wait here if you need to take me in," Jeff told him.

"No, I'll take care of it, you are not to worry. Tell Señora Garcia that I'll be by later to pay my respects."

"Thanks amigo," Jeff told him.

"Por nada," said Morales.

He returned to the living room to find Wilson standing there. "Where in hell did you go?" he asked Jeff.

"You're better off not knowing boss," Jeff told him.

Wilson motioned Jeff to follow him outside where the two women couldn't hear. "Okay, now I want to know, is that bastard dead?" he asked Jeff.

"Yes, said Jeff, but don't ask me anymore."

"Okay, okay, you had us worried sick. We thought we would be burying you along with Napo. That little girl almost went crazy, you should have taken some help."

"I know, but this was something I had to do on my own," Jeff told him.

"I understand," replied Wilson. "Still, you have friends. You know there is not a man in the office that wouldn't follow you to hell with a bucket of water."

"I know, but I didn't want anyone else involved, this was personal," Jeff replied.

Just then Chief Johns drove up. "How are you Jeff, Robert?" he asked.

"Fine Chief," said Wilson. "Is Mrs. Garcia available for visitors?" asked Johns.

"I believe so," said Jeff. " Come on in," and held open the door.

Chief Johns entered the living room with his hat in his hand. He walked to where Carmen was sitting and took her hand in his. "Señora Garcia, I'm so sorry for your loss."

"Thank you for coming Señor Johns," she replied.

"Is there anything you need or we can do for you?" he asked her.

"No, I just can't believe that Napo is gone. It feels like a bad dream."

"I hope they catch the man who did this," Johns told her.

Carmen started to say something, and then looked at Jeff, who shook his head. "I hope they will," she replied.

"Robert, could I have a word with you outside?" asked Johns. "Again, Señora Garcia please accept my condolences, Napo was respected by everyone who knew him." Wilson and Johns then made their way outside.

"Is there anything we can do for this family? Do you know when the funeral will be?" asked Johns.

"I don't believe so at this time. The funeral will probably be here at the church on Wednesday," Wilson told him.

"Well, let me know if anything changes," Johns said. He then drove off headed back to McAllen.

Wilson walked back into the house and went to where Carmen was sitting. "If there is anything you need, please let me know. I thought of Napo as a brother," he told her.

"I know, he thought the same way about you," Carmen stated as she stood up and hugged Robert.

"Please call if you need anything," he told her and left the room.

Jeff and Josefina stayed with Carmen, all plans for a honeymoon were forgotten for now. They were finally able to put Carmen to bed, then went to Josefina's room. They both undressed for bed, where Josefina finally saw that Jeff had been wounded. She insisted on changing the dressing and then he held her until she cried herself to sleep.

Tuesday the Mexican newspapers fully covered the murder of Napo. A side bar expounded on Mexican Customs finding the killer and his death while resisting arrest near China, Nuevo Leon. Comandante Morales was quoted in the paper. "This person was a paid assassin who tried to shoot one of my men." Nothing was said about how he found him or where the information came from.

On Wednesday, the day of Napo's funeral, it was bright and calm. There was a huge crowd in the streets and the church was full. The Governor of Tamaulipas was present, along with his bodyguards. A Mexican military honor guard was present and came to attention when Napo's casket arrived.

Six Federal Judicial Police carried Napo's body into the Church where two more soldiers flanked the flag-draped casket. Napo had been a Captain in the Mexican army, and had served twenty years with the Federal Judicial Police.

Jeff, Josefina, and Carmen, along with her father Cory O'Connor arrived on foot. They entered the Church under heavy guard by both

Federal Judicial Police and U.S. Border Patrol Agents. Jeff and Cory escorted the two women, their heads covered by lace veils, to the front. As Jeff walked down the isle, Wilson noticed there was a bulge under his coat and he had a slight limp. Wilson made his way down front and was invited to sit with the family. The eulogy was read by the Presidente of the Municipal (Mayor of Camargo).

Mayor Armando Cortez spoke of Napo's service to his country and of his many years as an officer with the Federal Judicial Police. Tears rolled down the Mayor's cheeks, as he recanted the years Napo had served as the Comandante of Camargo and his devoted service to the community.

When the service was over, Carmen, Josefina, Jeff, and Cory were left alone with the Priest and closed casket for several minutes. Finally Jeff and Cory escorted the two women from the Church, where a horse drawn military caisson was waiting. Six FJP agents carried out the flag draped casket. The soldiers came to attention, as it was placed on the caisson.

Six of the soldiers along with their sergeant formed in front. Another singular soldier carried the Mexican flag. Six more soldiers flanked the casket with two behind carrying Napo's Army unit flag along with the flag of the FJP. The six FJP agents walked behind with the family following.

Most of the town of Camargo brought up the rear as they walked the half-mile to the cemetery. The bright sun danced off the gleaming helmets of the honor guard. The crowd was deadly quiet as the procession made its way out of town to the soft beat of drums.

When they arrived at Napo's final resting place, seven soldiers and their sergeant marched to one side and formed to give a salute. After the priest had talked for a few minutes, the honor guard removed the flag from Napo's casket, folded it, and presented to their Captain. The Captain marched proudly over to Carmen, saluted her, and presented her with the flag. She clutched it to her breast and began to cry.

The order was given and seven rifles were pointed to the sky. When the first volley was fired, Jeff jerked and then held Josefina as she began to cry. Two more volleys crashed into the bright still sky.

Almost the entire town filed past to pay their last respects to their Chief of Police and his family. A group of children from the Camargo School approached Carmen and presented her with a bouquet of flowers. Carmen hugged each one, as tears streamed down her cheeks. One little girl handed Jeff and Josefina each a single rose. A few more tears rolled down his face as he thanked her.

When they finally arrived back at the Garcia's home, they discovered that neighbors had filled their kitchen with food. The back patio was full of people, talking in soft tones. Border Patrol Agents in dress uniform mingled with Federal Judicial Police.

Carmen escorted by her father, followed by Jeff and Josefina finally came out of the house. Jeff called for attention.

"Señora Garcia has something she would like to say to everybody here," Jeff told them.

A hush fell over the crowd and hats were quickly removed as everybody turned to Carmen and her father.

"I wish to thank each of you for your kindness and prayers. I don't want any more sadness here today. Napo is gone and he is now with God. Please eat and tell stories of Napo. He will always be alive in our memories, Mi casa es tu casa," she told them.

Josefina and her mother went back inside. Jeff and Cory made their way to an outside table loaded with food. He and Cory began handing out plates. Every person that passed by reached over and shook Jeff's hand or touched him in one way or another.

CHAPTER 10

On Friday, Carmen entered the kitchen where Jeff and Josefina were having breakfast. She sat down with them with her coffee.

" I want to talk to you of my plans."

Josefina reached out and took her mother's hand. "Mama, Jeff and I want you to live with us," she said.

"No, mi hija, I have decided to go back home with your grandfather. Since your grandmother's death five years ago, he has been very lonely. He needs me to help him run his hacienda. You two have your own lives to live, you don't need a third person right now. I want you to continue your honeymoon. You must put this behind you. It's what I want, and it's what your father would have insisted on. He had a good life, he was very proud of you, mi hija, and of you Jeff. He already thought of you as his son. He wouldn't want to be the cause of continued sadness and grief."

Just then Cory O'Connor entered the kitchen and poured himself a cup of coffee.

"Have you told them?" he asked.

"Yes Papa, I want them to go on their honeymoon," Carmen replied.

"Yes, I believe this is what Napo would have wanted," said Cory. "I have a wedding present for the two of you," he said and handed over a large envelope to Josefina.

(Cory O'Connor was a slim Irish man in his late sixties. He had married into the Mexican aristocracy and now owned several ranches, one near the town of Sierra Mojada. This ranch consisted of over four hundred square miles and was adjacent to the border of the States of Coahuila and Chihuahua.)

Josefina opened the envelope, took out several sheets of paper and a check, as Jeff looked over her shoulder. It was a deed to a ranch of over thirteen thousand hectareas. It was called "Rancho Las Palmas" and was near the town of Alicante, Coahuila, Mexico. The deed was in the name of Josefina Mercedes Garcia de Larson, along with a check for 150 thousand pesos. Jeff doing some quick figuring in his head suddenly realized that his bride was the owner of over fifty square miles of ranchland with a check for approximately $ 16,000.00 dollars.

"Abuelo mio, what is this?" she asked her grandfather.

"It's a little ranch I want you and Jeff to have. You don't need to live there now. I have an excellent majordomo (foreman) running it. But when you want it or you want to visit, it's yours," said Cory. Josefina went to her grandfather and hugged him with tears in her eyes.

"I want you and Jeff to be happy. The check is for your honeymoon. The ranch will be there anytime you want it."

Jeff stood up and grabbed Cory's hand. Cory hugged both of the young people to him. Jeff was stunned; he just realized that his new bride was a very wealthy young woman.

The following Monday, Josefina and Jeff packed his old pickup. She hugged her mother, grandfather one last time and they departed. They drove back to Jeff's house to pick up a few things and then drove east on Hwy 83. They drove to McAllen and crossed into Mexico at Reynosa and on to highway 97, south to highway 180 and followed 180 through Tampico and on to Vera Cruz. They checked into a beachfront hotel and ordered supper in their room.

The next day Josefina deposited her check and made arrangements to write checks for local purchases. Afterward they shopped for a while, returning to the hotel to swim. Josefina went into the bathroom and came out in her new bathing suit. Jeff's mouth fell open as she entered the room. The white one-piece suit, against her golden skin, and her long, light brown hair left him speechless.

"Where the hell is my gun, I'll have to fight every SOB that sees you," he told her.

"You like it?" she asked.

"What's not to like and I sure like what's in it," replied Jeff as he reached for her.

"Not now, let's swim first," she said.

"I'd better stay out of the water with this leg wound, but I'll watch you," Jeff replied. After Josefina swam for an hour, they returned to their room and made love for the rest of the evening.

The next few days they spent, walking the beach, shopping in town or making love in their room. Josefina turned golden with each day in the sun. Jeff was starting to acquire a nice tan. The two bullet wounds in his back had completely healed, but the one on his leg was still white.

A week of lying in the sun, and he started to get a faraway look in his eye. She could tell he was thinking of work or the murder of her father. He had told her that he blamed himself for Napo's death. Josefina had scolded him and told him he wasn't to blame. Finally she asked, "Do you want to go visit our ranch?"

"That's a wonderful idea, let's go," he told her. "We'll also visit your mom and grandfather."

They checked out and drove northwest to Ciudad Victoria. They spent the night in one of the old hotels downtown. Jeff was happy with the beautiful Josefina by his side. His old pickup didn't have an air conditioner, so they would stop every hundred miles or so. They would find a store or cantina for sodas or a beer. Josefina wore white shorts, halter-top, and sandals. Her long golden legs and bare midriff caused a stir in every place they went. A crowd of men and boys usually followed them to the truck to wave goodbye.

They left Ciudad Victoria and went to Monclova, Coahuila, Mexico where they again spent the night. The next day Josefina dressed in a long peasant skirt and red blouse. Jeff was disappointed and asked, "no shorts today?"

"No silly, we'll arrive at Abuelo's ranch tonight. He is still very old fashioned," Josefina replied. "We'll take highway 30 south to Sacramento and then we turn northwest to the town of Oso and Ocampo. From there we'll take a dirt road to Ranch Alegre."

They traveled through several small villages and Josefina pointed out the dirt road that led toward the ranch. After several miles they came to a turnoff with a large gate that extended over it. Burned into the wood were the name El Rancho Alegre and the brand of Cory O'Connor, a C slash O.

After driving for several miles they observed two riders on a nearby hill, watching them. Finally, they saw the sprawling ranch house in a grove of trees. When they drove into the front yard Carmen and Cory was waiting for them.

Jeff told Josefina, "those riders we saw must have some way of communicating with the ranch headquarters."

Josefina jumped out of the truck and ran to her mother who hugged her. Her grandfather walked over to the pickup as Jeff was getting out. "Welcome to El Rancho Alegre," he said as he hugged the young man.

Josefina came over and kissed her grandfather, "how are you Abuelo?" she asked.

"I'm fine mi nieta," (Granddaughter) he replied. "I'm so glad that you both have come. Come in, come in," he said and directed two servants to bring in their bags. After they had gone to their rooms and unpacked, they returned to the huge den, where Cory and Carmen were waiting.

"A meal is being prepared, how about a before dinner drink," Cory asked.

"That would be very nice," they both agreed. Cory poured the brandy and passed around the glasses.

"To my granddaughter and my grandson, you both look very happy," he toasted.

"We are Abuela," Josefina said as she hugged Jeff. "Vera Cruz was so beautiful, but so is Rancho Alegre. I remember many happy summers that I spent here and how Tio Arturo (Uncle Arturo) taught me to ride. Where is he?" she asked.

Cory burst out laughing. "He is the majordomo of your ranch," he replied.

Jeff spoke up asking, "Do your riders have a way of contacting you?"

Cory laughed aloud again replying, "yes, they each carry small walkie-talkies in their saddlebags. We have a relay tower and a man who monitors the radio. We knew when you had entered the ranch. You have sharp eyes mi nieto." (nieto; grandson, nieta; granddaughter)

One of the servants came in and announced that the meal was ready. Cory took Josefina's arm as Jeff took Carmen's and they entered the formal dinning room. When they were seated, the servants began serving.

Cory turned to Jeff and asked, "What are your plans?"

"Well sir, Josefina has decided that she wants to see her ranch," Jeff replied.

"Good, I'll radio Ranch Las Palmas and inform Arturo that the new owners are coming. I hope you will stay here for awhile, as your mother has missed you very much mi nieta," Cory stated.

Tears came to the young bride's eyes as she turned to her mother. "Oh Mama, I have missed you and Papa so much."

"Just remember mi hija, we are not that far from you," Carmen told her and wiped away her tears. "And your father still watches over you."

Jeff spoke up, "I have been thinking of transferring farther west to New Mexico. If I do, we will be closer or it will be a lot easier to travel here."

With the meal over, they sat out on the wide veranda. One of Cory's vaqueros walked up with his sombrero in his hand. "Perdone me Patron, may I have a word with you?"

"Certainly," said Cory and walked over to where the vaquero stood. A few minutes of low conversation and Cory returned to his seat with a smile on his face. When Josefina asked him what was going on, he replied, "wait and see. You and Jeff are in for a treat."

Around the corner of the hacienda came the families that lived on Rancho Alegre. Several of the vaqueros were on horseback and rode out on the large green lawn. One rode to one side and spurred his horse into a full run. When he came by he slid off to one side and all that could be seen was his hand holding the saddle horn. Another came by with his horse at full speed and placed his head in the saddle, with his feet sticking straight up. Another was twirling a rope around both himself and his horse as he raced by. Josefina was delighted and loudly cheered each one.

The vaqueros and their families came up to the veranda, where one of the women gave Josefina a beautiful embroidered shawl. The vaqueros gave Jeff a pair of spurs with the brand of Rancho Las Palmas worked in silver on the sides. The brand was a J lying on its side with a bar under it. Tears came to his eyes as he accepted the gift.

He showed the spurs to Josefina. "Your brand is the Lazy J Bar," he told her.

"No silly, our brand is the Lazy J bar," she corrected.

They spent several more days with her mother and grandfather before Jeff became restless again. Josefina was also anxious to see her ranch, so they packed their bags.

Saying their good-byes after getting directions to the ranch, they drove north to the town of Alicante. They were still several miles from town when they found the gate to the ranch. It too had a large arch over the ranch road with the name of the ranch and brand burnt into the wood.

They drove along the ranch road for several miles. Finally they could see the ranch house and out buildings surrounded by palm trees next to a low cliff. They saw several people waiting for them in the yard.

The first one was Arturo Mora. "Tio Arturo," cried Josefina as she jumped from the truck and flew into his arms, kissing his leathery cheeks.

"Mi hija, mi hija," he said as he hugged the girl to him and swung her off her feet. Jeff stepped down from the truck and Josefina pulled Arturo over to him.

"Tio, I want you to meet my husband, Jeff Larson. Jeff this is my Uncle Arturo."

(Arturo Mora was a stocky man in his early fifties. He had been in love with Josefina's mother for years, but had never spoken of his feelings. He had worked for Cory O'Connor for over thirty-five years and thought of Josefina as his daughter even though they were not related.)

Arturo looked at the young man Josefina had married and liked what he saw. He saw the steel behind brown eyes that was also taking his measure. As he shook Jeff's hand, he said, "I'm very glad to meet you."

Still holding Josefina he said, "your home is ready mi hija." He motioned to the hands to carry the bags inside.

When they entered the living room Josefina said, "it's so beautiful Tio."

"When you are ready and rested from your trip, I'll show you the ranch," Arturo told them. Josefina and Jeff walked through the house and into the master bedroom.

"Will you look at this," Jeff told Josefina as he opened the door to the bathroom. There was a large sunken tub trimmed in Mexican tile that over looked a small private patio.

"It is just so gorgeous," she explained

"Not as gorgeous as you," he told her as he took her in his arms. After a long kiss, he carried her over to the large bed and laid her down on it. He then started to remove his clothes.

An hour later when they walked outside, they found Arturo waiting for them. They walked around the outbuildings and looked at some of the cattle. "If you'll permit me, I would like to arrange a fiesta in your honor."

"Of course Uncle, whatever you want to do," Josefina replied. " This place is so peaceful, I never want to leave. I wish we could just stay here forever."

The next morning about 10am, they came outside and found Arturo waiting for them. "Please come this way," he requested. He led the way into the large back yard surrounded by palm trees and flowers. All of the ranch vaqueros and their families were present. The children were playing games and having fun.

There was a steer being slowly roasted on a spit over an open pit. A tub of iced Mexican beer, with several bottles of wine, brandy, and tequila were to one side on a large table. Arturo took Josefina and Jeff to each person and introduced them.

About 2 o'clock the cook announced that the meat as ready. Josefina said, "please, let's eat, I'm starved." Arturo led the way over to the main table where he seated Josefina at the head. Jeff took his seat beside her. After Jeff had stuffed himself on the food and Josefina had learned all of the children's names, Arturo rapped on his glass for attention.

Everybody stopped talking, "I have a wedding present for both of you." He motioned to two of the ranch hands and they left toward the barn. One soon returned leading a beautiful palomino mare. On her back was a saddle trimmed in silver, with a matching bridle. Josefina was speechless, as was Jeff. The other ranch hand came forward leading a palomino gelding also with a matching saddle.

"Los caballos suyos," (Your horses) Arturo stated.

"Oh Tio, they are just so gorgeous," she said. She went to Arturo and hugged him as she kissed his cheek. Jeff went to the gelding and ran his hand down his side as the horse nudged him looking for a treat.

"Tomorrow we will go riding and I'll show you your ranch," Arturo told them.

The next few days flew by as Jeff and Josefina spent their days riding the ranch with Arturo and making love at night. Soon it was time to leave, as Jeff needed to return to work.

The morning they were leaving, Arturo came to the house for breakfast with the newlyweds. He presented Josefina with a checkbook from a bank in Ojinaga, Chihuahua.

"When we sell our cattle, I'll continue to place the profit into this bank. You may use it as you wish. There is another account that I use to pay the hands and expenses. You may examine it, whenever you wish."

"Tio, I love you so much, you run this ranch as you see fit. I'll never interfere," said Josefina. "Jeff and I will return whenever we can."

Waving goodbye as they drove away to make the long trip back to Rio Grande City and back to the real world.

When they returned to Rio Grande, Jeff began working the river or sign cutting. He would arrive home in the evening to a hot meal and his beautiful bride. Josefina began to spade up a garden in the back yard.

Several days later he was working a trail of two aliens north through the thick brush. There were heavy low clouds and the planes were grounded. It was after 3pm before he was able to apprehend the two. He placed one in the back of the Scout and the other one in front with him. The guy in front would open any gates they came to.

He was talking to Jesus about Mexico and his family there, when Jesus stated that he had seen a strange sight. "What was that?" asked Jeff.

"When we were walking north we walked east to a ranch house for food. We didn't approach the house because of two men armed with rifles standing in the yard. There was a large truck parked in the yard and it was pulling a large tank. We saw a man enter the tank from underneath. We then returned to the fence line and walked north where you caught us," Jesus stated.

"How far back was this ranch?" Jeff asked Jesus. "About five or six kilometers south of where you found us," he stated.

Jeff removed a piece of paper from his pocket and said, "Put down your name and address, if I find what I think I'll find, you two may receive a reward." Jesus did as requested and gave Jeff back the paper. He later transported them to the bridge and gave Jesus what money he had in his pocket, eight dollars.

"This will buy you two something to eat and say nothing about what you have told me," he cautioned Jesus.

He returned to the office and relayed to Wilson what he had been told. They looked at a large map of Starr County. He could see approximately where he had caught the two wets. Drawing a line south for about four miles, they were able to find a ranch named El Conejo (the rabbit).

"I'll scout it out tomorrow from the brush," Jeff stated.

"Okay," Wilson said. "I'll try to find out who is using it. Don't go in without backup."

The next day Jeff approached the ranch on the same trail he had used the day before. Hiding the Scout in the thick brush, he eased his way to the fence that overlooked the ranch on foot. He found a good place to hide and settled down with his binoculars. He didn't see a truck parked in the yard.

After watching for several hours, he observed a man walking from the house to the large barn. The man opened the double doors and he could see a truck hooked to a large tank trailer. It appeared to be like the ones used to haul propane. The man unhooked from the tank trailer and drove off in the truck.

Approximately two hours had passed when Jeff saw the truck return, with two cars following it. He watched from concealment as the two cars backed up to the barn doors, which they swung open. They begin to unload bundles from the trunks and carry them into the barn. The truck driver had parked nearby and Jeff saw him crawl under the tank and disappear.

The two sedan drivers began to pass the bundles up into the tank. Jeff was able to count the bundles and estimated there were five to six hundred pounds placed in the tank. The man then crawled from the tank, got into the truck which he backed into the barn, and shut both doors. They then went into the ranch house.

Jeff eased out of his hiding place and returned to his vehicle. He drove to the BP station as fast as he dared. Once there, he advised Wilson of what he had seen. "There's no doubt it's a load of pot, the bundles were approximately 18 inches by 12 inches. There's no telling how much is already in the trailer," he stated.

Wilson agreed, "I'm calling Customs, let's get them involved.

Special Agent Beasley arrived in less than an hour and was quickly given the information. "How do you want to work it?" he asked Jeff and Wilson.

"I believe we'll need twenty-four hour surveillance from now on. We don't know how much is there, ready to go," replied Jeff. "I wasn't able to get a license plate on the two cars. They could have crossed anywhere along the river. I didn't recognize the drivers either."

"Okay," said Wilson, "Let's pull twelve hour shifts with radio contact at all times. From the location of this ranch the walkie-talkies can reach the repeater."

"They sure can, I tried one after I pulled out," Jeff stated

Wilson turned to Jeff and said, "I know you've worked all day, but could you take the first shift from six tonight until tomorrow morning?"

"Sure, let me run home and tell the wife I'll be working tonight, pack a lunch and a thermos of coffee," Jeff replied.

"I'll get things started on my end, its just Neil and I," said Beasley.

"Okay, do you want the morning shift?" Wilson asked. "You bet," Beasley replied. "I'll bring Neil with me he needs the experience.

Jeff took off for home where his new bride had supper warming on the stove. "I'll have to eat on the run mi amor, we have work to do."

"Please be careful," she said. "I'll die if anything happens to you."

Jeff pulled her to him and gave her a long kiss. "Nothing's going to happen. Don't you remember, Los Tecolotes tell me what's going on."

Josefina hit him with a flyswatter, "I said be careful and I mean it. Don't be telling me crap about some dumb owls." She quickly packed him a lunch and watched from the door as he sped away.

Jeff watched the ranch all night and was joined by the two Customs agents shortly after daybreak. The agents set up a spotting scope in case the vehicles came back. Jeff walked back where he had parked and drove home.

Josefina was up and had breakfast waiting for him as he walked in the front door. She placed a plate of machacado con huevos (crushed meat and eggs) and fresh tortillas along with a large glass of milk in front of him. "Wilson is right, they will call me Lobo Gordo if I keep eating like this," he said.

"You've been out all night, you need to eat or you'll get sick," she replied.

When Jeff awoke it was after 3pm and he walked into the living room where Josefina was ironing. "Robert called and said when you were up to give him a call," she told him.

"No need, he just drove in the yard," said Jeff looking out the window. He opened the door and invited Wilson in the home.

Josefina handed Wilson a glass of iced tea and set out a plate of cookies. Wilson picked up a cookie and said, "I've an informant over in Miguel Aleman who says there are ten guys from the State of Guanajuato trying to pay anyone to haul them north. He says they are soliciting people on the street with offers of three hundred dollars each."

"For that kind of money they'll soon find someone pretty soon," Jeff said.

"You're right about that. With us sitting on this load of dope we don't have time to dick around with these guys. We need to pick them up and ship them home," Wilson stated.

"The informant has told them he's waiting on his boss to pick him up and that he works on a large ranch in Oklahoma. I have a set of Oklahoma plates and I'll put them on my pickup. You drive over to the Lucky Seven and meet with Victor, he'll introduce you to them. I'll have one of the other agents take your place on the surveillance tonight. You do whatever you need to do, we have to catch these guys before they find somebody to haul them all north," Wilson told him.

"Okay boss, I'll get ready and go right after supper, that is if I get any supper," Jeff teased Josefina.

"Yeah, you sure look like you're starving. I'll have one of the guys bring my pickup out here and I'll be standing by at the port tonight. You call me as soon as you know something," Wilson told him.

After supper, Jeff dresses in jeans, boots, western shirt and cowboy hat drove to Miguel Aleman. He parked the Wilson's pickup on the street near the Lucky Seven and entered the dimly lit bar. He found Victor sitting at a table with three other men.

Victor jumped up and embraced Jeff, "Mi Jefe" he said. Jeff ordered a round of drinks for the table as he was introduced to the others at the table. One of the men asked Jeff if he would haul them north if they paid him.

Jeff refused, "No, I'm a rancher not a contrabandista" (smuggler). They continued to drink beer and swap stories.

One of the men told Jeff, "there are ten of us here and we'll pay three hundred dollars each for a ride north."

"No, " said Jeff, "I'm here to pick up my foreman," and slapped Victor on the back.

A few more beers and the man upped the price to four hundred dollars each. Finally, Jeff turned to Victor and asked, "how much fence do we have to build on the ranch?"

Victor dropped his head as if in deep thought and replied, "over three miles Jefe."

Jeff turned to the men, "if you guys will work for me building that fence, I'll pay you forty dollars a day each. I'll furnish your meals and when you are finished you can go where you want. The ride north to my ranch in Oklahoma is free."

The guy jumped to his feet and said, "Let me get the others."

"Not so fast," Jeff said. He turned to Victor and said, "if these guys want to go, show them where I pick you up near Roma on the US side and have them there by 11 o'clock tonight."

"Si mi Jefe," Victor replied.

Jeff left the cantina, got in the pickup, and drove back across the bridge at Roma. He found Wilson waiting at the Port of Entry and told him where the men would be hiding.

"Good work, go home and take the night off. You can go back on surveillance in the morning," Wilson told him.

Later that night, two BP vehicles checked the bridge west of Roma on the road to Fronton where they found ten illegal aliens hiding under it. Victor had made an excuse that he had to take a crap just before the agents arrived. When the agents brought the aliens into the office Wilson told them, "write these guys up for the airlift and let's get them the hell away from the border."

The next morning Jeff relieved the agent who had the night shift watching the ranch. He had been there about thirty minutes when the two Customs Agents arrived. They had just set up the spotting scope when they saw a pickup drive into the yard. Jeff looked through the scope as the person exited the pickup and entered the house. "Can you see who it is?" asked Beasely.

"Shit, its Eduardo, one of Carlos's men," Jeff replied. Just then two sedans drove into the yard and backed up to the barn. The agents watched as Eduardo and another man came out of the house and walked over to the vehicles. The man opened the barn doors while the drivers opened the trunks.

They watched as bundles were removed and carried into the barn. They could see the bundles being passed up into the large tank.

When they were finished, they could see one of the men spraying the tank with paint. Eduardo then returned to his pickup and left, followed by the two sedans. When the man had finished painting, he started up the truck and hooked up the trailer then pulled it out of the barn. He left the truck running and went back into the house.

"I think they are going to move," Jeff said.

"I believe you're right," Beasley replied.

"Neil, run back to the vehicle and get on the Customs radio, have them launch the plane from San Antonio."

"You got it," said Neil and took off running. After about thirty minutes the man walked out of the house with a small bag, entered the truck, and drove off.

Jeff and Cliff quickly ran back to their vehicles where Neil was waiting. "The plane is up and coming south, I gave him the description of the truck and trailer," Neil said as Cliff jumped in the car. Jeff quickly entered the BP sedan and sped down the dirt trail followed by the two Customs Agents. He got on the radio to Wilson telling him that the truck was moving.

"Kitchens is located on 649 north of El Sauz. I'll have him go north toward Hebbronville and wait until he sees the truck or you," Wilson stated.

Jeff pulled onto a dirt road running west to 649 still followed by the two Customs Agents. "We'll need someone on 1017 in case he goes that way," Jeff told Wilson.

"I'm heading north from Rio Grande and I'll have 1017 covered," Wilson said.

Jeff had given his walkie-talkie to Beasely when he had got to his unit. Now he could hear Beasely calling him on the radio over the roar of the sedan. When Jeff answered, Cliff informed him that the Customs aircraft was approximately eighty miles north of Hebbronville heading south over Hwy 16.

Kitchens came on the radio and stated that he could see the truck going through Guerra.

"Stay behind him and don't let him see you," advised Jeff. He asked Beasely if he had heard Kitchens and was advised that he had and that he had passed on the info to the aircraft.

Jeff slid his sedan onto Hwy 649 and watched as the speedometer climbed to 105 MPH. He looked in his rear-view mirror and could see that Cliff was still on his tail. As the two sedans sped north, passing through the small village of Guerra, Jeff requested an update from Kitchens.

"I'm about four miles south of Randado and the truck is a mile ahead," he replied.

"Where is the aircraft?" Jeff asked Cliff.

"He's almost to Hebbronville," Cliff replied.

"Gary, if he turns north on Hwy 16, back off," he told Kitchens.

A few minutes later Kitchens radioed that the truck had turned north on Hwy 16 toward Hebbronville, Texas. "Park your vehicle at the store and be ready to get in with me," Jeff told him.

"Where are you Rio Grande One?" he asked.

"On Hwy 1017 heading to Hebbrobville, I'll meet up with you there," replied Wilson over the roar of his engine.

Jeff slid to a quick stop and Kitchens jumped into the sedan. With tires smoking, he pealed out and was on Hwy 16 before Cliff and Neil arrived at the stop sign. Cliff came on the radio and told Jeff that the plane could see the truck still south of Hebbronville.

"Great, we can all slow down now," said Jeff as he relayed the information to Wilson.

"How do you want to work this?" he asked Cliff.

"We'll let the plane follow him wherever he's going. I'll have more Customs Agents from San Antonio waiting when he arrives," Cliff stated.

Wilson met them in Hebbronville and crawled in the back seat of Jeff's sedan.

"Where's the truck?" he asked.

"About five miles north," Jeff replied as he burned rubber pulling back on Hwy 16.

Two hours later they were in San Antonio and followed Cliff to an industrial section. They met with two other Customs Agents who told them that the truck had entered a warehouse. "We're getting a search warrant now, and as soon as we have it we'll go in," one of the agents told them.

An hour later another agent drove up and waved the search warrant. "Let's go," said Cliff. Four sedans drove into the warehouse yard as the Customs plane circled overhead. One of the agents had a large crowbar and used it to pry open a small door. When the agents entered the warehouse they found several men unloading the tanker. The truck was unhooked and parked nearby.

"Manos Arriba," (hands up) the officers shouted and arrested them all without incident. Then they unloaded the rest of the bundles of marijuana. The San Antonio Customs Agents using a scale determined that the tanker was loaded with over 5,000 pounds of marijuana.

The men in the warehouse and the truck driver were placed in jail after being processed by the agents. The truck driver was found to have a long record of dealing in narcotics.

Eduardo was nowhere to be seen and none of the men would talk. All wanted lawyers.

CHAPTER 11

Eduardo Escobedo was south of the Mexican town of Cerralvo at a ranch when he received the news. He flew into a rage about losing the marijuana. "Who snitched off this load?" he demanded.

"We don't know Jefe," stated Arturo. "Javier heard it on the news that Customs had made a large arrest in San Antonio and seized over five thousand pounds of marijuana."

Eduardo turned to Javier, "make some calls and find out all the information you can. I talked Cisneros into giving us this chance and promised him we could deliver." Eduardo had been Carlos's lieutenant and was very short tempered. He knew that his life was forfeit when Cisneros learned of the loss of the drugs.

Javier returned late in the evening with a San Antonio newspaper. It showed pictures of the tanker truck and the warehouse. The attached story gave the names of several of the officers involved. Listed among them was the name Jeff Larson. Eduardo again went into a rage. " I want this Cabrone dead, do you hear me? Dead."

Javier, Modesto, and Arturo all looked at each other, "I don't know if that's a good idea, Jefe. You know what happened to Carlos."

"Yes, and I also know what happened to Gustavo. Do you think Cisneros is going to leave you or me alive when he learns about the loss of the moto. But you are right about one thing; we must think this out very carefully. We need to get Lobo Verde on this side of the river," Eduardo stated.

"But how, Jefe? He comes into Camargo, but we never know when he coming."

"Can you find out where he lives? I may know of a way to do it easy," said Eduardo.

"Sure," said Javier. "I'll find out. Let's go Arturo."

❃❃❃

Jeff had returned to sign cutting duties and was busy on a trail of three near Roma along with two other agents. They had stopped for a break under some mesquite trees and were eating their lunch. "How far ahead of us are these guys?" asked Kitchens.

"I'd say about two hours, we should have them soon," replied Jeff. Just then a large rattlesnake sounded off that he had been disturbed.

"Damn, where's he at?" asked Parker.

"Right over there," Jeff stated. He reached into the scout and removed a .45 auto. Taking aim he shot the head off the snake. "Do you want his rattlers?" he asked Kitchens.

"Sure do, when he stops moving around," Kitchens replied.

"Where did you get that pistol?" asked Parker.

"It was a wedding gift from Comandante Morales," Jeff stated.

"Let me take a look at it," Parker requested and Jeff handed over the pistol to him. He looked at the Colt Combat Commander with silver and gold Mexican grips. "Damn, that's a nice weapon," he told Jeff.

"Thanks, it sure shoots good," replied Jeff.

They located the three they had been tracking two miles north where they had taken a siesta. The three men were sound asleep when the BP arrived. They were loaded up in the scouts, taken to BP office, and processed.

***

Javier returned to the ranch, telling Eduardo they had found where El Lobo lives. "His house is just west of Rio Grande and north of Midway crossing," Javier stated. "The house is about a kilometer or a little more from the river. We've seen him leave the house each morning before 6 am," he finished.

"Very good," said Eduardo. "Tomorrow we'll give El Lobo something to worry about. I want one man to stay at the river crossing. Javier you and Arturo will be with me, we're going to hit El Lobo where he lives. We'll see how big he is after this."

The next day Jeff left the house just before 6 am and drove to the BP station to begin his tour of duty. There were no trails that day, so at ten o'clock he requested leave and returned home. He planned to take Josefina shopping in McAllen.

When he drove into the front yard, he noticed that the screen door to the kitchen was open. Josefina did not come out to meet him, as was her practice. He walked into the kitchen and found two chairs overturned with broken glass and spots of blood on the floor. "Josefina, where are you?" he cried.

A quick search of the house revealed no one was at home. He returned to the kitchen and noticed a note lying on the kitchen counter. He picked it up and saw it was written in Spanish. The note said, "We have your woman and we want our mota, be on the square in Camargo tomorrow morning." The note was unsigned. Jeff quickly called Wilson and told him what he had found.

"I'll be right out, you stay there," Wilson stated.

Wilson arrived in a few minutes and walked into the house. Jeff had changed from his uniform to civilian clothes while waiting. He was still in shock as he handed Wilson the note. "Okay, what's the plan?" he asked Jeff.

"Well, I can't get the dope back from Customs and I wouldn't if I could," he told Wilson. "I'm going to Camargo to try and find out where they may be holding her."

"Not without me, let me change clothes. Pick me up at my house in fifteen minutes," Wilson said as he left. Jeff quickly loaded a few items into his pickup and then drove to Wilson's house. Picking up Robert he drove to Camargo and to Jesus Castillo's house.

"Who is this guy?" Wilson asked him.

"He was a friend of Napo's. Napo once told me if I ever needed help to come see him and I sure as hell need help now."

He and Robert walked to the door and were admitted by Jesus. "Come in please," he said. "Welcome to my home, may I get you some coffee?"

"No, Señor Castillo, Napo told me if I ever needed help to come see you. Some narcotics smugglers have taken Josefina, and I need to find out where they are holding her."

"Who could do such a thing?" asked Jesus.

"I believe one is named Eduardo. He was seen on the other side where they loaded the narcotics," Jeff told him.

"Of course, he was one of Carlos's men. His name is Eduardo Escobedo and he has a small goat ranch south of the town of Cerralvo. The ranch is located off highway 54 about thirty-five kilometers south of Mier," Jesus told the two agents.

After getting good direction to the ranch from Jesus, they drove west from Camargo. They picked up highway 54 and turned south. They located the dirt road to the goat ranch and drove down it a short ways. Jeff then found a place off the road to hide his pickup.

They both prepared for the walk into the ranch. Jeff placed the Colt Combat in a SOB (small of the back) holster under his jacket. His Colt 1911 was placed in his waistband on his right side. Both weapons were loaded with eight rounds of 230-grain slugs. He placed several more loaded magazines in his pocket and picked up a pair of binoculars. The last item he removed was a crossbow and several bolts for it from behind the seat. Wilson had on his S&W .357 and removed a chrome-plated shotgun from the pickup.

"Let's go, Jeff said, but slow and easy."

"I'm right with you," Wilson said. "I hope you're not going to shout manos arriba (hands up) or any shit like that are you?" he asked Jeff.

"Hell no, going after me is one thing, but when they pick on my family they are bought and paid for," Jeff replied.

"Good, we're thinking alike then," said Wilson.

They walked in the brush along side the road that led to the ranch. Jesus had told them it was about three kilometers off the main highway. As they neared the ranch, the two officers moved very carefully among the mesquites and cactus. Finally, they could see the shack backed up to a small bluff. Jeff pointed out a guard sitting near the road under a tree. He was in good cover and would not have been seen by anyone traveling the road.

Jeff using the binoculars told Wilson, "I can't see anybody inside, and they have a burlap sack over the only window." Jeff whispered and laid out his plan. "I'll ease over to the left side of the house. See if you can get to the right, behind that large rock. You'll be about forty yards from the front door and about twenty-five from the guard."

"Watch for my signal and then fire these right at the front door." Jeff handed over two firecracker charges loaded in twelve gauge shotgun shells. "Don't hit those two gas cans to the right of the door," he cautioned.

"You be careful," Wilson warned, "let me have that crossbow and I'll take care of the guard."

***

Josefina had just finished washing the breakfast dishes when she heard a small noise behind her. She looked over her shoulder and saw two men enter the house through the kitchen door. She threw a glass at the first one, hitting him between the eyes and ran toward the bedroom to get her revolver.

The second man tackled her in the living room and fell on top of her. It knocked the breath out of the slight girl and the two had her on her feet before she could regain it. Her arms were jerked behind her and tied with a cord. A gag was placed in her mouth and tied. Her housecoat had come open and Javier grabbed her right breast through the thin cotton tee shirt she wore.

"Let's get a little of this before we go," he sneered.

Eduardo slapped him and grabbed Josefina's arm. "Not now, pendejo. We'll have plenty of time later for that," he said. He was still trying to stop the blood where the glass had struck him.

The two men rushed Josefina from the house, where she saw another man standing near the driveway. The three pushed the girl along a path to the river where another man and small boat was waiting. They threw her into the boat and quickly paddled to the Mexican side.

When they arrived at the shack she was thrown on a filthy bed in one corner. Eduardo turned her over on her stomach and removed the cord from her hands and the gag. Before she could recover, he turned her on her back and quickly tied her arms and feet to the bed spread eagle. Her housecoat was open and she lay exposed to the men in the thin shirt and briefs. Eduardo stood back and admired the view.

"You are too good to be with that cabrone, you need a real man," he laughed. "We'll have to see that you get one while you're with us."

"Hijo de la puta," (son-of-a-bitch) Josefina screamed. "El Lobo era matar por eso." (El Lobo will kill you for this)

Eduardo slapped her and grabbed a bottle of tequila. He took a drink as he watched the blood seep from the mouth of the helpless girl. He turned to Arturo. "Get outside on guard duty," he ordered. "Modesto, fix us something to eat."

"Let's make her fix the meal," Modesto suggested.

"No, I like looking at her the way she is," stated Eduardo. "It's time she learned a few things and we'll be the ones to teach her."

Javier came over to the bed and looked at Josefina. "Soon, mi novia, soon," he bragged.

Tears came to her eyes but she squeezed them shut. I'll not let them see how scared I am she vowed. Oh Jeff, where are you? She cried to herself. Lying there she closed her eyes tight and started to pray. She could smell the sweet odor of marijuana and had seen several bundles stacked in one corner of the shack.

Eduardo and the others were drinking as they ate their meal. "Take Arturo something to eat," he told Modesto. As the day wore on the men continued to drink, secure in the belief that no one knew where they were.

Javier finally stood up and said, "I'm going to get me a little of that," motioning to Josefina. He walked over to the bed where Josefina was tied.

"Sure, go ahead, your little dick won't hurt her," said Eduardo as he laughed loudly.

Javier reached down and tore the tee shirt from her body baring her breasts to his leering eyes. She screamed in fear as he ripped off her briefs and undid his belt, letting his trousers and pistol fall to the floor. "Now you'll have a real man," he said.

Two small thumps were heard at the front door and suddenly there was a loud explosion. Eduardo fell out of his chair and Modesto jumped up. They both started for the door while Javier was trying to get his pants up and his pistol off the floor. The side door was kicked in and Eduardo saw a figure step through that made his blood run cold.

Jeff had slipped along through the brush until he was at the side of the shack. The cactus grew almost to the side door and he could hear a radio playing. He heard some loud laughter coming from the shack. He waved to Wilson that he was ready and then heard Josefina scream.

Wilson raised the crossbow and sighted on Arturo under the tree. When Josefina screamed Arturo turned toward the shack and the bolt hit him in the throat. He grabbed his throat with both hands and fell over, his feet kicking.

Jeff quickly ran to the side door and removed his pistol from the right side. He switched the weapon to his left hand and drew the Combat Commander with his right, removing both safeties.

Wilson raised the shotgun and fired the two firecrackers at the front door. When they exploded, Jeff kicked in the flimsy door, stepping inside with both pistols ready. His eyes took in the whole room and time seemed frozen. Eduardo and Modesto were near the front door. Javier was at the foot of the bed, trying to pull up his pants. He saw Josefina naked on the bed, and believing Javier had just raped her, shot him twice with his left-hand pistol.

The first slug hit Javier in the groin and doubled him over. The next round went in the top of his head and he fell dead at the foot of the bed. Jeff fired twice with his right-hand pistol at Eduardo, who was moving and missed. Eduardo pulled his pistol and started firing at Jeff, but he too missed.

Modesto screamed in fear and ran out the front door. Jeff now turned both pistols on Eduardo. "You assholes never could hit anything," he shouted as he fired both automatics. The heavy bullets knocked Eduardo off balance and against the wall. Then with both pistols blazing Jeff walked toward Eduardo. When his right foot hit the floor he fired the right weapon, the same with his left.

The heavy bullets pinned Eduardo against the wall, the last two shots were fired from less than a foot away and the slides locked open on the .45's. They were empty. Jeff quickly reloaded both weapons and walked over to Josefina.

Wilson was walking toward the front door from the side when Modesto came running out with a gun in his hand. He was about ten feet away when Robert fired both barrels into him. The heavy load of buckshot knocked him off his feet and he was dead when he hit the ground. Wilson quickly reloaded his shotgun.

He could hear the sudden burst of gunfire from the house and it seemed to go on forever. Then it became very quiet. He came in the front door with his shotgun ready, but could hardly see for the gun smoke and dust. Two bodies were lying on the floor in pools of blood.

Jeff was standing at the bed, cutting the cords from Josefina hands and feet. The girl was crying with great sobs as Jeff wrapped her housecoat around her naked body. He picked her up and carried her outside, motioning Wilson to follow him. They walked down the road past the dead Arturo and Jeff set her down on her feet.

"Robert take Josefina to the pickup and wait for me. Let me have your escopeta." (shotgun) Wilson wrapped his arm around the crying girl. Saying, "Don't be long."

When Robert and Josefina were no longer in sight, Jeff walked over and picked up Arturo's rifle. He tucked it and the shotgun under his left arm. He grabbed Arturo by his shirt collar and dragged him into the shack. He leaned the shotgun by the front door, and dragged Modesto in also.

He went out, picked up both five-gallon gas cans, and carried them inside. He poured the gasoline over the bundles of marijuana, the bed, and dead bodies. When they were both empty he tossed them to one side.

Jeff picked up the shotgun and walked down the road. When he was about fifty yards from the shack, he loaded another firecracker charge in the shotgun. He fired it through the open door and when it exploded the gasoline ignited with a loud roar, blowing out the single window. Huge clouds of black smoke billowing into the sky. Holy shit, we had better get the hell out of here, he thought.

When he arrived at the truck, Josefina and Wilson were waiting for him. Jeff started the vehicle and they quickly left the area. Jeff wanted to stop at Dr. Kesler's office and have Josefina checked out. She refused, "I'm all right. They didn't harm me other that a slap and rope burns on my hands and feet. You arrived just in time."

"I'd still feel better if the doctor looked you over," Jeff stated.

"All I really need is a good hot bath, please take me home," she begged.

Jeff dropped Wilson off at his house and then drove home. When they were inside he started the bath water for Josefina, while he fixed something to eat. When Josefina came out of the bathroom, she had her hair wrapped in a towel. She was wearing Jeff's bathrobe, as she had thrown her old one in the trash. Jeff had some soup ready and pulled out her chair. "How do you feel, now?" he asked.

"I'm fine, that smells so good," she replied. She picked up her spoon and started eating.

Later, after she had gone to sleep, Jeff lay awake thinking how he could protect her.

The next day was one of Jeff's days off. He had been up early, fixed Josefina her breakfast and served her in bed. She was delighted. "I'll have somebody kidnap me again if I'm going to receive this much attention."

Jeff sat down on the side of the bed. "Sweetheart, I want you to go live with your mother or go to your ranch for awhile. It's too dangerous here right now."

Josefina looked up at Jeff. "No way," she said, and continued to eat.

"I mean it," Jeff said. "Its too dangerous here right now."

"I do too," she replied. "If you think I'm running home to mother, because of this, you've got another think coming. My mother didn't leave my father and I'm not going, and that's the end of it."

There was a knock at the front door and Jeff went to answer it. Wilson was there with a bouquet of flowers for Josefina. "Come in Robert, you can help me talk some sense into a stubborn female," he said.

"Maybe I should come back later," Wilson replied, not wanting to get in a domestic.

"No, please stay," said Josefina who had walked into the living room. She had on one of Jeff's long tail white shirts and with her bare long golden legs looked very sexy.

Wilson handed her the flowers. "Thank you Robert," she said, hugging and kissing him on the cheek. Wilson turned bright red and sat down on the couch. "I'll put on some fresh coffee," she said.

"I'm trying to talk Josefina into living with her Mother and Grandfather until it settles down around here," he told Wilson.

"Might be a good idea," replied Wilson.

"Don't you two gang up on me," she stated. "I've already told Jeff, I'm not going and that's it," she said stamping her foot. Both men were taken back by the sudden anger and determination shown by the young bride.

"Sweetheart, I just want you to be safe," Jeff said.

"Then teach me to shoot and I'll keep my gun on me at all times," she replied.

Jeff looked over at Wilson, "I guess I lost this argument."

"I believe so," Wilson replied.

Later that day Jeff got several boxes of 38 wadcutters (a low velocity target round) and some targets that he loaded into his pickup. He walked back into the house and told Josefina, "let's go practice."

They drove through Rio Grande City to the firing range on the east side of town. Jeff put up a bullseye target and had Josefina stand about twenty feet away. He watched her load five rounds of the wadcutter ammo into her Colt revolver. " Okay, I want you to aim at the target and fire all five rounds double action," he stated.

Josefina placed her right foot slightly behind and raised her right arm. She cupped her right hand with her left and starting shooting. When she had emptied the revolver, Jeff walked down and looked at the target. Three rounds were in the ten ring, with two just outside in the nine ring.

"Shit, where did you learn to shoot like that?" he asked her as he walked back.

"My father taught me," she replied as she loaded five more rounds in the weapon. "It shoots a little to the right," she said. She again raised the weapon and firing as fast as she could, put all five in the ten ring.

"Damn, I'm going to win some money on you," stated Jeff. "Just wait until I sucker one of the guys into a contest."

"Oh no you don't, she said, I won't do it."

"What was that bullshit about teach me to shoot?" he asked her.

"Well, at first I was going to act like I didn't know anything, so you could teach me. But then I changed my mind, you're not mad at me are you?" she asked.

"Hell no, I should've known Napo would have taught you to shoot," Jeff stated. "Let's see how good you can shoot with your left hand."

Josefina changed the pistol to her left hand, cupping it with her right and slowly fired off five rounds. Four were in the ten and one was in the nine ring.

"Let me put up another target. I want you to try something," Jeff told her. He replaced the bullseye target with one of a person in silhouette. He walked back where Josefina was standing as she reloaded.

"Turn your back to the target and when I give the command, face the target and fire all five rounds. Are you ready?" he asked her. Josefina just nodded her head, pointing her pistol at the ground, her back to the target.

"Go, go," hollered Jeff. Josefina spun like a cat on her right foot and when her left hit the ground, went into a crouch firing all five shots. They sounded almost like one.

Jeff walked down to the target. One shot had hit a little low with the other four in the middle of the chest area. "Damn, that's good shooting," he said. "I still like for you to shoot against one of the guys."

"No, Papa told me never show up a man unless I had too," she replied.

"Here, try your father's .38 super," he said as he handed the girl the heavy automatic.

Josefina took the auto with her right hand, opened the slide slightly to check if it was loaded. She turned toward the silhouette target and emptied the auto in one continuous roar. Jeff's mouth fell open, as all ten rounds were centered in the head of the target.

"Damn, don't let me make you mad," he joked.

"You just remember that buster," she laughed.

"Well, that's enough for today, let's go have some lunch at the Catfish Inn," he said as he hugged his bride to him. As they drove into town, Jeff said, "reload your pistol with those special bullets I gave you and put it in your purse. I want it with you at all times."

"Okay Jeffie, I will." Jeff had taken several 38 special rounds and drilled a small hole in the nose of each one so they would spread better. He watched as she put five into her weapon and placed the gun in her purse. They parked in front of the café and walked into the cool interior with Josefina carrying her purse, where they ordered lunch.

"I'm violating the law, aren't I?" she asked.

"Yes, replied Jeff, but don't worry about it. I had rather you be caught with it, than without it. There is an old saying, "better to be judged by twelve that carried by six."

Josefina looked confused not understanding the colloquialism. "It means it's better to be in court with a jury of twelve than be carried to your grave by six pallbearers," Jeff told her.

"Oh, now I see," said Josefina. "Let's eat, shooting always makes me hungry."

The next day Wilson called Jeff and told him to come to work in civilian clothes. When he walked into the office at 5pm Wilson was just finishing some of the never-ending paper work. "What's up Boss?" he asked.

"Well, we have information that the aliens are trying something new. It seems they are walking the highways at night, but are getting off and hiding when they see a car coming. One of the truck drivers hauling bricks told me he saw three different groups trying to wave him down on 649 last night. He thinks they see the clearance lights on the cab and run out on the road trying to get a ride."

"Shit, no wonder we don't have any trails leading north," Jeff said.

"I want you to drive the truck sector sent us and see if you can lure them out on the road. I'll have a couple of the guys waiting at Randado to take any that you pick up."

"Okay, I'll wait until its good dark before I leave," Jeff stated. The two agents came in and wanted to eat before they left for Randado. Jeff told them he had already eaten but would have coffee with them. When they came out of the restaurant, Jeff saw a local farmer motion to him.

"Excuse me guys, I'll see you later." He walked over to where Angel Sanchez was standing and shook hands with the old gentleman. Mr. Sanchez farmed a small piece of land along the river that had belonged to his family for over a hundred years and was a good friend.

"Señor Jeff, I wonder if you could help me?" he asked.

"Certainly Tio," Jeff replied. "How can I be of service?"

"I have about forty acres of cotton on the river and some mojados are coming over and stealing it at night. I have tried to catch them but they run back to Mexico using that old abandoned pipe that crosses the river," Sanchez stated.

"I have an assignment for this evening, but let me think on it and I'll see what I can do."

"Thanks Señor how is your new bride? My wife and I want you to bring her to visit us soon," Sanchez told him.

"I will, she would enjoy that very much, Adios amigo," he told Sanchez.

Jeff returned to the station thinking about the problem. If we just apprehend the wets and return them to Mexico, they'll be back tomorrow, he thought. I doubt if I could get them on an airlift. What I need is to make an impression on them. He suddenly laughed aloud as he thought of something. Wilson in the next room asked, "What's going on in there?"

"Nothing Jefe," Jeff said. "I better get on the road and see if I can pick up some wets. I'll have a walkie-talkie with me so I can call the guys if I have any." Before he left town he stopped by one of the stores and picked up a large picture of a wolf.

Jeff drove the flatbed truck with solid sideboards west on highway 83, then turned north on 649. He'd traveled about ten miles, when he suddenly saw a man run out on the highway waving his arms in the headlights. Jeff pulled over to the side and the guy ran up to him, asking if he would give him and his friends a ride north.

"Sure, Jeff replied in Spanish, hop in the back." He watched as four more ran from the brush and all five climbed in the back. A few miles up the road he saw another man waving him down. This time he picked up three and drove on toward Randado.

When he was about three miles from the location he quietly radioed the agents and told them he had eight customers. "I'll make a rolling stop at the intersection, then you can pull me over."

The agents agreed. "We'll cuss you out for hauling them and then let you go."

After the agents had relieved him of his passengers, Jeff drove on to Hebbronville. He then took FM 1017 and FM 755 back to Rio Grande City. When he arrived at the station, the two agents had already returned the illegals to Mexico and were going off duty. Jeff looked around the garage until he found a gallon of used motor oil. He placed it in one of the scouts and drove east of town.

He drove down several back roads until he was a mile from the Sanchez farm. Parking the scout he walked along the riverbank until he could see Sanchez's cotton field in the moonlight. He watched for a few minutes and could see three men in the field picking cotton by hand.

He slipped down to the river to the big abandoned pipe that crossed the Rio Grande River. The pipe was about two feet in diameter and Jeff walked out in the middle. He started pouring the motor oil on the pipe as he backed toward the US side. When he was finished he returned to his vehicle and waited until it was daylight. Just as it got light he drove toward the field. The three men saw him coming and started running for the pipe still carrying their cotton.

He floored the vehicle like he was trying to catch them and saw the first one reach the pipe. The guy was running so hard he was several feet out on the pipe when he hit the oil. His feet went over his head and he fell into the river. The other two were right behind and they too cartwheel into the water. Jeff had stopped the scout and was laughing so hard tears came to his eyes.

He watched the three climb out of the water on the Mexican side without their stolen cotton and run into the brush. He got out of his vehicle and taking the picture of the wolf, he attached it to a stick and stuck it in the ground near the pipe.

That'll warn them El Lobo protects this field, he thought. Still laughing he drove back to town then went home.

When he arrived Josefina started his breakfast, while he told her of last night's events.

She asked, "Do you think they'll return?"

"Not when they see the wolf's picture I put near the pipe," he replied.

"Eat your breakfast, you're going to need your strength," she stated with her eyes twinkling.

CHAPTER 12

In the weeks following Josefina's abduction, Jeff was busy in routine patrol duties. He had driven the flatbed truck twice more and picked up a total of thirty illegals. Now the trails had again started up as the mojados were driven off the highways.

He had been checking the vacancy announcements that were posted in the office and noticed one for Deming, New Mexico. It stated that Deming was a satellite station. The main station was in Columbus, which was a small village on the New Mexico border with old Mexico. The town's one claim to fame was that the Mexican bandit Pancho Villa had raided it in 1916 and almost destroyed it. He filled out the paper work and mailed it off.

When he arrived at home, he told Josefina what he had done and they both looked up Deming on a map. They quickly realized that it would be much easier to travel to Josefina's ranch through El Paso.

"Oh Jeff, do you think you'll be selected?"

"I believe I'll have a good chance, as they want experienced agents working there."

While they were eating supper, the telephone rang. Josefina got up and answered it, then called Jeff to the phone. When Jeff came on, the caller who lived on highway 649 near Randado told Jeff that three wets had come to his house looking for work.

"They are walking north on the highway right now," he said.

Jeff called the station and found out the two agents on duty were processing a smuggling load. "I'd better get a sedan and run up there," he told Josefina who told him to be careful. "Not to worry, I'll get back in time for dessert," he replied.

In less than an hour he arrived where the aliens had last been and drove slowly north. About two miles up the road, he saw a flash of color on the right side. He pulled over and ran into the brush, where he could see several pair of legs hidden.

"Come on out of there," he commanded in Spanish. Heads started to pop up all around him and he saw there were a lot more than three. All of the men were small in statue and were from the Mexican State of Michoacan. A quick head count revealed that he had apprehended eighteen illegals in one group.

Now, how in hell am I going to get them back to the station? "Guys its like this," he told them. "We have fifty miles to go and only one vehicle. Do you guys think you'll all fit in?"

One of them spoke up, " seguro que si Jefe." (For sure boss) Jeff walked over to the 69 Chevy, opening the doors and trunk. The men placed their small bags in the trunk and then started to climb inside the vehicle. Soon Jeff was alone standing by the trunk, which he shut. As he slid into the front seat, he saw that three guys were in the front with him and the other fifteen were in the back seat. The sedan was almost dragging its rear bumper as they started for Rio Grande City.

Jeff joked with the men in Spanish as they drove south on highway 649. When they arrived at the station the two agents were standing at the front door. "Did you catch those three you went after?" they asked.

"Sure did," Jeff replied as he opened the doors. It soon appeared to be a crowd standing around the sedan waiting for their bags to be unloaded.

"Holy shit," said Ed Cook. "You just beat all. We've worked our butts off catching a load of six and you go out and get an army all by yourself."

"Naw, just a few friends," Jeff replied, opening the trunk and handing out the bags.

With Ed and Kitchens helping, the processing went fast. They had called sector and had a detention guard with a bus sent to the station. The guys would be airlifted to Leon, Guanajuato, Mexico in the hope that they would return home instead of the border. As they were loaded the guys from Michoacan wanted to shake hands with Jeff. They were waving from the windows as they left for the Detention center at Port Isabel, Texas.

Jeff called home and found that Josefina had a fresh baked apple pie waiting. Jeff called to the agents, "since you guys helped me out, there is a pie waiting at the house."

"You'd better drive fast or we'll run over you," Ed shouted. Jeff jumped into his pickup and roared out of the parking lot. He could see the BP scout right behind as he drove toward home.

Josefina, wearing her white shorts and halter made a bigger hit than the pie. Soon the stories started as the two agents tried to out do each other telling stories about Jeff in the Border Patrol. Jeff tried without success to change the subject. With the beautiful girl laughing and egging them on the two agents continued to embarrass Jeff.

"Did you ever hear the story about Jeff and the mortar simulator?" asked Ed.

"No, please tell me," she replied. " But what is a mortar simulator?"

"It's a device that the military uses in practice combat. It has a pull string and when it's pulled, it whistles for about three seconds, and then explodes. It's like a quarter stick of dynamite," Ed continued.

"Well, it seems we had a smuggler that was leading wets away from the river, using several different trails. We tried to catch him, but were unable to. So Jeff gets the mortar simulator from God knows where. He picked one of the trails and ties this thing to a small tree. He then runs the pull string across the trail and goes home. Later that evening we hear this loud explosion."

"Several of us hot foot it to the trail and find the small tree completely blown down. We find a wide path going right through the cactus and brush back to the river. There were hats, water jugs, trique bags, and clothes strewn all the way to the river. You could see where some of them ran right through cactus patches. That smuggler never used that place again."

Josefina was laughing, "oh please tell me more," she begged.

Kitchens spoke up, "I'll tell one. When I first came here as a trainee, I worked several weeks with Jeff. When we caught any wets, Jeff would shoot holes in the plastic water jugs. He told me this was to discourage them from returning. Well, one evening I was working with SPA Hayden on the river. We were about 300 yards apart when I caught two wets crossing the river. Both were carrying jugs, so I shot the jugs. Here comes Hayden running up thinking I'm in a gunfight. Talk about a dressing down, I've never heard so many cuss words before or since. I didn't tell him about Jeff shooting the jugs and Jeff paid for my lunch for a week."

"What about the time we pulled over a smuggling load and all the wets bailed out and ran into the brush," said Ed. "Jeff drives up just as the last guy goes through the fence. He pulls out his sawed-off shotgun and fired several of those firecracker charges he carries around into the brush. We had wets hollering, 'Don't shoot, we give up' and running back to the road."

Josefina cut them another piece of pie with lots of whipped cream and refilled their coffee cups. "Please tell me another story," she pleaded.

"Well, we'd better go," said Ed with his mouth full of pie. "Jeff is staring holes in me now. Maybe another time," he said.

"The pie was delicious," said Gary as they left. "Thanks for having us out."

"You're both welcome anytime, especially with some more stories," she said.

"What a bunch of blabber mouths," Jeff said with a grin as they both got ready for bed.

Jeff was up early the next day and stopped by the office. He picked up a letter from Regional Headquarters addressed to him. He opened the letter and read that he had been selected for a transfer to the Deming, New Mexico station. The letter advised him to call in with his EOD date. (Entry on duty)

Jeff quickly drove back home and ran into the house. Josefina was in the kitchen when he walked in. "We've got it," he shouted. "We're moving to New Mexico." He picked her up and swung her around and around.

"Put me down," said the laughing girl. "Let's call Mama and tell her about it."

It took about twenty minutes to place a call to Rancho Alegre. Cory answered the telephone. After talking to her grandfather for several minutes Carmen came on the line.

"What's this mi hija? You're moving to New Mexico," she asked.

"That's right Mama, Jeff received his transfer. We'll move in about a month mas o menos," (more or less) said Josefina. After a few more minutes of conversation she told her mother, "You and Abuelo take care," and hung up the telephone.

The next day Jeff returned to work. After sign cutting all morning with no trails, he returned to the office. Wilson was catching up on paper work when he walked in. "Hi Boss," he said.

"No trails today?" asked Wilson.

"Not a single one," Jeff replied. "I do need to show you this," and handed Wilson his letter from Region.

Wilson read the letter and handed it back. "Damn, I hate to see you go."

"Me too, but I need to get Josefina away from here before some other asshole decides he can pull the same thing that Eduardo tried," Jeff stated.

"When are you leaving?" Wilson asked.

"I haven't given my EOD yet, maybe next month," Jeff replied.

"You let me know, we're going to have a party," said Wilson.

Several days later, Jeff told Wilson he had decided on May 19 as his EOD date. Wilson said, "I'll contact Region and give them the date. I'm going to set up the party for the 10th of May," he continued.

"Whatever you want boss, you know I'll always be grateful for all of your help and support. You have been a true friend, Josefina and I have already decided to name our first born son after you."

Wilson walked over to the window and looked out so Jeff couldn't see the wetness in his eyes. "Well, you aren't out of here yet, so get to work," he stated.

"Sure thing boss," said Jeff as he left the office. His eyes were also wet and after he was outside he wiped them with his sleeve.

On May the 10th the party started at 6pm with kegs of beer on the patio of the Catfish Inn. Jeff was in the Rio Grande dress uniform. (blue jeans and a white shirt) Josefina was dressed in tight black slacks with a white silk blouse. Wilson was already half in the bag as he was in charge of the beer.

People were still arriving at 7pm and the party was in full swing. Suddenly Josefina gave a squeal, which made Jeff reach for his hidden pistol. She had seen her Mother and Grandfather walk in the front door. She quickly ran into her Mother's arms, with Jeff close behind.

"Mama, we didn't know you and Abuelo were coming."

"Robert called us and we wanted it to be a surprise," said Carmen, as she hugged her daughter. Cory O'Connor was beaming as he shook Jeff's hand and then pulled the young man to him in the Mexican abrazo. Carmen then hugged Jeff as Josefina kissed her Grandfather.

"Come out on the patio and let me get you two something to drink," Jeff told them. He took Carmen's arm while Josefina escorted her Grandfather.

Later, after everyone had eaten, Robert rapped for attention. The room quickly quieted down and they all turned toward the head table. "You all know that these two young people are leaving us for greener pastures," Wilson stated as he stood behind Jeff and Josefina.

"I know that all of us are sorry to see them leave, but we wish them the very best. Jeff, all of the agents in the sector have chipped in on a going away present for you and Josefina. Josefina you are first because you're so much prettier than Jeff."

With that Robert handed her a small wrapped package. She quickly opened it and removed a gold chain with a large ruby attached, the size of a hummingbird's egg. She placed it around her neck and Wilson fastened it for her. The ruby dropped down to her cleavage.

"Oh Robert," she cried, hugging and kissing him. Wilson turned a bright red but still held the girl to him as he picked up a large package leaning against the wall.

"Jeff, this is for you and you had better not try kissing me," he stated.

Jeff opened the package and removed a Winchester Model 1894 pre 64 rifle in 30-30 caliber in mint condition. Inlaid on the stock was a brass plate. Engraved on the plate were the words, 'Presented to BP Agent Jeff Larson (El Lobo Verde) from the Agents of the McAllen Sector.'

Jeff just stood there for several minutes. He then looked up, "I don't know what to say. Josefina and I will never forget you. You're the best bunch of people in the world. Thanks from the bottom of our hearts." He then sat back down beside Josefina with tears running down his face.

Wilson turned away and wiped his eyes. Then said, "okay that's it, let's all have a drink and wish these two the very best."

"Hear, hear," said Hayden, and lifted his glass, "to the Larson's." The party finally broke up about 3am when Jeff and Josefina left for home accompanied by Carmen and Cory.

The next morning Jeff was up early and had fixed breakfast. Carmen, Cory and Josefina sat at the table while Jeff dished out the machacado con huevos. After talking for the rest of the morning, Cory and Carmen left for the ranch. Jeff had promised to come visit as soon as they were settled at the new station. Josefina was still wearing her necklace and refused to take it off even in the shower.

Jeff still had a few days to work and Wilson had told him to work wherever he wanted. He drove into the river area just down river from Roma, Texas. He walked slowly along the river keeping to the brush. After he was a mile down river from the port, he found a huge log near the edge of the brush and sat down behind it.

The river was shallow here and one of the favorite places for wets to cross. He had been hidden behind the log for an hour when he saw two men walk out of the woods on the Mexican side. He lay down behind the log where he could still watch the two guys. They slowly looked around and one walked to the water's edge and looked up and down the river. They both sat down near the river and removed their clothes. With their clothes held up high, out of the water, they slowly waded to the US side. They were like two deer as they eased up on the bank where they stood for several minutes.

They then walked over to the log where Jeff lay hidden and sat down on it. They sat there for several minutes then started putting on their clothes. When they were fully dressed, Jeff could hear them talking softly about finding work. He rose up just behind them and leaned over the log.

"Ya pescado," (I caught you) he says as he grabbed both by their belts. The two men tried to run, but were held firm. One gave a startled cry until he realized that Jeff was a Border Patrolman.

"It's El Lobo Verde," he said. "I thought it was a bruja (witch) that had caught us."

The two appreciated the joke played on them. They were still teasing each other when they arrived at the sedan. Jeff drove to the station where the two were processed and given back their possessions as they walked across the bridge to Mexico.

Later that evening after he and Josefina had finished supper, he received a call from an informant. The man told him that ten illegals were crossing the river and would cross the highway two miles west of where Jeff lived soon after dark.

Jeff called the station and found only Parker was working. "Pick me up at my house and I'll go help you," he told Parker. He put on his BP shirt and tucked it into his blue jeans. He then slung his gunbelt around his lean hips and went outside to meet Parker.

They drove west for about two miles where Jeff had Parker let him off with a radio.

"Go down about a mile and I'll call when I see anything," he told him. He walked into the grove of trees that paralleled the highway. After he was through the trees he could see an open field. There was a small tree about thirty yards out in the field and Jeff could see several men sitting under it in the moonlight. He walked quietly over to the tree and could hear the men talking in low Spanish. They were busy watching the field to the south and didn't see Jeff until he sat down with them.

"It's La Migra," one of them said. They all laughed and one said, "Well you have caught us, let's go."

"No," said Jeff. "Let's wait a few minutes until your friends get here."

"What friends?" one asked.

"The other five guys who crossed with you," replied Jeff. He was watching the open field and could see another group of men running toward the tree.

When they arrived they sat down out of breath and failed to see Jeff. One of them asked, "are we all ready?"

"No, we're not," he replied in Spanish.

"Why not?" the man asked.

"Because we're waiting for the car."

"What car?"

"The Border Patrol car," Jeff replied. Just then the man noticed Jeff's green shirt and badge.

"La migra otra vez," (The Border Patrol once again) he exclaimed. One of the first men thought this was the funniest thing he had ever encountered and fell over laughing.

Jeff radioed Parker asking him to drive in and pick them up. They loaded the men into the sedan and drove to the station where he helped Parker with the paper work. When they were finished Parker told him, "go on home, I'll wait for the bus to haul these guys to camp." Jeff called Josefina and had her drive into town for him.

The next day Jeff and Josefina drove to McAllen and rented a U-Haul truck. They returned to Rio Grande where they finished packing their belongings. The next morning after breakfast they had just started to load the truck when the entire BP station arrived to help. In Less than two hours the truck was loaded and Jeff's pickup was attached to the truck by a tow-bar.

Jeff thanked all of the guys while Josefina rewarded each with a kiss on the cheek. Jeff then slowly walked over to where Wilson and Hayden were standing. "So long amigos," he said around the lump in his throat. Josefina came over and kissed both supervisors with tears running down her face. She then ran to the truck and jumped in crying. Jeff hugged both saying, "you guys come see us."

"We will," they both replied.

Jeff drove out of the yard and turned west on highway 83. They drove for about fifty miles each with their own thoughts. Then Jeff turned to Josefina, "well sweetheart one part of our life is over, but we have a new one starting." Josefina smiled and moved over beside him, they stayed that way through Laredo.

Josefina asked, "didn't you travel to Laredo to testify in Federal Court?"

"Sure did, several times," he replied. "I remember one time Ed Cook and I caught forty pounds of marijuana in the trunk of a car at Randado. We came here to court and we both testified that the vehicle appeared to be heavily loaded. The guy was bound over for trial. Later as I entered the elevator, the Federal Judge also got on."

He looked over at me and said, "That vehicle appeared to be heavily loaded did it Officer?"

"Yes Sir, I replied, wondering where he was going with this."

"You Border Patrol Agents have the most amazing eyesight of any group of people that I know. I had one of you testify one time that a car appeared to be heavily loaded and they found six ounces of dope," he told me.

"What did you say?" Josefina asked.

"There was nothing I could say except, Yes Sir."

"I heard about another case in front of the same judge. One of the agents from Hebbronville was testifying on a dope case and when he said the vehicle appeared to be heavily loaded the defense lawyer jumped up."

"Heavily loaded, heavily loaded. Every time we have a Border Patrol Agent testify, the first thing out of his mouth is that the car appeared to be heavily loaded. I want to find out when he first noticed that the car appeared to be heavily loaded."

"The judge looked over at the agent and then said to the attorney, Go ahead and asked him."

"The attorney then asked the agent," "When was the first time you noticed that the vehicle my client was driving appeared to be heavily loaded?"

"Well sir," replied the agent, "when he first came into Hebbronville and crossed the railroad tracks."

"And why did my client's car appeared to be heavily loaded?" asked the attorney."

"He knocked off his gas tank when he crossed the tracks," the agent replied.

"They said the judge declared a recess so no one could see him laughing," Jeff told her.

Northwest of Laredo, they picked up US 277 at Carrizo Springs. They stopped in Del Rio, Texas for the night. The next morning they were on the road early and at noon turned west on Interstate 10 at Van Horn, Texas. They stopped for a quick lunch and were on the road again headed west.

Josefina was the first to spot El Paso in the distance. They could see the Franklin Mountains to the north of the city. They stayed on I-10 north out of El Paso and crossed into New Mexico in a few miles. They again turned west at Las Cruces, New Mexico on Interstate 10 and soon crossed the Rio Grande River.

Jeff said, "If we had crossed this river about fifty miles back we would be in Mexico. It seems we're leaving everything we know."

"I hope the people and the other agents will like us," Josefina said.

"They'll love you, I don't know about me," he replied.

"How many agents are stationed in Deming?" she asked.

"There will be one line supervisor and four agents. We're a backup station, which will check local farms and ranches for illegal workers. The main station is in Columbus and I believe there are about eight or nine agents assigned to it."

Late that evening they arrived in Deming and checked into a local motel. Jeff unhooked his pickup and they drove around town for an hour or so. They went to supper at a local steak place, "The Branding Iron" east of town on the old highway.

The next morning after breakfast, Jeff drove over to the BP station at the airport. The old building had once been a control tower for the airport when it was a military base during World War II.

Jeff walked in and met Cody Dunbar the Deming supervisor. After talking for a few minutes Dunbar suggested that they get some coffee. Jeff followed the BP jeep to the Best Western Motel where they both went inside. Jeff told Cody that he would like to go to work the next morning and Dunbar agreed. "Where are you staying?" he asked Jeff.

"Right here," he replied.

"I'll pick you up here at 6am and take you down to Columbus," Dunbar stated.

"That'll be just fine. I'll see you tomorrow then," Jeff told Dunbar as he left.

The next morning Josefina insisted on getting up with Jeff and going to the café with him. They had just finished their meal when Dunbar walked in and came over to their table. Jeff introduced him to Josefina and invited Dunbar to join them. Cody asked if they had found a place to buy or rent. "Not yet, Josefina plans to look around today."

"How would you like it if my wife Leeza went with you?" Cody asked Josefina.

"I would like it very much," Josefina replied. "We're here, in room twenty-two."

"We're staying next door at the Ramada. We'll stop by on the way out and I'll have my wife come over in about two hours, if that's okay with you," Cory told Josefina.

"That will be perfect," Josefina told him.

Jeff kissed her goodbye and left money on the table for the meal. He and Dunbar drove next door, where Dunbar went inside. Jeff stayed in the vehicle listening to the traffic on the radio. Cody came back out and they drove south on highway 11 toward Columbus.

"They tell me there are a hundred illegals crossing every day," Dunbar stated. "They also tell me there are about forty illegals in those mountains to the east. They are called the Florida Mountains," he continued.

Jeff was amazed, as they had only caught about fifty for the whole month in Rio Grande City. "Why don't they go in and get them?" he asked.

"They say its too much trouble. They just try to catch as many as they can, because there'll be a fresh batch crossing tomorrow."

They arrived in Columbus and met the Station Supervisor Joe Reynolds. Reynolds was a large man around fifty with a head of white hair. They followed him over to a local coffee shop where Jeff met the other Columbus Agents, who seemed a bit standoffish. Dunbar had Jeff go with one and they tracked down several illegals that day.

During the next few days Jeff rode with one of the Columbus agents and opened any wire gates they encountered. Josefina had located a ranch house for rent in the gap between the Big and Little Florida Mountains. Jeff arranged for two days off so they could unload the U-Haul truck. They did the work by themselves as no one came to help. The first night at the old house Jeff cooked some steaks outside on the grill and they enjoyed the quiet solitude. They watched several quails running to the water tank near the house.

The next week Jeff was assigned to work the Columbus area. A week later the Deming station received scouts and sedans of their own. Jeff then asked Dunbar, "Why don't we track north of I-10?"

"Reynolds says you can't track them out in those flats," Dunbar replied.

"Well, I never liked to tell a supervisor he's full of shit, but he is you know," Jeff said.

"I think so too, so why don't you take Hoffman and see what you can do out there. I'll tell Reynolds I'm having you two checking some of the ranches north of town. You might stop in at some of them if you get the chance."

"You've got it Jefe. You ready Stan?" Jeff asked.

They started east along the railroad tracks just north of I-10 and about twelve miles out of town cut a trail of fifteen. They quickly caught them near a windmill where they had sat down to rest and nap. The men were surprised to see the BP vehicle. On the way to the station, one of them said that they had been told that after crossing the big highway they wouldn't be caught.

"Well, you can pass the word that there are some new people in town who will follow you to Albuquerque if need be," Jeff told him.

In the next few weeks Jeff and Stan Hoffman each with his own vehicle began to catch more and more illegal aliens north of I-10. They were joined by Dunbar and later by another agent who had been assigned to the Deming station. The first full month they were able to work north of I-10, they apprehended more aliens than Columbus.

The next month Jeff was assigned to observe traffic on highways 180 and 26 north of Deming from 6pm to 2 am. He patrolled the highways and apprehended three aliens trying to hitch a ride five miles out of town. After processing, they were placed in the Luna County jail to be picked up the next day and Jeff returned to patrolling.

He heard the agents in Truth or Consequences come on the radio to sector, saying they had apprehended a load of narcotics. Sector requested information on where the load had originated and was told Arizona. Jeff pulled over to the side of the road and got out the map of New Mexico. He could see that highway 26 cut off about forty miles from I-10 to I-25. I'll bet that load went right through here, he thought to himself.

The next night he drove about nine miles out of town and parked by the side of the road. Suddenly he observed an older sedan with Illinois license plates go by and could see it appeared to be heavily loaded. He pulled up behind the vehicle and turned on his red lights.

The sedan pulled to the side of the road and the driver got out. Jeff identified himself and asked the driver his citizenship. The man stated he was a United States citizen born in Illinois, but appeared to be very nervous. His hands were shaking and he was sweating even though it was a cool night. Jeff then requested the driver to open the sedan's trunk for an inspection for illegal aliens.

Jeff detected, when the trunk was opened, a strong odor of marijuana. He could see several paper wrapped packages in an open bag. He reached over, stuck his finger in one, and saw a green leafy substance. Jeff placed the driver under arrest and called for assistance. Dunbar and Hoffman came out and Stan drove Jeff's sedan while Jeff drove the load vehicle with the marijuana back to the station.

After giving the driver his rights, he agreed to talk and told them he had picked up drugs at the Pancho Villa State Park in Columbus. The marijuana was weighed and found to be one hundred sixty pounds in two bags. Customs Agents were notified and took custody of the subject and narcotics.

The next night Jeff drove down to Columbus and met with one of the agents assigned there. He informed him of the dope load and what the man had said.

"Yea, we know anytime you want a dope load, all you have to do is find some hippie staying in the park," he told Jeff.

"Why don't you check the park then?" Jeff asked.

"Oh, we do from time to time," replied the agent.

"Well, I'm going to take a drive through now," stated Jeff and the Columbus agent got in with Jeff.

As they drove into the park and down along the west side, Jeff saw a pickup pulling a pop-up camper parked in one of the spaces. "That's funny," he said.

"What's funny," asked the other agent. "They are always folks camped here."

"Yes, but the camper has not been raised and no one is around. I'm going to call one of the Customs Agents and tell them about it," Jeff stated. A quick call and Jeff returned to the park alone, while the Columbus agent went to the port for coffee.

Jeff found a good hiding place and in a few minutes saw three men walk out of the brush and place some bags in the camper. He watched them leave headed toward Mexico about three miles away. About an hour later the two Customs Agents arrived and he filled them in on what he had observed.

The three lawmen settled down to wait. The Columbus agent called Jeff and asked if anything was going on. Jeff quickly told him what he had seen and the agent drove in and hid on the east side. Another hour went before Jeff saw the three guys arrive back at the camper and put more bags inside. They watched while the men lay down in the bed of the pickup and went to sleep.

Jeff turned to the Customs Agents, "how do you want it to go down?"

"When they leave, let them go up the road about three or four miles, then you make the stop," the Resident Agent in Charge told him.

It was getting light in the east when they saw the three men get out of the bed and into the cab. They started the motor and let it warm up for a few minutes. As they pulled out of the park, Jeff radioed to the other agent on how Customs wanted it handled. Jeff let the unmarked Custom sedan go first then he and the other BP unit fell in behind.

When they were about five miles up highway 11, one of the Customs agents motioned to Jeff. He floored the BP sedan and quickly pulled in behind the pickup and camper. When he turned on his red lights the vehicle pulled to the side of the road and Jeff exited his unit with his weapon drawn. He commanded the three subjects to come out on the driver's side one at a time.

As each one came out, he made him lay face down on the ground. When they were all out, he walked over and searched them while the other agents kept them covered. One of the Customs agents opened the camper and saw the bags of marijuana.

"I'll bet there is at least three to four hundred pounds here. Damn good work," he said.

One of the hippies spoke up. "I've never seen anything like this. We came down to some God forsaken place in the middle of nowhere to get our dope and spend the whole night carrying it from Mexico. We lay down and take a short nap and when we leave, the whole damn park leaves with us."

Both Customs Agents and Jeff had a good laugh.

CHAPTER 13

The next few months had Jeff busy either tracking, checking farms in the Las Uvas valley or observing traffic on the highways north of Deming. He made several arrests for narcotics smuggling during this time.

He had asked one of the Columbus Agents about the three airplanes he had seen at the dirt strip in Columbus. The agent had told him that the owners flew people on fishing trips in Mexico. Something didn't seem right about it to Jeff, and he made a mental note to look into the operation at a later time.

Jeff was tracking a trail of three, north of I-10 along with Dennis Mitchell. They had been joined by one of the BP aircraft until about 2 o'clock when he returned to El Paso almost out of fuel. The tracks were hard to follow, but they had finally followed them to the bluff on the Nunn Ranch.

He and Dennis had agreed that this was the hardest trail they ever tried to follow. Jeff was on foot going up the side of a steep bluff following turned over rocks. When he was about half way up he came across a little old man hiding behind a yucca plant. Jeff asked, "Where are you from?"

"Oaxaca Señor," he replied.

" Where are your two friends?" asked Jeff.

The old man stood up and pointed to a large boulder that Dennis was standing by about a hundred yards below them. "They are hiding under that rock, Señor," he replied.

"Hey Dennis, this guys says the other two are under that rock," he shouted.

"Bull shit," replied Dennis. "I haven't cut any sign near here."

"How about calling your two friends out," Jeff commanded.

"Juan, Jose," the old man hollered. Dennis turned toward the boulder, when dirt started moving as the two dug their way out from under the rock.

"I'll be damn," he told Jeff when he and the old man arrived. "I'd have bet money no one was here."

Jeff, Dennis and the three wets walked about a mile to where the vehicles were parked. Dennis took two of the wets with him, while Jeff had the old man sit up front with him in the scout. As they drove to Deming Jeff learned that he was named Demetrio Urbano. Demetrio told him this was the first time he had ever been caught by the Border Patrol, even though he had been crossing for years.

He then started talking about his lucky monkey, and how his luck had failed. Jeff thinking he had a pet monkey at home asked his name. "Oh no Señor, I have my monkey here with me." He then pulled a small salves tin from his pocket and opened it. He passed it to Jeff, inside was a peach seed carved into a monkey holding his tail. Demetrio then insisted that Jeff keep it when he tried to return it. "You are the first Migra to ever catch me and I want you to have it."

Jeff pulled a five-dollar bill out and gave it to Demetrio saying, "Have supper on me in Palomas tonight."

After the three were processed at the station, Jeff volunteered to haul them to the port at Columbus. When they arrived and he had given them back their bags, Demetrio shook hands with Jeff. "If I had to be caught I'm glad it was El Lobo Verde who did it," he said.

Jeff had a shocked look, "who told you I was called El Lobo Verde?"

"No one Señor, you match the description, and only El Lobo could have tracked me. But they told me you lived in Texas," replied Demetrio in Spanish. "When did you move here?"

"About three months ago," Jeff replied.

"Then I'll cross in Texas from now on," laughed Demetrio. "Adios Señor Lobo."

"Vaya con Dios, Demetrio," Jeff replied.

Jeff drove into Columbus and parked for a few minutes near the old train station. I wonder what it was like when Pancho Villa raided here in 1916, he thought. Just then he heard aircraft engines and watched as the three Cessna airplanes took off from the dirt strip and headed toward El Paso. Hauling people fishing my ass, he thought. He drove back to the Deming Station, parked the scout, and drove home to Josefina.

The next few days the trails were light so Jeff took a sedan and scouted some of the roads north of Deming. He took one road toward Cook's Peak and found a ranch over a low hill on the east side. As he drove to the ranch house in a small basin, he could see two men painting the barn. He saw the owner walk out of the house and drove over and introduced himself. He was invited inside for coffee where he met the rancher's wife. Jeff noticed that she appeared to have been crying, as her eyes were red.

As they sat in the kitchen, the rancher stated he was glad to meet Jeff, but it sure was a bad time. "You have a problem," he asked.

"Yes, we are giving my parents a surprise party this weekend for their fiftieth wedding anniversary. I sure do need those guys," the rancher stated.

"You mean the two painting the barn?" asked Jeff.

"Yes Sir," the rancher replied.

"Won't they be here next week?" Jeff asked.

"Yes, they sure will," replied the surprised rancher.

"Fine, I'll come back next Thursday," Jeff replied.

The next week Jeff returned to the ranch and picked up the two workers. From then on he would receive a call every time some illegals came through the ranch on the way north. This proved a point to Jeff; if you try to be nice it will be returned.

Several days later Jeff was again in Columbus where he met one of the Agents. The Agent told him that he had found some footprints at five-mile road west of town. "They go to the road and then return to Mexico," he told Jeff.

"Sounds like the smuggling operation has moved from the State Park to Five-mile road," he told the agent. They drove out to the location and Jeff could see where two people had indeed walked to the highway and then returned south.

"There is no telling when or what time they are doing this," the agent told Jeff.

"I have an idea. Do you have an old flashlight, some insulated wire, and some ignition points from a car engine?" Jeff asked.

"I can get them," the agent replied.

"Let's go then," Jeff stated. An hour later the two agents returned to the location, where Jeff wired up the flashlight and placed a long hood over the lens. He placed it about fifteen feet off the ground on a nearby electric pole and pointed the lens toward Columbus. The insulated wire from the flashlight was run through the brush to a fence post that paralleled the dirt road coming from the border. The car points were then attached to the post and a small piece of plastic was inserted between the points.

"Now, all you need is a piece of black thread tied to the plastic. You run it across the road and tie it to a bush. When someone walks up this road they'll pull the plastic out and the flashlight will come on. We should be able to see it from Columbus," Jeff stated. They then drove back into Columbus for coffee.

Just after dark they returned to the dirt road where Jeff let Kurt off at the intersection to look around. Jeff drove a short distance down the dirt road to where the sensor was located and parked the sedan. He could hardly see because it was now full dark with no moon. He tied the thread across the road to a bush and returned to the BP sedan. He could see a vehicle traveling west on the highway so he waited for it to pass the location. The vehicle stopped at the intersection and slowly turned around. Jeff could hear the motor revved up several times and then heard the driver give a loud whistle.

Well shit, thought Jeff and gave a loud whistle back. He saw the vehicle start to move and heard Kurt holler, "Stop, stop." He jumped in the sedan and floored the engine. As he drove onto the highway he could see Kurt had a man around the neck with his left arm and his weapon pointing at the driver who was still in the vehicle.

Jeff pulled the unit in front of the other sedan and jumped out with his weapon in his hand. "What's going on?" he asked as he removed the driver, who had a death grip on the steering wheel.

"The guy I have here just threw two packages into the back seat, after the driver gave a whistle. I heard someone whistle down the road toward you. Then I saw this guy come running over the old railroad bed and throw in the packages. I grabbed him before he could get away," said Kurt.

"That was me returning his whistle," Jeff replied. Suddenly there was a loud explosion as Kurt's weapon went off into the pavement. "Shit," hollered Jeff, jumping on the driver's back and pulling his .357. "What the hell happened?"

"My gun went off," said Kurt. They quickly handcuffed the driver and the other subject, placing them in the back seat of the BP sedan. Kurt then went over the old railroad bed where he found another illegal alien hiding in the brush.

Later at the office while they were waiting for the Customs Agent to come down, the driver asked, "was that a warning shot out there?"

"Hell no, my gun went off when I lowered the hammer," Kurt replied.

"You sure scared the crap out of me," said Jeff.

"Me too," the driver replied. "You guys knew I was coming didn't you?" asked the driver who had been given his rights.

"We can't say anything about that," Jeff quickly stated. He winked at Kurt where the driver couldn't see him.

"I know I was set up," the driver replied. He then told who had sent him to pick up the forty pounds of marijuana. The Customs Agents arrived, signed the I-44 for the drugs and subjects then departed.

Kurt left for Columbus and Jeff finished the paper work, and then drove home. Josefina was waiting up when he arrived and he told her all about the seizure. "That guy still thinks somebody snitched him off. He doesn't know it was dumb luck that he got caught."

The next night Jeff drove to Columbus, where he and Kurt started to five-mile road just after dark. When they were about a mile from the intersection, they saw the headlights of a vehicle stop at five-mile road. The car then made a U-turn and started westbound on highway Nine. "Shit, we've had another picked up, put your foot in it

Kurt," Jeff said. As the BP unit picked up speed through the curves, they lost sight of it. When they topped out on the other side they saw the vehicle pull back on the highway from the side of the road and quickly pulled it over.

While Kurt checked the driver's identification, Jeff ran back down the road where the vehicle had been parked. With his flashlight in one hand and his weapon in the other, he followed some footprints to the old railroad bed. He located a subject hiding behind a large yucca with two bags of marijuana. Jeff made him roll over on his stomach and handcuffed him, and then walked him back to where Kurt was with the driver.

Both subjects and the thirty pounds of marijuana were released to the Customs Agents. "How about that partner," Jeff said. "We've caught two loads with our flashlight sensor and haven't even got it set up."

A few days later Jeff and Kurt were notified that they had to travel to Albuquerque for a hearing on one of the smugglers before a Federal Magistrate. They were both in civilian clothes but driving a marked unit for the trip. Near Belen, New Mexico about thirty miles south of Albuquerque, the railroad tracks paralleled Interstate 25 and are about ¼ mile to the east of the highway. Jeff looking out the window spotted four illegals walking the tracks. A quick call on the radio revealed that a detention officer was departing Albuquerque heading south. He agreed to take the aliens to the T or C station for processing.

Jeff and Kurt drove over to the railroad tracks at the next crossroad and apprehended the four men. They had a very dejected look when they saw the Border Patrol sedan and realized they were caught. Jeff winked at Kurt and made the men show the soles of their shoes to him. "Yep, you guys crossed near Columbus didn't you? We've been trailing you for six days," Jeff told them.

"Ay mierda," (oh shit) "we've been walking for eight days," one of the men replied.

After turning the men over to the detention officer Jeff and Kurt continued on to Albuquerque and testified at the hearing. The narcotics smuggler was bound over for trial.

A few days later Jeff is again working in Columbus with Kurt, both in separate vehicles. Jeff observed sedan acting suspicious near the park on highway 11. The vehicle drove by the big ditch near the park several times and then stopped on the road. Jeff by this time was on foot near the road when he saw a person run out of the brush and jumped into the vehicle. He called Kurt on his walkie-talkie and had him stop the car and arrest both the illegal alien and the driver.

He started back to his unit when he heard some movement in the nearby brush. Using his flashlight he located a subject lying on the ground about fifteen yards off the road. Jeff reached down and dragged the man to his feet. The guy grabbed Jeff by both wrists and they tugged at each other for a while. To hell with this Jeff thought, I'll put a little karate on him.

Jeff threw the guy over one hip to the ground. Thinking he had knocked the fight out of the subject reached down and dragged the man back on his feet. The guy took a swing at him and hit him in the chest. Well damn, he thought to himself and again he grabbed the man and threw him to the ground. This time the guy hangs on and pulls Jeff down with him. Jeff was finally able to get a headlock on the guy, but couldn't get up.

Jeff hears Kurt calling him and finally got enough air to shout, "come help me with this carbon." Kurt walks over where Jeff is still struggling on the ground with the alien.

"Hey pendejo pararse," Kurt says. The guy keeps fighting until Kurt reached down and hit him with his flashlight. Batteries go every which way and the guy folds up. That ended the fight. Jeff is finally able to get up and bring the man to his feet where he was handcuffed. Kurt tells Jeff, "the driver says he was going to get fifty dollars each for a ride to Silver City." They transport all three subjects to Deming where they were placed in the Luna County jail to await prosecution.

The next two months were routine tracking and sign cutting north of I-10. Jeff had just finished processing several illegals at the Deming office, when Dunbar said, "telephone Jeff, its your wife."

Jeff walked into Dunbar's office and picked up the telephone. "Jeff, Mother just called and she needs us at the ranch as soon as possible. Something is wrong, but she won't tell me what it is over the telephone," Josefina told him.

"Let me arrange some time off and I'll be right home," Jeff told her. Jeff turned to SPA Dunbar, "I need some annual leave my mother-in-law has a problem in Mexico."

"Just fill out a slip for what you need," Dunbar told him.

"I'm not sure how much I'll need, I'm going to put in for a week right now," Jeff said.

"That's fine, said Cody, if you need more just call in."

Jeff quickly drove home, where he found a distraught Josefina. "What did Carmen say?" he asked.

"She was crying and would only say that she needed help. I asked her if Abuelo was okay. She kept repeating, hurry please hurry. I packed our clothes while I was waiting for you."

"Good girl, let me hide my weapon in the truck and we'll be on the road," he told her.

"I have a better idea," Josefina told him. "I'll place it in the suitcase under my panties. Mexican men do not like to go through women's underwear."

"Damn, you're smart," he told her.

"No, I just know how the males are in Mexico."

Jeff and Josefina quickly departed Deming en route to Rancho Alegre. "The quickest way is east on I-10 to Van Horn, then down to Presidio, Texas. We can cross there, go through Ojinaga and take highway 18 southeast to La Perla. I believe we can find a dirt road that will take us to Sierra Mojada," Jeff told her.

Five hours later, they drove into Presidio, picked up some hamburgers to go and filled the tank with gas. They didn't have any trouble with Mexican Customs and were soon on highway 18. By this time it was very dark and Jeff slowed the truck down. "We have to be careful about livestock on the road," he said.

When they arrived in the village of La Perla it was about 4 o'clock in the morning and everything was closed. "We better take a short nap in the truck and I'll ask about directions in the morning," said Jeff. He wedged a pillow against the door and leaned back on it. He placed his legs out across the floor and pulled Josefina against him. Both were very tired and quickly went to sleep.

A loud rooster in a nearby yard woke them just as the sun was rising over the hills to the east. They found a small café where Jeff ordered breakfast while Josefina used the bathroom. Jeff also got directions to Sierra Mojada. As they were eating he relayed the information. "We keep going south to San Fernando and take a dirt road east. The owner here says it will go through the hills to Sierra Mojada. When we are finished with breakfast, I'll top off the gas tank, if you'll pick up a few things to take with us."

While Jeff filled the gas tank, Josefina walked to the next block where there was a Tienda de Abarrotes. (Grocery Store) She returned shortly with a sack of eats and two sapares as the morning was very cool. They drove south out of town and found the narrow dirt road leading to the east. Jeff turned to Josefina and said, "you better get my pistol out. There is no telling what we'll come across on the road."

It was slow going, as the road was rough with places washed out. About noon they forded a small creek and saw a goat herder nearby with several goats. Jeff pulled the pickup under a large tree and called to the man, "que tal ?"

"Buenos Dias Señor," replied the goat herder. He saw Josefina get out of the truck and quickly removed his sombrero. As Josefina removed the sacks of eats, Jeff invited the man to have lunch with them. In a few minutes Josefina had him talking about the condition of the road as she handed out the goat cheese and other items she had purchased. He introduced himself as Jesus Ortal and had lived near here all his life.

As they were eating their lunch, Jesus told them he had been seeing strange things at night. When Jeff inquired what he had seen, he reported strange lights in the sky to the southeast. He also stated that he had been seeing more vehicles on this road than usual. Jeff and Josefina bid him goodbye and gave him the rest of the cheese. As they drove off Jeff said, "I believe we are no more than twenty miles from the ranch."

In less that an hour they entered the sleepy village of Sierra Mojada. They quickly turned on the road that led to the ranch, but this time Jeff did not see any riders. When they drove into the yard, Carmen and Arturo Mora came out of the house to meet them. Jeff saw that Arturo was carrying a pistol under his short jacket. Carmen hugged Josefina, then Jeff as Josefina hugged Arturo.

"What's going on Mama?" she asked.

"Come inside and I'll tell you all I know," Carmen replied. When they were seated around the large table, Carmen drew a ragged breath. "Some strange men came last week to see your Grandfather. They talked for about thirty minutes in his office, and then Papa ordered them off the ranch. I've never seen him so angry. When I asked him about them, he would only say they were "zopilotes."

"He called them buzzards?" asked Jeff.

"Yes, that is his term for any lowlife worthless person," continued Carmen. "Yesterday morning he left here to make a quick trip into town and never returned. We found his truck near the gate and there were spots of blood on the seat. There was also this note," which she pulled from her pocket.

Jeff and Josefina quickly read the note written in Spanish. It said: "we have O'Connor. Do not contact the Police if you want to see him again. Do not go into the land south of the Red Buttes." "It was then I called Arturo and you two. What are we going to do? I'm worried sick for Papa," Carmen said.

Jeff turned to Arturo, "what do you think amigo?"

"Last night I rode a horse to the other side of the butte. There is an old adobe house located there near a dry lakebed. I didn't get too close, but I was able to see some lights at the house. They may be holding El Patron there. There will be a quarter moon tonight about 11 o'clock," Arturo told him.

"Okay, first we all need to get some rest, then if you can have two horses ready about 9 tonight, you and I'll take a little ride," Jeff stated.

"Until tonight then," said Arturo. Josefina followed him outside, but returned in a few minutes.

Jeff turned to Carmen. "Does Cory have any firearms here on the ranch?"

"Sure, follow me," Carmen said. She walked into Cory's office to a large bookcase. She pulled at one side and it pivoted out away from the wall. Jeff saw a recessed door, which was unlocked and opened by Carmen. Just inside the door was a light switch and stairs leading down below the office. Jeff and Josefina followed her down into a large basement.

"I never knew this was here," said Josefina.

"Your Grandfather intended to tell you and Jeff when you were married, but there was so much confusions, Carmen replied. Jeff looked at the walls, which were covered with all types of rifles, shotguns, and pistols. Shelves below held all types of ammunition.

Jeff walked slowly over to the rifles both bolt action and lever action. Further down were shotguns, then pistols. "I don't believe this, look at this, it's a Thompson MIAI."

Josefina walked over to where Jeff was holding the weapon. "What is it?" she asked.

"This was used in World War II. It shoots the .45 ACP, the same bullet my pistols uses and can be fired on full automatic." Jeff located spare magazines for the weapon and boxes of ammo.

Josefina walked further down where the pistols were hanging. "Look Jeff, Abuelo has a Colt .38 Super just like the one of Papas."

Carmen said, "yes, your Grandfather purchased both of them at the same time and gave one to your Father after he became the Comandante." Carmen then handed Jeff a key to the door. "Take anything you need or want," she told him.

"We need to get some sleep and later Arturo and I will take a little ride," Jeff stated as he and Josefina followed Carmen upstairs. The two young people went to their room and were quickly asleep.

When Jeff woke about 5 o'clock in the evening, Josefina was already up and gone. He found her and Carmen in the kitchen. They were placing plates on the table for the evening meal. Arturo came into the house through the back door. "Is everything ready?" Jeff asked.

"Si mi Jefe," replied Arturo.

"No, I'm not the Jefe we're partners on this," he told Arturo.

"You two sit down and eat," Carmen told them. While they ate Jeff and Arturo talked about the land and trails south of the buttes. Arturo told Jeff there were no cattle were in the area.

"What kind of pistol are you carrying?" he asked. Arturo reached under his jacket and handed over his weapon. Jeff saw that it was a Colt single action in .38-40 caliber. "Very good," Jeff stated and handed it back to Arturo.

"Some of the vaqueros want to help," said Arturo.

"I understand, but I believe you and I need to scout it out first," Jeff stated.

"As you wish," Arturo replied. The two then walked into the office, where there was a large map of the ranch on one wall. Arturo pointed out where the old adobe house was located and the trails leading there. They talked for another fifteen minutes, and then Arturo left to get the horses.

Jeff using the key Carmen had given him went down into the basement. He picked up the Thompson and two extra magazines for the weapon along with several boxes of ammo. Locking the door behind him, he went to the bedroom for his jacket and pistol.

As he walked into the kitchen, Josefina came from one of the back rooms. Jeff almost didn't recognize her. She was wearing tight black pants, a red silk shirt with a short black jacket. Her hair was tucked up under a flat crowned hat. He could see an automatic pistol tucked under her belt on the left side with the butt forward. She had a double barrel hammerless shotgun with the barrel cut down to twelve inches and the stock sawed off behind the pistol grip in her left hand.

"Where the hell do you think you're going?" he asked.

Josefina stopped about a foot away, her eyes flashing. "I don't "think" I know where I'm going. That's my Grandfather out there and I'm going with you or without you. You decide," she stated.

"Now sweetheart," Jeff began.

"Don't you dare try sweet talking me Jeff, it won't work. I love you very much, but I'm going and you might as well get use to it." Just then Carmen walked into the kitchen behind Jeff and he turned to her.

"Can't you reason with her?" he asked.

"She's her Father's daughter, you may as well try moving a mountain, you'd have better luck," Carmen replied.

Jeff stood there looking at Josefina for a minute. She looked him straight in the eye and said, "I know what I'm doing Jeffie."

"Okay, it's a hell of a man who can't control his own wife," he replied.

"Don't try making me feel guilty, that's not going to work either," she stated.

Jeff finally grinned at her, "Let me see that thing you're carrying." Josefina handed over the shotgun and Jeff broke open the barrels. He pulled out the two shells and looked at them. Both were marked 00 buck. He replaced the shells and handed the weapon back to her. "Where did you get that thing?" he asked.

"Abuelo gave it to me when I was about 17, he said I couldn't miss," she replied.

"He was sure right about that, if you're close enough," Jeff said. There was a rawhide cord looped through the stock and she placed it over her shoulder. "Let's go," he said and hugged her to him briefly.

A small tear ran out of one of her eyes as she looked up at him. "Thank you," she whispered. She then hugged her mother who said, "you two be careful."

They both walked outside where three horses were saddled and waiting along with Arturo. He had on a gun belt with the loops filled with ammo and a rifle in a saddle scabbard. Jeff looked at the three horses then at Arturo who grinned back at him. "You too?" he asked. Arturo just shrugged his shoulders and gave one set of reins to Josefina. Jeff took the other set, placing the extra magazines and ammo in the saddlebags, then swung up on the horse. The Thompson was over one shoulder on a sling. Arturo led the way south in single file.

After riding for about two hours they rode up on a small hill. Arturo pointed out where the house was located. They could see fire burning in the front yard. "There is a dry creek at the bottom of this hill, it runs by the house about a half a kilometer from it. We can ride the horses that close. There are some small trees where we can tie them," he stated as he led the way down.

They slowly made their way up the creek, being careful not to make any noise. When they had reached the place Arturo wanted, he reined up and dismounted. Jeff and Josefina also dismounted and they tied the horses to some trees. With Arturo leading the way, they walked up to the top of the bank near a large tree. From there they could see the fire in the yard and several men around it. They could also see a dim light in one window.

Jeff removed his spurs and said, "You two stay here while I see if I can get close enough to find out if Cory is there."

"You be careful," whispered Josefina.

"You know I will," Jeff said as he disappeared into the darkness.

Arturo turned to Josefina and in soft Spanish said, "You married a good man."

"I know," she said. "But sometimes he thinks women should stay home and shut up."

"Mi hija, if I thought it would have kept you at home I would have taken his side, but I know how you are. You are more like Napo than Carmen," Arturo replied.

"Thank you Tio, there are four men I love, one has passed to a better place. The other three are still here. I'll do what needs to be done to keep them safe," Josefina stated.

Jeff returned in less than an hour. His sudden appearance caused Arturo to reach for his gun. "Easy amigo," he told Arturo.

"What did you find out, mi amor?" Josefina asked.

"There are five around the fire and one more on the porch by the door. I could also see one moving around in the house. I believe that Cory is in the house as I overheard one talking about El Viejo." (the old one)

"What did he say, Jeff?" asked Josefina.

"They were talking about him not eating very much and about a plane coming in the morning to carry him away," Jeff stated.

"How do you want to do this?" asked Arturo.

"I don't believe we can wait for more help. I think we're it," Jeff said. "Give me thirty minutes to get in back of the house. Be ready to ride, when you hear me cut loose. Make a quick pass shooting at anything that moves then ride back here. I'll get Cory out the back door and meet you. We should have brought another horse for Cory, but we'll make do," said Jeff.

He walked down to where the horses were tied and removed the Thompson slung from it's sling on the saddle horn. He placed the two extra magazines under his belt. He walked over to Josefina and kissed her. "I don't guess it would do any good to ask you to stay here," he stated.

"Not whatsoever," she replied, as she hugged him.

"Then keep your head down," he said and left at a trot.

Arturo turned to Josefina and said, "let's be ready to go." They untied their two horses and made sure that Jeff's was securely tied. His mount wanted to go with theirs. They walked the horses to the top of the bank and waited under the tree.

CHAPTER 14

Cory O'Connor was sitting on the front porch when two men drove up in a new black GMC pickup. The driver was about forty, two hundred pounds wearing tan pants and a light brown windbreaker. The passenger was in his mid fifties and he was nicely dressed, with several gold chains around his neck. As they walked up to the porch, Cory met them at the steps.

"Are you Señor O'Connor?" asked the older man. "Si Señor," Cory replied.

"May we have a few minutes of your time to discuss some business?"

"Of course, please come in," he replied. The older man introduced himself as Felipe Salinas and the driver as Joel Sosa. Cory led the way into his office and asked one of the maids to bring coffee and some sweet bread. Cory sat behind his desk, while the two were seated in leather-covered chairs to one side. The coffee was served and they talked for several minutes about the price of cattle and feed, Salinas came to the reason for the visit.

"Señor O'Connor, I represent a gentleman that would like to lease the land south of the Red Buttes and the old abandoned house. He would pay very well."

"I'm sorry you had a trip for nothing. No part of my ranch is for lease," Cory told him.

"Señor, you don't understand. This gentleman would pay you more for this lease than you can make raising cattle."

"I'm still not interested, but I'm curious of what he would use the land for," Cory replied.

Salinas then made his first mistake. "He needs a place for a fuel stop for his aircraft, what he does after that, needn't concern you," Salinas stated.

It suddenly dawned on Cory that these people wanted the use of his ranch to smuggle drugs into the United States. He stood up and in a voice edged with anger and eyes blazing said, "I must ask you to leave my house and ranch, this meeting is over."

Salinas then made his second mistake. "Señor, you do not want my patron as an enemy."

"You're threatening me in my own home?" He looked at them as if they were cockroaches needing to be stepped on. O'Connor opened a desk drawer and removed a long barrel pistol. "You will leave my land and do not come back," he replied in a firm voice.

The two walked outside with Cory following behind. Just before they entered the pickup Salinas turned to Cory. "We'll be back," he said

Cory raised the single action Colt and shot out one of the headlights on the pickup. "I'll be waiting," he said. Both men jumped into the pickup and quickly drove off. Cory turned to his foreman who had run around the corner of the house when he heard the gunshot. "Pass the word if any rider sees that pickup on the ranch again, shoot the driver," Cory told him.

"Si mi Jefe," the foreman replied. Just then Carmen came out of the house as she had also heard the gunfire.

"What's going on Papa?" she asked.

"Just getting rid of some zopilotes," he replied. They watched the cloud of dust from the speeding pickup as it left the ranch.

"What did they want Papa?" she asked.

"Nothing to get concerned about," he replied his voice still tight with anger. Carmen could see that he was very pissed off and wisely decided not to ask any more questions.

***

Several days later Cory and Carmen were having breakfast. "I'm going to town today to pick up some horseshoes I ordered. Is there anything you need," he asked.

"Yes, please pick up some hand soap for me. Don't you want one of the vaqueros to go with you?" she asked him.

"No, they have plenty of work to do around here," he replied. He walked into his office and removed his pistol from the desk drawer. He placed it under his jacket, got his hat and left the ranch in his pickup. When he arrived in town, he removed the pistol and laid it on the seat of the truck. He first picked up the horseshoes he had ordered from the Ferreteria. (Hardware store) He then walked across the street to the store for Carmen's hand soap. As he left the store he met two friends and they went to the nearby café for coffee.

One asked if some men had come to see him last week. "Yes," Cory replied, "but I don't think they'll be back."

"Who were they?" his friend asked.

"Just some lowlife smugglers. If you see General Huerta in town, tell him I would like to visit with him at his convenience." The three friends talked for about an hour then Cory left for the ranch.

As he left the café and entered his truck he saw a small dirt bike leaving town. He failed to see the black van that pulled out behind him and stayed about a half-mile back. As he approached the gate to his ranch he was startled to see the dirt bike lying in the road with the driver in the nearby ditch. It threw him, he thought to himself. He quickly stopped the truck and ran over to the rider, who was face down. When Cory gently rolled him over to check for injuries, he suddenly found himself looking into the barrel of a pistol.

"Don't move," the rider commanded.

The black van pulled up and three men jumped out with weapons pointing at Cory. When one of the men got in front of the others to search him, Cory pushed him into them and ran for his pickup. He was reaching for his pistol lying on the seat when he was hit on the head. Cory fell on to the front seat, where one of the men grabbed his belt and pulled him outside. Cory fell to the ground with his head bleeding and was handcuffed. One grabbed his pistol while the other two loaded him into the van, while the rider picked up his dirt bike. With the small motorcycle leading the way, they left the area.

Several miles down the road they turned off the main road on an unused dirt road and made their way to an abandoned house with several outbuildings. There was a dry lakebed a quarter of a mile south of the house. Cory was still unconscious when they carried him into the house. There was an old bed with just the springs on it in the front room. One of the men opened a bedroll he was carrying and spread it out on the springs.

"Put him here," he said. There was an iron eyebolt sticking out of the wall near the bed with a chain attached. One end was padlocked around one of Cory's ankles. "Now you can remove the cuffs," he stated.

When Cory regained consciousness, he tried to sit up. His head felt like it was coming off and he was very dizzy. One of the men brought him a glass of water and Cory mumbled his thanks, still unsure of what was happening. It became clear when the door opened and in walked Salinas.

"How are you feeling?" he asked Cory.

"Like hammered shit," replied Cory.

"Well, you brought it on yourself," Salinas replied.

"What is it you want?" Cory asked.

"We have what we want now, you should have taken the money," Salinas laughed. "We have a plane coming through headed north tomorrow. When it returns, you and I will take a little trip down south," stated Salinas.

Joel Sosa came in carrying a bag of groceries and placed it in the kitchen. He came out and walked over to Cory. "You're not the big man now without your pistol, are you Viejo?" He pulled back his jacket and Cory could see his own pistol stuck in Sosa's pants.

"I'm going back to town and notify El Jefe. You're in charge, see that he doesn't get away," Salinas told Sosa.

The day passed slowly for Cory. When he needed to use the bathroom, he was unchained and under heavy guard walked outside to a small privy. Later that night, one of the men cooked supper, but Cory didn't have an appetite and only drank some coffee. The men built a fire outside near the front porch. He could see several men around it drinking, but someone always stayed in the room with him. Salinas returned late in the evening.

The next morning he was able to eat a little and drank some more coffee. His head was still throbbing and he thought he might have a concussion. Late that evening near sundown he heard the sound of an airplane. He heard Salinas tell Sosa, "I'm going with the plane and should be back early in the morning. When we do, he will go with us," pointing at Cory. Cory watched as Salinas and several of the men drove off in one of the vehicles. Sosa had walked outside and he was left with one guard.

"Where are they going?" he asked.

"Shut up," snarled the guard.

Later that evening, the fire was again built in the front yard and Cory could see Sosa passing around a bottle. His guard was sitting in a chair near the front door. One of the men had brought him some beans and tortillas for supper, but he was only able to eat a few bites. I must not lose hope, he thought to himself.

***

Jeff had made a detour around the house and approached it from the rear through the brush. When he was within fifty yards of the house, he stopped to check his weapons. His .45 automatic was in a holster on the left side with the butt forward. A round in the chamber cocked and locked. Two more magazines for the pistol were in his left jacket pocket. The spare magazines for the Thompson were tucked under his belt.

He checked the Thompson and made sure that both levers on the left side were in the forward position. This meant that the weapon was on full automatic and the safety was off. He pulled the bolt back in the open position and made sure the magazine was fully seated. He slipped by the outbuilding and to the rear of the house.

Jeff eased up to the back door and pushed it open. The door opened into the kitchen, which was empty. He could see light from a kerosene lamp in what he believed to be the front room. He walked quietly to the connecting door and took a quick look inside. He saw Cory sitting on the bed with his head in his hands. A dirty white bandage was tied around his head. He saw the guard seated in a chair near the front door looking out the window. He could see the fire in the front yard through the window and men moving around it. He eased into the room keeping out of sight of the window. He pointed the Thompson at the guard and said, "Phsstt."

The man looked over his shoulder and his eyes grew wide as he saw the figure in the door. "Tenga cuidado," (be careful) he told the guard. Cory looked up from the bed.

"Jeff!" he said and jumped to his feet.

When Jeff looked at Cory, the guard made his move. He fell out of the chair to the floor, pulling his pistol as he fell. Shit, thought Jeff and touched the trigger on the Thompson. A five round burst chewed up the floor and three of the heavy slugs hit the guard in the chest, killing him on the spot.

Cory was pulling on the chain, but was unable to get free. Jeff could see several of the men start toward the house. "Get down Abuelo," he shouted and triggered a burst through the window. He then fired another burst through the door, killing the man that had been running toward it. Cory had dropped to the floor and Jeff changed magazines in the Thompson.

Arturo and Josefina had been walking their horses toward the house and were only about two hundred yards out, still in the dark when they heard the gunfire. Josefina slammed her heels into her horse's side and came into the yard at a hard run, riding like a bat out of hell. She had lost her hat and her long hair was blowing in the wind.

One of the men near the fire turned toward her, aiming his pistol. He hesitated when he saw she was a girl and it cost him his life. Guiding the horse with her knees, the reins in her teeth, she pointed the shotgun at him and fired both barrels. The charge from the first barrel straightened him up and the other barrel knocked him down.

Then she was through the light from the fire, bent low in the saddle. Her heels were drumming her horse into even greater speed, his hooves throwing up little chunks of dirt, as she disappeared into the darkness, dust hung in the night air.

Arturo was about fifteen yards behind Josefina and was firing his single action Colt as fast as he could while leaning low over his mount's neck. One man had almost reached the porch when he was hit by a bullet from Arturo and fell. He was crawling toward the porch when a burst of .45 caliber slugs from inside the house knocked him over on his back. He twitches a few times and is still.

A man near the pickup was firing a full automatic weapon at Arturo, who fired back at him and missed. Just then his horse took several slugs in the chest and fell near the fire. When he felt his horse falling, he kicked his feet loose and went into a roll. He came up on his feet with three men still shooting at him. He ran back to his dead horse through a hail of gunfire and jumped behind the body, where he reloaded his pistol.

Josefina looked back and saw Arturo's horse fall. Sliding her horse to a stop, she broke open her shotgun and quickly reloaded it as she turned back toward the fire. Again she slammed her heels into the horse and he took off like his tail was on fire.

The man near the pickup was hidden from the house and was taking careful aim on Arturo when Josefina came riding back into the light. The man who was trying to shoot Arturo took both barrels from her shotgun as she raced into the yard.

Sliding her horse to a stop, she fell as she dismounted and dropped the shotgun. One of the men decided he had enough of this and was trying to shoot at the house and start the pickup at the same time. Jeff stepped through the front door and fired a full magazine from the Thompson into the truck. That ended both the man's shooting and starting the truck.

The other man was shooting at Josefina as she lay on the ground. Josefina rolled over twice and pulled her Grandfather's .38 Colt. She fired six times just as Arturo stood up fanning the hammer on his .38-40. The man appeared to be dancing as the heavy slugs hit him in the chest. He was dead when he finally fell to the ground.

Suddenly the night was quiet and still. Arturo reloaded and stepped from behind his dead horse with his pistol cocked. He walked over to where Josefina was getting up and helped her stand.

"Are you all right, mi hija?"

"Yes, I'm okay, where's Jeff?" Josefina replied.

"I'm here," said Jeff as he and Cory walked out of the house. Jeff had found the key to the padlock in the pocket of the guard he had killed in the house.

"Abuelo," cried Josefina as she ran to her Grandfather and hugged him. "Are you okay?" she asked looking at the bandage.

"I'm fine now, thanks to you guys. You are a sight for sore eyes," Cory stated.

Jeff said, "Well, we have a small problem. We have four people and two horses. This truck won't run, it got a slug through the distributor. Plus how in hell are we going to explain all this? Especially this thing," holding up the Thompson.

Cory looked at Jeff and then laughed. "Not to worry nieto," he said. "Just let me get to a telephone and I can take care of this," he said motioning around the yard. "First, let me get something." He walked over to where Sosa lay by the porch and rolled him over with his foot. They saw him reach down and pick up a pistol from the dead man's hand. Cory came walking back.

"Just wanted my old pistol," he said, placing the old Colt in his belt.

Jeff turned to Arturo, "Take Josefina's horse and pick up mine where we left him. Get Abuelo home and cared for, then you can return for us."

"I'll come back by the road just as soon as I can," Arturo replied. He had Cory mount Josefina's horse, and then got on behind him. "You two be careful until I get back," Arturo stated.

"Until we get back," corrected Cory.

After they were gone, Jeff turned to Josefina, "I thought you were to ride through one time only. I just lost ten years of my life, when I saw you come riding back in and fall."

"Well, when I looked back I saw Tio's horse go down. I was coming back to pick him up and couldn't see him. He was hidden behind the horse. When I dismounted, I tripped and fell on my ass, if you must know," she said dusting herself off.

"Just as long as you're okay," Jeff said hugging her to him. They put more wood on the fire and looked around the yard. Jeff found a turned over coffeepot and refilled it with water and set it on the fire. He pulled up a small log and he and Josefina huddled together in the crisp night air.

The sun was just coming up over the low hills to the east, when Jeff heard the sound of an airplane. They watched as the plane made a low pass over the dry lakebed, then turn toward the house.

"Shit, that must be the plane returning. Cory told me they were going to move him to another location. Well, there's nothing we can do. I can't move that dead horse and they'll see the bodies."

Jeff watched as the low flying twin-engine airplane came toward them. When it was about a hundred yards away, he brought up the Thompson and fired his last loaded magazine at it. He saw the plane fly into the stream of bullets and pieces of Plexiglas came off. The plane made a violent maneuver away from the house and start climbing. They watched as it disappeared into the rising sun.

"Did you see any tail numbers?" he asked.

"No, they turned too quickly," Josefina replied.

By 10 o'clock, Arturo and Cory returned in one of the ranch's pickups with four armed vaqueros riding in the back. They pulled up by Josefina and Jeff and all stepped down.

"I called General Huerta and he should be here very soon," Cory told them.

"Well, your plane came back, but didn't land," Jeff said.

"To bad you didn't shoot it down," Cory replied.

"I tried," stated Jeff. "I did hit it, as some pieces came off, but it was still climbing when we last saw it."

Jeff walked over to the ranch pickup and placed the Thompson behind the seat. As he walked back to them, he stopped to listen. "I hear some helicopters coming," he said.

"That will be the General," replied Cory.

They watched as two military helicopters swept in and made a circle around the house. Both pulled up and landed about fifty yards away in a cloud of dust. Armed solders jumped out and formed up. Cory walked toward them and was met by a Captain, who escorted him to meet the General.

Jeff, Josefina, and Arturo watched as the General embraced Cory then started toward them. When they walked up Cory said, "General, I would like to introduce you to my granddaughter, Josefina and her husband Jeff Larson. My grandson is a Border Patrolman, stationed in New Mexico."

General Huerta made a low bow to Josefina as he took her hand in his. "I knew your father and was very saddened to hear of his death."

"Thank you," she replied.

General Huerta then turned to Jeff. "So, I finally get to meet El Lobo Verde himself," he stated as he shook Jeff's hand. "Coronel O'Connor tells me that you are a great pistolero," he continued.

"I'm afraid my grandfather exaggerates sometimes," Jeff said.

"I have known El Coronel for many years, he never exaggerates," stated the General. "Why don't you all go home and leave this mess to my men, he said. "They will take care of everything. You are not to worry."

"As you wish my General," said Cory. "If you have time, please stop by the ranch."

"A later time perhaps. I must report this to Ciudad Mexico as soon as possible," the General replied. "We need to determine who these people are."

Arturo motioned the vaqueros into the truck and climbed under the wheel. Cory talked quietly to the General for a few minutes off to one side. When he was finished, he then came over and slid in next to Arturo. Jeff sat by the door with Josefina on his lap. "Let's go home," said Cory. "Carmen will have dinner ready."

The next morning Jeff and Josefina slept late. When they finally entered the kitchen Cory, Carmen, and Arturo were having a last cup of coffee. "Here's the two pistoleros now," Cory said. "We were just talking about you."

"How are you Abuelo?" asked Josefina as she hugged him.

"I'm just fine this morning," he replied.

"I've been trying to get him to see a doctor. But he's just as hard headed as always," replied Carmen.

"I don't need any doctor. They just hit me upside the head and it feels much better this morning," Cory stated.

EL LOBO VERDE

"I wanted to ask why the General call you Coronel ?" asked Jeff.

"Because I hold a commission of a Colonel in the Mexican Army," replied Cory. "It's just an honorary title, but it does permit me to have a firearm on me when I leave the ranch and travel to town."

"That reminds me, I need to clean your Thompson," Jeff said.

"No need, Arturo has taken care of it," said Cory.

Josefina spoke up saying, "Well, I still have your .38 super."

"Keep it if you want to," Cory replied.

"She still has Napo's at home. We smuggled in my .45 when we came down," Jeff said.

As the maids served Josefina and Jeff their breakfast, Cory excused himself and left the room. Carmen reached over and touched her daughter's hand.

"I was so frightened for you last night mi hija, I had visions of one of you shot."

"You should have seen her," Jeff spoke up. "She came riding in like a wild Indian shooting that shotgun. Talk about being scared when I saw her come back and fall, I just knew she had been hit."

"I told you I just tripped," Josefina replied.

"You tripped mi hija?" asked Carmen.

"Yes, I tripped when I slid off the horse and fell on my butt. I just knew Jeff was going to laugh about it," she replied.

"I was too scared to laugh then, but now looking back it is kind of funny," said Jeff.

"They shot my best horse, I've had him since he was a colt," stated Arturo.

Cory returned to the kitchen and said, "Carmen, we're having four people for dinner tomorrow. General Huerta and three of his officers will be here."

"I'll have the cook prepare something very special then," she replied.

Arturo stood up and said, "I'd better get back to the ranch. You never know when the owners may show up and fire me."

Josefina laughed and hugged him, "thank you and be very careful Tio."

"As always mi hija." He then shook Jeff's hand. "You two come by if you can," he said as he left.

"Vaya con Dios, amigo," Jeff told him.

The next day a little after noon, Jeff heard the sound of a helicopter. When he walked out on the wide veranda, he saw a military helicopter landing on the huge front lawn. As the pilot shut down his engine, Cory walked out and was greeted by General Huerta and his aide. They were soon joined by the two pilots and walked toward the house. Jeff could see that the three officers were armed with what appeared to be model 1911's. The General was carrying a 380 Beretta, model 1934 in an open holster.

"You remember my grandson Jeff, General," said Cory.

"Of course, how are you Señor," inquired General Huerta.

"I'm fine sir," Jeff replied.

"Allow me to introduce my officers," the General continued. "These are Capitains Adan Zavala and Ariel Ubaldo, my pilot and copilot. This is Teniente Angel De La Rosa, my aide." They all shook hands.

Then Cory said, "please come inside, we'll have drinks before dinner."

"Just a small one for us," replied Zavala motioning to himself and Ubaldo.

When they entered the den, Jeff was surprised to see both Carmen and Josefina were already dressed for dinner. They were dressed in identical long green dresses with bare shoulders. Both had their hair piled on top and held with silver combs. Josefina had on a pair of ruby earrings given to her by Carmen that matched her necklace. Jeff was struck by the fact that they looked more like sisters, instead of mother and daughter. Cory introduced the officers to Carmen and Josefina. The General had known Carmen since she was a little girl.

The three military officers were very taken with the two beautiful women. After several minutes of conversation a maid announced that dinner was ready. The General requested the honor of escorting Carmen and Captain Zavala asked Jeff if might have the privilege of escorting Josefina.

"Of course Señor, you are our guests," replied Jeff. He and Cory followed behind as they entered the dinning room.

Cory insisted that the General sit at the head of the table with Carmen on one side and Josefina on the other. General Huerta assisted Carmen with her chair while Captain Zavala did the same for Josefina who rewarded him with a smile. Zavala then seated himself next to her while Captain Ubaldo was seated on the other side next to Carmen. Jeff was seated next to Ubaldo and across from Lt. De La Rosa with Cory at the end.

All through dinner the two Captains were taking in every word that Josefina said. Her flashing eyes and smiles lighting up the room. Jeff thought to himself, if these two hang around very long, I'd have to shoot them.

After the meal Cory suggested that the men go into the den for cigars and brandy. Carmen and Josefina excused themselves saying they would join them later for coffee. When they were all seated in the den, General Huerta asked his aide for the paper he had been carrying. Da La Rosa removed an envelope from his jacket and handed it to him.

"My good friend Cory tells me that you had to smuggle your pistol into Mexico to help him. I have had several conversations with Comandante Morales in Miguel Aleman about you. He tells me that you were the one who avenged Napo's death. With that in mind, I would like to present you with this commission as a Lieutenant in the Mexican Army."

Jeff was speechless as he accepted the commission. He thought if the Border Patrol ever finds out about this, I'd be fired. The letter stated that Jeff was one of General Huerta's aides and authorized to carry firearms in the Republic of Mexico.

"I don't know what to say, Jeff stated. Except thanks."

"Think nothing of it," stated the General. "With that letter, you will no longer need to smuggle your weapon into Mexico. Now I would like to hear about the rescue of my friend Cory. We have not found the aircraft at present," he continued.

"You should have seen it my General," said Cory. "My grandson here came in the back door and shot the guard when he pulled his pistol. Meanwhile my granddaughter and Arturo came riding into the front yard like a cavalry charge. Arturo told me she shot two of them and put lead into a third.

The two Captains could not believe that they were talking about the beautiful young girl at dinner. Captain Zavala finally spoke up. "You are saying your granddaughter killed two of the bandits. Two of them were killed with a shotgun."

"That's right," stated Cory. "She came into that yard with her horse at a dead run. The reins were in her teeth and she shot one as she went by. When she saw Arturo's horse fall she reloaded, came back and shot another one. Arturo told me she finished another one off with my .38 automatic."

The three officers shook their heads. It was hard for them to picture the slender girl firing a pistol, much less a shotgun. The General who had known her father was less surprised.

Jeff stated, "Maybe we can get her to put on a little demonstration."

"I would really like to see that," Zavala stated.

"So would I," replied the General.

Just then Josefina and Carmen came in with coffee and desert. "Your grandfather tells me that you are a great pistolera," said General Huerta to Josefina.

"Well, sometimes I can hit the ground," she laughingly stated.

Jeff hugged her and said, "General Huerta would like to see you shoot. Would you please?" he asked her and showed her the commission.

"If it would please the General," she replied.

"Nothing would give me greater pleasure that to see the daughter of my late friend Napo and her husband **both** put on a demonstration," said General Huerta.

"Then excuse me while I change into more appropriate clothing," she said.

Jeff followed her out and to their room. "I know you don't like to show off, but the General did give me this commission. I just hope the Chief doesn't find out about it."

"I don't mind as long as I'm not shooting against someone," Josefina replied.

"Maybe when those two Captains see how well you can shoot, I won't have to shoot the bastards," Jeff told her.

"Are you jealous?" she asked.

"Hell yes, you could have given them a horse turd for dinner and they wouldn't have noticed. They were too busy eye balling you."

"You're so very sweet," laughed Josefina.

She quickly changed into tight pants and a red blouse. She took her hair down, fastened it into a ponytail, and placed her flat brimmed hat on her head. Jeff picked up his Colt .45 and the .38 Colt Super of her grandfathers.

"Let's go put on a show for them," he said, as he also picked up a box of ammo for each weapon. The last thing he picked up was a small hand mirror from the dresser.

They walked out near the barn where Cory had a shooting range with a low hill for a backstop. The range had a covered bench where Cory and the General were sitting, drinking coffee. The three officers and two of Cory's vaqueros were placing silhouette targets on two moveable stands. When the targets were ready they walked back to the shooting bench. Jeff pulled one of the vaqueros over to one side and had a brief conversation with him. He quickly left in the direction of the horse corrals.

"With your permission my General," Jeff said. The General gave a nod and Jeff along with Josefina walked to about fifteen yards of the two targets. Jeff handed her another loaded magazine for the .38. "Let's shoot one magazine center of mass and the other in the head," Jeff whispered to her.

They dropped their arms to their sides then Jeff softly said, "Go." He and Josefina brought up the weapons firing with a continuous roar of sound. When the slides locked back, Jeff beat her on the reload and was shooting first. Josefina was a half-second behind. When both weapons locked open again, they walked back to the bench and laid the weapons down. The vaquero quickly removed the targets and brought them to Cory and the General.

Jeff's target had one huge hole in the center and six holes in the head with one near miss. You could count all ten rounds in the center of Josefina's target. The nine rounds she had fired at the head, two were near misses with seven in the head. The army officers all agreed that it was good shooting.

Jeff had the vaquero put up another target. He walked to about fifteen yards of the target and turned his back to it. Using the small hand mirror to line up his sights, he started firing slowly over his shoulder. When he was finished the vaquero brought it to the General. Six of the seven shots fired were in the head, with one near miss. When the General saw the target he said, "bravo, bravo."

Just then the other vaquero came up leading a horse. Jeff met him and took the reins while the ranch hand replaced the target and turned it sideways. Jeff motioned to Josefina to join him. He quickly reloaded the .38 Colt Super with nine rounds in the magazine and one in the chamber.

After a whispered conversation with her, she placed the automatic in her belt. She mounted the horse and rode about fifty yards to one side. The horse seemed to know that this was for show as he pranced sideways with the slender girl on his back.

Jeff walked back to where the others were seated. When Josefina turned the horse back toward the target, Jeff waved his hand. She kicked the horse into a hard run coming toward the target and drew her weapon. The horse was running with his head stretched out, his tail flying in the wind, with Josefina bent low over his neck. When she was approximately twenty-five yards from the target, she started shooting. The last shot was fired just before she passed the target with the horse at a full run. She was finally able to get him stopped in about a hundred yards and turned back.

Again he seemed to know this was for show, as his tail was up and he pranced along with the girl sitting up on his back. By the time she rode back to the men, the vaquero was showing them her target.

Seven rounds were center of mass, two shots were in the head, and one had missed by less than an inch. Josefina jumped down and patted the horse, which was taken by the vaquero and led away.

General Huerta picked up her hand and stated, "I would like to have you as my bodyguard if you would take the job."

"You are so very kind, but it seems I must look after my husband," she replied. She was still tickled that Jeff had gotten jealous about the two Captains.

The two Captains gawked in disbelief at her target and were much more subdued. This tickled Jeff, now you two butt holes know we can shoot, he thought.

The General stood up saying, "we must get back. Thank you so much my friends for the wonderful dinner and the entertainment," as he shook Jeff's hand. "I would be very pleased to have you and your lovely bride visit me and my wife."

"It's very kind of you mi General," said Jeff. "We'll do that the next time we come down to the ranch."

With that the General pulled Jeff into an abrazo, then hugged Josefina. "Your father would be so proud of you. You are so beautiful," he told her.

They walked around to the front of the house, where Carmen met them. "Thanks for the lovely meal," said the General.

"It's our pleasure, please come again," Carmen replied.

"I have invited Jeff and Josefina to come visit. I would be honored if you and Cory would come with them," the General continued.

"You are very kind General Huerta," she said. "When Jeff can arrange more time off, we'll try to make it."

The two pilots had walked out to the helicopter and were going through the pre-flight. Cory walked out to the aircraft with Huerta. They talked for a few minutes, and then shook hands. The General entered and his aide closed the door. The rotors started to move, picking up speed. In a few minutes the helicopter lifted off the ground. The nose dropped and it accelerated away from the ranch.

The next day Jeff and Josefina loaded their pickup and said goodbye to Cory and Carmen. "We're going to drop by and see Tio for a couple of days," Josefina told them.

Cory hugged both of the young people. "I can never repay you for what you have done," he said.

"We're family," said Jeff. "Nobody fools with our family." They both entered the truck and drove off with Josefina waving her arm.

***

Felipe Salines and the pilot had left the ranch with the dope load flying north. They stayed low and entered the United States in the Big Bend area. They flew on north of Hobbs, New Mexico with Salines watching for a light. Suddenly he and the pilot could see a flashing strobe on the ground. A set of headlights came on showing the dirt road. The pilot came over the headlights and landed on the remote road and stopped the aircraft. Two pickups drove up and the marijuana was quickly loaded into the camper shells on the pickups.

With the plane empty, they peeled off the tape covering the US registration numbers and using the lights from one of the trucks was soon back in the air. They flew back south and landed for fuel at Carlsbad, NM. While refueling the plane, they passed themselves off as businessmen en route to Arizona. After paying for the fuel and parking the aircraft on the ramp, they slept for a few hours in the plane.

Just before dawn they took off flying southwest toward El Paso. When they passed Whites City the pilot dropped down close to the ground and they headed south toward Mexico. "Watch out for wires," Salines cautioned.

"No, look for poles," replied the pilot. "You can't see the wires. But sure as hell if there are two poles, some bastard put wires between them."

A few hours later when they approached the ranch with flaps and gear down to land on the lakebed, Salines noticed something odd. "Don't land yet, get the gear up and fly by the house," he commanded. The pilot who was on final, increased power to the engines and raised the gear. The plane was still low as he turned toward the house. As they approached the house, Felipe saw what had caught his attention. There was a dead horse lying in the yard. He could see two people standing nearby. Suddenly one of them raised something to his shoulder and smoke poured from it. "Shit," Salines hollered, "they're shooting at us." He and the pilot heard a hammering as the slugs hit and the window blew out next to Salines.

The pilot jerked the aircraft over on one wing and started to climb, as he slammed in full power. When they were several miles away he looked over at Salines who was holding his chin and blood was dripping from his hand. "Are you okay, Jefe?" he asked.

"I'm okay, just a piece of Plexiglas hit me. Let's land at the Saltillo airport and get the window replaced."

"Who in hell was shooting at us," the pilot asked Felipe.

"I don't know, but I'm sure going to find out. Are the engines okay, " he asked.

"All of the instruments are in the green," the pilot replied.

When they landed at the airport, Salines told the pilot to taxi over to a maintenance hanger. Salines had wiped the blood from his chin and used the first aid kit. After making arrangements for the repairs to the aircraft with a hefty bonus to the mechanic for his silence, they caught a taxi downtown. When they were in a hotel room, Felipe placed a call to Cesar and told him about being shot at.

"I thought we had this all wrapped up, Cesar stated.

"I did too Jefe. I'll send one of our people from Sabinas to Sierra Mojada to see what he can find out," said Felipe.

"Just get it done," Cesar stated as he hung up.

A week after returning to Columbia, Salines had finally learned who had freed O'Connor. He walked into the den where Cesar was having a drink. "Jefe, its seems that O'Connor, in Sierra Mojada is the grandfather of Larson's wife. His daughter was married to the Comandante in Camargo that Alejandro killed. She called Larson and he came down to the ranch. O'Connor is also a good friend of General Huerta who is the Military Comandante of Nuevo Leon. I just got off the telephone with General D La Fuente. He suggests that we stay out of Huerta's area, as he is very straight and will not take bribes."

Cesar sat drinking for a few minutes. "Very well, we need to move further west with our operations. I've been talking to a man in Agua Prieta and he has a friend in Douglas, Arizona who operates a cement plant. They claim they can dig a tunnel under the border. If they are successful, we'll run a couple of loads of yerba. (slang for marijuana) Then we'll switch to cocaine. One of these days I'm going to get my chance at that damn gringo, Larson."

CHAPTER 15

After spending two days at their ranch, Jeff and Josefina returned to Deming. Jeff reported in and was told to be at the station the next morning at 6 am. The Station Senior at Columbus wanted to have a big raid in the Uvas Valley, he was told.

Jeff was at the station before 6 o'clock and was drinking coffee when Cody Dunbar came in. "What's up boss?" he asked Cody.

"Reynolds wants to raid the farms in the Uvas Valley. They have labor buses coming in from El Paso, Texas and he says there are a lot of wets on them."

"Yeah, and they also return to Juarez every night," Jeff replied.

"Ours is not to reason why," Cody said. Just then the guys from Columbus drove up and the Deming agents went outside to their scouts. They drove north on highway 26 to the turnoff for the Uvas Valley. As soon as they crossed the railroad tracks, the BP plane started a sweep of the farms. The radio came alive with "they're running." Scouts were peeling off in different directions as the agents tried to catch the fleeing Mexicans.

After over three hours of searching in the ditches and crops, they had caught thirty-five illegals. Jeff and Cody were loading one van with as many of the workers as they could get inside. "Well, this was sure a lot of fun," sneered Jeff.

"You think this is bad. Reynolds wants to raid the west farming area tomorrow," Cody said.

"What the hell for?" asked Jeff. "They'll just be back that evening."

"Reynolds said they have over a hundred working out there," Cody replied.

"That sounds like Columbus's problem to me," Jeff replied. "I think we're catching too many on trails up here and Reynolds wants to slow us down," he continued.

The rest of the day was spent processing the workers and returning them to Mexico. By the time Jeff got home he was in a pissed off mood, until Josefina teased him out of it. When supper was ready they sat down and ate, then later moved to the front porch. As they sat watching the lights in the Franklin area Jeff said, "it sure is pretty up here. Well I'd better get to bed, I have to be up early in the morning." The two walked inside with their arms around each other.

The next morning, when the Deming agents reported for work Cody said, "Let's go get some coffee at the Ramada." When they had their coffee sitting in the back away from the other customers, Cody laid out the plan. A Border Patrol pilot who had flown in from El Paso and parked his Super Cub near the office was with them.

"They want us to drive down Hermanas Grade and come in from the west. When we get close, we'll call on the radio and the Columbus Agents will came in from the east. They want to hit the fields about 9 am. Jeff will you lead this group?" asked Cody.

"Sure, Boss if that's what you want," he replied. "Okay guys, if you're finished with your coffee let's go." The agents went out to their scouts while Cody drove the pilot back to his plane.

Halfway down the grade the Super Cub overtook them. Jeff laughed as the plane flew along side his vehicle just over the brush. The plane flew on south until he was about a mile ahead then and turned back up the road. The pilot timed his flight, so he flew over Jeff just as his scout dropped into one of the dips on the road. Crazy bastard, Jeff thought.

When they reached highway 9 west of the farming area, Jeff called the Columbus Agents on his radio. They replied that they were just over the hill, east of the farms. He watched the plane fly south as the scouts picked up speed for the dash to the border fence. He heard the pilot calling, "they're running for the fence." He and the other Deming Agents arrived at the border fence in time to catch six of the slower men.

Jeff could see that about eighty workers had made it back to Mexico and sat in the grass about twenty-five yards south of the border. They acted as a cheering section for the ones that were not as fast. SPAIC Reynolds drove up accompanied by one of the Columbus Agents named Jesus Rodriquez. "We got about five of the slow ones," he bragged to Jeff.

"Yea, we really earned our money today," Jeff replied. "While we're dicking around here, over a hundred have gone north."

Rodriquez a heavy Hispanic with an attitude smirked at Jeff. "I didn't figure an Okie would understand. After all, ain't Okies just Texans who escaped across the Red River?"

"And where might you be from Heysus?" asked Jeff, deliberately mispronouncing Jesus.

"I was born in Kansas, that makes me a son of Kansas," Rodriquez replied.

"Well," said Jeff, "I always thought there were only three kinds of suns in Kansas. Sunshine, sunflowers and sons-of-bitches."

Rodriquez turned bright red and started for Jeff. "Hold on there," hollered Reynolds. "Larson, I think you owe Agent Rodriquez an apology."

"Piss on him," replied Jeff. "You won't find anybody named Larson on that plaque by the Alamo." Jeff then drove off while Cody Dunbar tried to keep from laughing.

Later at the Deming station, Cody came in while Jeff was finishing his paper work. "Boy did you piss off Rodriquez," he told Jeff. "He was still mad when I left."

"What an asshole," Jeff stated. "Son of Kansas my butt. If he was born in Kansas, you can bet his mother swam both the Rio Grande and the Red River."

"Hell, he was still complaining to Reynolds when I left Columbus. With all the Columbus Agents around, I felt like a proctologist in a room full of assholes," said Cody.

The next several months saw many changes. The Customs Agents and the Bureau of narcotics and dangerous Drugs were merged into one agency. The newly created Drug Enforcement Agency was to do all narcotics investigations. One of the two Customs Agents in Deming was transferred to El Paso and the other retired.

Customs brought back the old Customs Patrol that had been abolished about 1945 so they could have people on the border. The

Border Patrol finally obtained sensors that were placed along the international border. Some of the sensors were placed in the gates that had been cut in the barbed wire fence that was the line between Mexico and the United States.

Jeff had met one of the pilots for the New Mexico State Police named Darby Livingston at the airport in Deming. Over coffee they started talking about the aircraft based in Columbus. Darby asked Jeff what he knew about them. "The guys at Columbus say they haul people fishing in Mexico," Jeff stated. "But I think that is a load of crap. Those planes are too nice for that kind of use."

The tall lanky pilot gave a raspy chuckle, "shit, they are hauling dope in by the plane load. They land them all over the damn place. I've tried to follow them several times, but the State Police doesn't have enough money in our budget to buy the fuel."

"Is there anything I can do?" asked Jeff. "I'd really like to catch the bastards."

"Keep your eyes and ears open," Darby replied. The two officers talked for a few more minutes and Jeff watched as the Cessna 206 with Darby at the controls left heading north.

A month later Jeff was contacted by one of the State Narcotic Agents named Ruben Molina, while he was working nights patrolling north of Deming. "Livingston told me that you would want to get in on this," the agent said. "We've had wire taps on the guys with the planes in Columbus and they are running a load tonight."

"Hell yes," said Jeff. "Where do you need me?"

"There are about seven planes following them, and after they unload they want us to arrest them when they return to Columbus," the agent replied. "We need some people in uniform just in case they try to shoot it out."

"There are three other BP Agents working tonight. I can get them to help if you want."

"Okay, you round them up and meet me in the State Park in Columbus about 10 tonight. Keep the details off the radio," the Narcotics Agent requested.

"You bet," Jeff replied. Jeff called the other Deming Agent and asked that he meet with him at the office, where he told him was going on. They both got in the same vehicle and drove down to Columbus where they found the two Columbus Agents. The four lawmen drove into the State Park and parked their vehicles. Several New Mexico State Narcotics Agents along with two DEA Agents soon joined them.

"Here's the plan," stated Molina. "We have several planes and one helicopter following these guys. We believe they will drop their load west of Socorro and then return here. Our job is to arrest them when they land, we don't believe they're armed, but you can never tell. We are in contact with our planes and they'll notify us when they have seized the dope load. Stay out of sight because they have ground-to-air radios in their houses and one of the wives may came out to have a look around."

The lawmen slipped across the highway and hid in the mesquite near the dirt runway. Molina along with Jeff hid near the small building at the side of the runway. While they waited, Molina told Jeff how they had obtained funding for the operation.

"When they formed DEA they placed a lot of funds in the kitty. We were able to get a grant from the Feds to put this bunch out of business. We've had the wiretaps in place for about two weeks and you would not believe all of the stuff we've heard. I think we should give these pricks copies of the transcripts. They would kill each other if they heard all that been said."

Just then Molina answered his walkie-talkie. "One of the planes is on its way back," he told Jeff. Forty-five minutes later they could see the navigation lights of an approaching aircraft. Molina and Jeff watched as the plane turned on its landing lights and touched down. The plane taxied near the building and the engine was shut down. The hidden lawmen watched as two men exited the aircraft and walked to the shed where one unlocked the door and both went inside.

"Come on," Molina whispered to Jeff. The two officers quickly ran to a location near the door. They were standing with weapons pointing at the door when the two men came out carrying the rear seats for the plane. "Police, don't move," commanded Molina. The two men had both arms around the seats and could only stare at the two lawmen. The pilot however pissed his pants when he looked into the bores of the pistols.

"He said don't move," Jeff stated.

"I'm not moving," replied Workman the pilot.

"Something is, it's running down your pants leg," Jeff said with a belly laugh.

The two were quickly handcuffed and moved into hiding with the other officers. They could see another plane approaching the airfield. They watched in the cold night air as it turned on its landing lights and landed. The plane pulled up by the other one, gunning its engine as it turned and then shut down. The officers watched as the door opened and the pilot got out. He then opened the rear door and removed a fuel barrel, which he started to roll toward the shed.

When he was twenty yards away, Molina stepped out of hiding with Jeff beside him. "State Police, don't move Logan," Molina again commanded with his weapon drawn. The pilot, his face stricken starts to run in place. The officers could hear his feet pounding the ground, but he wasn't moving.

"If you try to run, I'll kill you Logan," stated Molina.

The pilot was finally able to get his body under control and his feet to stop moving. His hands went into the air as Jeff and Molina walked to him. He was quickly cuffed and stuffed with the other two arrested smugglers nearby. Molina told the officers guarding them, "If they make a sound, knock the shit out of them."

Molina and Jeff walked to the aircraft. "All we need now is for their leader Mark Hamlin to land. I sure would like to know if he calls in from the plane," Molina said.

"Hell, we can turn on the radio. They probably left it on the frequency they use," Jeff stated. He opened the door and making sure the switch for the lights were off, turned on the master switch and the radio.

A few minutes later they heard Hamlin call his wife on the radio. "Have the guys been by the house?" he asked.

"No, I heard them land a few minutes ago, but I haven't seen them," she replied.

"Well shit, get out and round them up, we need a meeting. Something is very wrong."

"Okay, I'll get dressed," she replied.

The two lawmen could now see the approaching plane. Molina hid in the brush between the plane and the shed while Jeff pulled the door closed and hunched down out of sight. A few minutes later with his weapon drawn, he heard the plane pull up beside him. After Hamlin had shut his engine and passed the aircraft where Jeff was hiding, he eased the door open. He saw Molina step out and throw down on Hamlin.

"State Police, you're under arrest Mark." Hamlin stopped, and then looked over his shoulder as Jeff walked up behind him. "Your plane is seized for narcotics smuggling," Molina stated.

Hamlin gave a little bow. "There it is, help your self," he stated. Jeff patted him down and handcuffed him. The two officers walked him over to where the others were being held.

One of them asked, "What's going on Mark?"

"Damn if I know guys," he said in a calm voice.

Jeff turned to Molina, "I'll say one thing, he sure is a cool prick."

"Yea, he is," replied Molina. "Let's see how he is after five to ten years in the pen." He and Jeff walked over to one side where Molina could use his radio without being overheard. He was finally able to make contact with one of the law enforcement aircraft near Socorro, New Mexico.

"Please tell me you have some dope seized up there," he requested.

"Stand by," he was told. A few anxious minutes later, Darby's voice came over the radio. "We have the load, I repeat, we have the load." They could hear cheering in the background. Molina turned to Jeff and shook hands. "Thanks partner," he said. "Let's load these assholes up and carry them to Las Cruces."

During the months following the arrest of the air smugglers, the Border Patrol made several narcotics seizures on the ground. Two tank trucks were seized west of Columbus with over 10,000 pounds of marijuana.

Jeff was working alone near Deming when he heard the El Paso Sector call for a Lordsburg unit. They notified the unit of an intrusion west of the Antelope Wells Port of Entry per the installed sensors.

The Antelope Wells is an eight-hour Customs Port of Entry located in the boot heel of Hidalgo County and staffed by a two Customs Inspectors who lived there.

Jeff listened as the unit stated he was the only one working and he was in Silver City. Jeff could hear the roar of the agent's engine as he tried to get in position to head off the suspected vehicle. Jeff picked up his mike and radioed the Lordsburg unit. "Lima 10, Delta 3"

"Go ahead Delta 3," the Lordsburg unit responded.

"I can be in Hachita in about forty-five minutes if you want me there," Jeff told him.

"Go for it, I'll back you up just as soon as I can."

Jeff hit the red lights and siren and turned west on I-10. After a few miles Jeff could tell that the big trucks were on their CB radios telling the other trucks to clear the inside lane. The BP sedan was doing over 110 miles per hours when the turn off to Hachita appeared in his windshield. Jeff slowed for the exit and then slid the sedan in a hard left turn. After making the turn, Jeff got comfortable with both feet flat on the floor.

As the sedan turned south Jeff could see a slow moving pickup traveling the same direction. He hit the siren and saw the farm truck move over to one side. Just as he passed the pickup, he saw a coyote hunting along the fence line for mice and rabbits about two hundred yards ahead. He hit the siren again and laughed when the coyote picked up speed traveling south. Just as he went by with the siren screaming, he saw the coyote run over the top of a jackrabbit as he dove through the fence with his tail twisting wildly. Jeff still laughing thought, I guess he now knows what it's like to be chased. Forty-four minutes after leaving Deming, Jeff was slowing for the intersection of highway 9 coming west from Columbus.

"Lima 10, Delta 3, I'm at the town and will go south about six miles and wait for you," he told the Lordsburg agent.

"Roger that, also be advised that Lima 8 is in his private aircraft headed for the border," replied Lima 10.

Jeff drove south of Hachita as the road headed toward the Big Hatchet Mountains. He pulled off the highway onto a dirt road leading to a dry dirt tank. About twenty minutes later the sedan driven by Joe Anders (Lima 10) came roaring up to Jeff's location. He pulled his smoking vehicle to the side of the road and got out. "Hi Jeff, nothing yet?" he asked.

"Not a soul," Jeff replied.

Just then both agents heard Lima 8 calling on his walkie-talkie. When Anders answered him, Lima 8 advised, " I can see only one truck coming from the direction of Antelope Wells. It's a large two-ton truck with white sideboards. I can't see anything in the bed and it's about eight miles from your location. I called the Customs Inspector and he reports that he's had no vehicle traffic through the port this morning."

Jeff opened the trunk of his sedan and removed a stop sign. He and Anders set it up in the middle of the road facing south. "We now have a checkpoint," said Jeff. Both agents could see the aircraft high in the air near the purple peak of Big Hatchet Mountain.

The two agents watched as the truck finally approached the stop sign. Both had their hands near their pistols. Jeff was behind his vehicle while Anders took cover behind his own. The truck came to a stop and Anders told the driver to get out of the cab. While Anders was talking to the driver, Jeff stepped up on the left side to check the cab. Finding it empty, he walked to the rear of the truck checking it over closely. He finished on the same side where Anders was talking to the driver. He motioned to Anders to join him.

After handcuffing the driver for officer's safety, he walked to where Jeff was standing.

"Well what do you think?" he asked Jeff.

"Do you see anything odd about this truck?" Jeff asked.

"It looks like they have been hauling cattle, judging by all the cow shit that's on it," replied Anders.

"Yea, but take a look. Some of the cow shit is on the outside of the boards and is six foot high. I never saw a cow that could shit that high, much less take a crap on the outside of a truck," Jeff stated. "There has to be a false bed or something."

Jeff walked to the rear and started to closely examine the bed. After a few minutes he walked over to his sedan and removed the jack handle from the trunk. He returned to the truck and pried two of the floorboards apart. "Hey, Joe, take a look at this," he said. Anders quickly walked over to Jeff. Looking over his shoulder he could see wrapped packages under the boards.

"This damn thing does have a false bed. Stick a knife into one," Jeff requested. Upon cutting into the package, both agents could see a green leafy substance and smelled the acrid odor of marijuana. "Read him his rights Joe, we have a load."

While Anders was giving the driver his rights, Jeff walked over to his sedan and radioed Lima 8, who was circling overhead. "We have a load, looks like about a thousand pounds," he told him.

Anders walked over to Jeff with the driver in tow. "How about you taking this guy in your vehicle and I'll drive the truck to Deming. Call Lima 8 and ask him if he can fly over to Deming and pick me up. He can then fly me back here for my unit," he told Jeff.

Jeff loaded the handcuffed driver into the front seat and pulled in behind the truck as Anders drove north. "Lima 8, Delta 3," Jeff called to the circling aircraft.

"Go ahead Delta 3."

"We're taking the load to the DEA office in Deming and Lima 10 is requesting that you pick him up and fly him back here for his unit."

"That's 10-4," replied Lima 8. Just then there was a loud roar as Lima 8 buzzed the sedan and truck.

"Damn," Jeff said on the radio. "That looks like fun, I've got to learn to fly."

"It's a lot of fun, almost as good as sex," replied Lima 8.

Jeff followed the marijuana-laden truck to the Drug Enforcement office in Deming. The driver had remained silent and sullen for the trip. Jeff had radioed ahead and the DEA Agents were waiting as the truck pulled in and Anders backed it up to office door. Agent Dean walked over where Jeff was getting the prisoner out of his unit.

"Did he say anything?" he asked Jeff.

"Nope, not a word," Jeff replied. "I'm not even sure if we have his right name."

"That's too bad, I'd hope that he would cooperate. Anyway this'll be the last load at this office, Headquarters is moving us to Las Cruces tomorrow," Dean stated.

Dean walked the driver inside while Jeff, Anders and two DEA agents started ripping up the truck's floorboards. Jason Cole (Lima 8) arrived after hitching a ride from the airport and helped with the unloading. They weighed the packages of marijuana and initialed each one for court, Dean then signed for the dope and the prisoner. Jeff, Anders and Cole then left and met with Cody Dunbar for coffee.

"That was a damn good bust you guys caught today," Dunbar stated. "I've already called the chief and he said to pass on the "Atta boys" to you guys."

"Yea, well remember one "oh shit" wipes out a hundred atta boys," Jeff replied. "You know damn well if Reynolds and his sidekick Rodriquez have their way, I'll probably get an "Oh Shit" out of the load," he told Dunbar.

The next day Jeff was scheduled to sign cut east of Deming. When he went 10-8 on the radio, he was informed by Sector to go by the local Sheriff's Department. When he arrived and walked inside the first thing he noticed were two young boys sitting in the lobby. Jeff could see that they had been crying and walked over to them.

"Hi guys, how are you doing," he asked.

Both boys looked up and one asked, "can you please help us, they don't believe us?"

"About what," Jeff asked.

Just then a railroad detective stepped out of an office. "Don't pay any mind to what these lying little shits have to say," he stated. Jeff turned to the railroad detective his eyes suddenly cold.

"What's going on?" he asked the detective.

"We got these two boys out of the trunk of a car being hauled west on the train. They're telling some bullshit story about some guy locking them in and abducting a girl. They're both runaways from El Paso that got themselves locked into a trunk by accident, is what I think," the detective continued.

"You don't mind if I have a word with them, do you?" Jeff asked.

"Knock yourself out," replied the railroad detective with a sneer.

Just then one of the deputies came out of an office. "Thanks for coming," he said. "These two boys said they heard the girl scream about thirty minutes before the train arrived in Deming. We would like for you to check the tracks east of town. The railroad police say even if the story is true, she couldn't survive being thrown from the train," the deputy stated.

"Do you mind if I talk to the kids?" Jeff asked.

"Not at all," the deputy stated.

Jeff bought two sodas from the machine and asked the two boys to step outside with him, where he handed them the cold drinks. "Guys, I'm not with the police. I'm a Border Patrol Agent, will you tell me what happened?" Both boys readily agreed as they drank deeply from the sodas.

"We all ran away from home in El Paso. We caught the train on the west side and crawled into one of the car haulers. We were in the front seat of a car and Maria was sitting in back, when suddenly this man appeared and grabbed us. He put Jimmy and me in the trunk and kept Maria with him. We could hear her fighting him and then we heard her scream. That's all we heard until the train stopped, then we started beating on the trunk and hollering."

"How old is Maria?" asked Jeff.

"She's thirteen," Jimmy said. "Please see if you can find her, she's our friend."

"Are you guys telling me the truth?" Jeff asked.

"Yes Sir," they both replied.

Jeff escorted both boys back inside to the deputy. He quickly walked to the marked BP Dodge pickup and sped out of town. When he was about ten miles east of Deming on the old highway, he radioed sector and requested an aircraft. He told sector he was looking for a young girl that may have been thrown from a train.

Jesus Rodriquez came on the air stating, " Sector, we have a lot of trails and we need that aircraft down here."

Sector came back on the radio, "a Zulu unit will depart in ten minutes, and you guys make up your minds where you want it."

Rodriquez replied, "send the aircraft to Columbus. That girl, if she exist, is dead."

Jeff grabbed his mike, "Sector, send that aircraft to my location, my authority. I guess it never dawns on some idiots that she could be laying out here somewhere with broken arms and legs."

There was silence for about two minutes, then the El Paso Sector radio replied, "Delta 3, sector."

"Go ahead sector," replied Jeff.

"The aircraft will depart in three minutes for your location."

"That's 10-4 sector, have him fly the railroad tracks from Sunland Park west," Jeff stated.

Jeff arrived at Akela and drove east along the railroad tracks. The road dipped and weaved along side the tracks as he sped along. He was ten miles east of Akela when he saw the aircraft in the distance. Suddenly he saw the aircraft pull up sharply.

"Delta 3, Zulu 5, Delta 3, Zulu 5," called the plane.

"Go ahead Zulu 5, I have you in sight," replied Jeff.

"I have your girl right below me, she just waved. She's walking west on the tracks and I'm going down to take a closer look."

"Rodger that, ETA five minutes." Jeff had the Dodge pickup up to 70 MPH on the rough road and was fighting the wheel to keep it on the road.

"Delta 3, Zulu 5, she appears to be okay but I can see blood in her hair."

"Rodger that," said Jeff. He could now see the young girl standing on the tracks watching the plane. Jeff slid the BP unit up beside her and jumped out. "Are you okay?"

"I'm very thirsty," she replied. Jeff could see that she had wrapped her sweater around her bare legs and was only wearing a thin blouse. Jeff helped her into the unit and handed her his canteen.

"Just a sip for now," he told her. He could see matted blood in her hair and decided the best thing to do was get her to the hospital.

Jeff turned the unit around and sped toward Deming forty miles away. The aircraft had notified sector that the young girl had been found and turned toward Columbus.

"Thanks a lot Zulu 5," Jeff radioed the plane.

"Anytime Delta 3, sometimes it's all worthwhile," replied Zulu 5.

Sector came on the radio, "Delta 3, we've notified the Sheriff's Office and they are requesting that you bring her to the SO."

Jeff looked over at the girl, just in time to see her trying to nod off. "Wake up honey, don't go to sleep, take another sip of water." Jeff was concerned that she had suffered a concussion from the fall.

Sector came back on the radio, "did you receive the last transmission Delta 3?"

"Yes I did, tell them to stuff it. I'm taking her to the hospital," Jeff said. After a minute of silence, sector came back.

"That's 10-4 Delta 3, the SO will have a unit at the edge of town to give you an escort to the hospital."

Jeff looked back over at the girl and again found she was trying to go to sleep. He started talking to her, "tell me what happened."

"My friends and I ran away from home, planning to travel to California. We had crawled into one of the new cars and were having fun, when suddenly this man appeared. He locked my two friends in the trunk of the car. Are they okay?" she asked

"They're fine. They sent me to look for you," Jeff told her.

"After he locked Jimmy and Alberto in the trunk, he tried to rape me. He pulled off my skirt and I kicked him in the cojones. (Balls) That's when he threw me from the train. I thought I would never stop rolling."

Jeff could see that both her bare legs and arms were badly scratched and bruised. She had wrapped her sweater around her waist for modesty. He was fast approaching the edge of town and could see the SO unit waiting for him. He hit the siren on the BP unit and saw the SO unit turn on his red lights, leading the way into town. City Police units were stationed at busy intersections blocking the traffic. When Jeff pulled up at the hospital, several nurses and a doctor were waiting.

They rushed the girl inside as the deputy walked over to Jeff. He and the deputy waited for about thirty minutes until the doctor finally came out. "She's fine," he told the two officers. "She just needs rest, we'll keep her overnight."

"That's fine doctor," replied the deputy. "We've notified the family, they'll be here this evening." He then turned to Jeff, "thanks a lot for finding her. I guess the boys were telling the truth."

"Yea, be sure you let that railroad prick know that, okay," Jeff said.

Jeff left the hospital and went back to work sign cutting east of Deming. He tracked down a group of eight illegals and transported them to the Deming office. While he was processing them to be returned to Mexico, Dunbar came into the office.

"What did you do to Reynolds?" he asked.

"Not a damn thing," Jeff replied. "I did call his ass kissing buddy Jesus an idiot, which he is," Jeff stated.

"He wants to write you up," Dunbar continued.

"What the hell for?" asked Jeff.

"Well, he maintains that you're prejudice against Hispanics. He also stated that you had no business going out looking for that girl," Dunbar said.

"Does the silly son-of-a-bitch know I'm married to a Mexican? He's got more wind than a bag full of farts" Jeff stated.

"There are a whole lot of damn good Hispanic agents in the Border Patrol," Jeff continued. "Rodriquez ain't one of them. He's an asshole. He'd be an asshole if he were a gringo, purple, or green. Color is only skin deep, stupid goes clear to the bone. As for that girl, that was a request from a local agency. I can see the headlines now. Border Patrol refuses help, girl dies in desert."

"That's kind of what I told Reynolds. I also told him I was contacting the Chief about this and that really frosted his butt. He and Rodriquez drove off to lick their wounds," Dunbar said.

"I'm getting awful tired of this shit," Jeff stated.

"Don't let it get you down Jeff," Dunbar continued. "You have two days off, go on home and relax. Get drunk, shoot rabbits or something."

"I know who I'd like to shoot," Jeff said. "Some people are alive, just because it's against the law to kill them."

CHAPTER 16

When Jeff arrived at home, Josefina met him at the door. One look at his face and she could tell she had a pissed off gringo on her hands. "Que paso, mi Amor?" she asked.

"Same old shit, different day," Jeff said as he hugged her. "The Columbus agents have their tails over their backs like an old mad cow."

"What's the matter with those pendejos now?" she asked.

Jeff told her the story about the young girl and what Dunbar had told him. Jeff got two beers from the refrigerator, handed one to Josefina, and walked out on the porch. He slowly drank the beer while Josefina rubbed the tension out of his neck.

"You know sweetheart, I think I'll go see what Customs has to offer. I think it's about time I pulled off this green uniform." Just then the telephone rang and Josefina went in to answer it.

"Jeff it's for you, it's Mr. Livingston."

Jeff took the telephone, "what's up Darby?"

"I was just checking to see if you were home and if I could come out," Darby told him.

"Hell yes, the beer is cold," Jeff replied.

A few minutes later Darby arrived and Jeff handed him a beer. "Josefina is fixing supper, you'll stay, right?" he asked.

"Sure," Darby replied. "I never turn down cold beer or food. He and Jeff sat on the porch drinking the beer watching the quails come in for water.

"The reason I came out, I'm quitting the State Police and going over to Customs as a pilot. One of the guys I've talked with also asked me to contact you. They want to know if you might be interested in going over to the Customs Patrol."

Jeff laughed, "I was just talking to Josefina about that very thing before you called."

"Great, let me call the man and he'll meet you tomorrow at the Ramada Inn," Darby said.

Just then Josefina opened the door. " Supper is ready," she told them.

The next day Jeff met with the Customs Patrol Director who had a filled out SF 171 for him to sign, if he agreed to the transfer. He talked to the Director for an hour, signed the form and left the café. He picked up some steaks and beer for a cookout then drove home. Josefina met him in the yard when he drove up.

"How did it go?" she asked.

"Okay, I guess. I met the Customs Patrol Director who had my paper work already filled out. All I had to do was sign the darn thing," he replied. Josefina had started the mesquite fire and there was a nice bed of coals waiting for the steaks. After supper, they sat on the porch watching the quails come in for water.

When Jeff returned to work, he asked Cody Dunbar to have coffee with him. After their coffee was served, he told Cody about applying for a position with Customs.

"Damn, I should have seen this coming. Is there anything I can do to get you to change your mind?" asked Dunbar.

"No, I don't think so. I know Customs will have some buttholes, but I want to work narcotics smuggling cases. I believe it's just a matter of time until they abolish the Customs Patrol again. Then we'll have Customs Agents working narcotic smuggling cases along with DEA on the border."

Three weeks later, Jeff drove to El Paso and turned in his Border Patrol equipment. After lunch, he drove to the Bridge of Americas where he met with the Patrol Director. Jeff was sworn into the Customs Service, issued his badge, credentials, and sidearm. The Director instructed him to report to the Station Supervisor at the Deming Office the next day.

"Let's go have a beer Jeff," he invited. Jeff followed him outside where they drove a few blocks to a small cantina. When the cold beers were served, the Director raised his bottle.

"Absent companions," he said.

"I'll drink to that," Jeff replied.

"You'll find that Customs is not as hard ass in some things as the BP are. You were hired because you show a lot of initiative and you have a lot of contacts in Mexico. This part of the border is going to see a sharp increase in smuggling. I'm depending on you to help get a handle on it."

"I'll do what I can," Jeff replied.

"Is it true that your wife owns a ranch in Mexico?" asked the Director.

"Yes, she has a small place in the state of Coahuila, about fifty square miles," Jeff said.

"You call that small? That's a good size spread even by Texas standards," replied the Director. "Well, I better get you back to your vehicle so you can go home. Report to Glenn Perry, the Station Supervisor tomorrow and he'll issue the rest of your gear. Glad to have you on board."

"It's good to be here, I'm ready to go to work," Jeff stated.

Jeff returned home to again find Josefina waiting in the front yard. "Let's drive down to Palomas and I'll buy supper," he told her. She ran inside and returned in a few minutes in a skirt and blouse.

"I'm ready when it means I won't have to cook tonight."

They drove east until they encountered highway 11 where they turned south. Thirty some miles later they drove by the Customs Port of Entry and into the Republic of Mexico. Jeff parked his truck in front of the restaurant, where he gave a dollar to one of the street kids to watch it.

While waiting for the meal, they were serenaded by three musicians. After eating, they returned to the pickup and got in line to enter the United States. After clearing Customs & Immigration they drove north back through the village of Columbus. Jeff pointed out the State Park named for Pancho Villa to Josefina.

" Pancho Villa almost burned this town to the ground in 1916. I don't believe it's recovered yet," he told her.

The next morning Jeff reported to the Customs Patrol Office on South Gold. Perry opened the gunroom and told Jeff to pick what he wanted. Jeff selected a military Colt MI6 along with several magazines. He also picked up ammo for the rifle and his S&W model 66 in .357 magnum. Perry then told the firearms instructor to take Jeff out to the gun range for qualifications.

When they arrived at the dirt bank near the airport, the instructor parked about twenty-five yards away. He had Jeff load the rifle magazines, then told Jeff, "see that beer can on the backstop? Let's see you hit it with your pistol."

Jeff pulled the S&W up to eye level and quickly fired. The can leaped into the air and then rolled a few feet. "Now let's see you hit it with the rifle." Jeff holstered the pistol and charged the MI6. He moved the selector lever from safe to semi-auto, quickly signed and fired. Again the can leaped into the air.

"Okay, you're qualified," said the instructor. "I never met a Border Patrolman that couldn't shoot. Let's go get some coffee."

The following weeks passed quickly for Jeff as he learned the ropes of his new job. He and another of the Customs Patrol Officers worked the boot heel of Hidalgo County. They checked the international fence for cuts and signs of smuggling activity.

Occasionally they would stop at the Antelope Wells Port of Entry to visit with the Customs Inspectors. This was an eight-hour Customs Port of Entry staffed by two Customs Inspectors who lived nearby. Usually they had some type of information on smuggling in the area. Plus they always had on the coffeepot.

After six weeks Jeff was notified that he was to attend an Interdiction School in Washington, D.C. Josefina decided to visit her mother and check on her ranch while Jeff was gone for the six weeks school.

When Jeff returned from D.C., Josefina met him at the El Paso airport. They checked into a nearby motel and tore each other's clothes off. The next morning after a nice breakfast they drove to Deming. Josefina told him all about the ranch and how much her mother would like to see him. "Abuelo sends his love," she told him.

"I would like to visit, but with this new job I don't know when I'll get any leave."

"I know and they are so proud of you and so am I," she said as she squeezed his leg.

"You'd better stop that or I'll run off the road," Jeff stated.

"Okay, I'll wait until we get home," she said.

The next several months found Jeff working long hours as he was placed in charge of the Customs sensors. These were old military type sensors left over from the war in Viet Nam. Jeff was trying to place them on roads where the Border Patrol didn't have any or where smugglers were cutting the border fence. Several dope loads were apprehended due to the sensors Jeff had placed along the International border.

Early one morning Jeff received a radio call from Customs pilot, Darby Livingston requesting a meeting at the Deming airport. Jeff was the first to arrive and he parked by the fixed base operations. He saw a Cessna 337 land and taxi up to the fuel pumps. Darby was alone in the plane and walked over to Jeff while it was being fueled.

"How are things going Jeff? How are you liking Customs?" he asked.

"Finer'n frogs hair Darby, I like it. Where in hell did you get that plane?"

"Customs received some ex-military aircraft and this is one of them. It was a "02" in the military," Darby told him.

"It looks like it's held together with bailing wire and chewing gum," Jeff laughed.

"Just about, how would you like to take a ride with me? I've some info I want to check out and I need an extra set of eyes."

"Sure, let me get my rifle," Jeff told him.

He walked over to his unit and removed his cased M16. He placed it in the aircraft while Darby paid for the fuel. When both were seated and belted in, Darby fired up the engines on the push-pull aircraft. He taxied to the active runway running up both engines and making sure the gages were in the green on the way. He then pulled onto the active runway and applied power.

When the plane reached takeoff speed Darby pulled back on the yoke and the wheels left the runway. He cycled the landing gear up and turned toward the Florida gap. Keeping the aircraft at about six hundred feet above the ground, they flew through the gap between the big and little Florida Mountains.

"There's my house," said Jeff pointing out of the right side.

He could see Josefina hanging clothes on a line to dry. Darby circled the house so Jeff could wave at her. After they were through the gap and out over the desert, Darby dropped down to about a hundred feet. Jeff watched jackrabbits run for cover as the plane passed over them, bumping along in the hot desert air. Twice he saw coyotes slinking from bushes.

After a few minutes, Darby asked, "Do you know where the border is?"

"Sure," Jeff replied. "Arenas gate, which is on the International border is at your 2 o'clock five miles."

"Then shut your eyes, we're going into Mexico Pard," Darby said.

"Oh shit," was all Jeff could say.

"I've got info that about twenty miles south of the border there is a dry lakebed. The informant tells me that smugglers are using it to refuel planes carrying narcotics," Darby continued. "I want to see if we can find it."

"Sure hope the engines don't quit," Jeff stated. "It'll be a long walk home."

"Just watch for the damn lakebed," replied Darby. He adjusted the fuel mixture as the border fence went under the plane.

"Damn, now you've got me thinking the engines are running rough," he said tapping on one of the gauges.

When they were about fifteen miles in Mexico, Darby said, "I'm taking her up, keep your eyes peeled." The aircraft made a hard climb until they were at a thousand feet.

A minute later Jeff shouted, "lakebed! 10 o'clock, three miles."

"I see it now, you have good eyes partner." Darby dropped the plane back down near the ground and turned toward the lakebed. As they sped over the ground Darby said, "look at all the plane tracks down there."

"There is something over on this side Darby," Jeff told him.

Darby turned the yoke and stomped the right rudder, standing the aircraft on its right wing. Both officers could see what appeared to be barrels covered with netting near some brush. He turned the plane back level and climbed to two hundred feet.

"Do you see anybody around," he asked.

"Nope, not a soul, just a couple of running jackrabbits," replied Jeff. "Watching the dust kicked up by the rabbits, the wind must be out of the north," he continued.

"Hang on, we're going to land," Darby stated.

He turned the aircraft north and reduced power. When he was slow enough, he dropped the landing gear. The Cessna 337 touched down on the dry lakebed and was taxied over to the barrels. Leaving the engines idling, both agents walked over to inspect what they had seen from the air.

Jeff pulled back the netting and unscrewed a cap. "It's avgas," he said. The two lawmen stood there for a moment then Darby looked over at Jeff.

"Are you thinking what I'm thinking?" he asked.

"Sure am, let me get my rifle," Jeff stated.

He removed his M16 and charged the weapon while Darby got buckled in. He removed another magazine loaded with all tracers from the case and stuck it in his pocket. Darby taxied the aircraft about a hundred yards upwind from the stored fuel. Jeff walked about fifty yards and turned, bringing the weapon to his shoulder. He moved the selector lever to full automatic and emptied the thirty round magazine into the stored fuel.

When the M16 locked open, he inserted the other magazine loaded with tracers as he walked to where Darby was parked. "You ready," he hollered to Darby.

Darby nodded and applied power, holding the aircraft with the brakes. "Let her rip," he hollered back over the roar of the engines. Jeff aimed the rifle at the barrels and sprayed the tracers into the leaking drums. There was a loud whoosh as the fuel ignited and Jeff leaped into the plane.

"Let's get the hell out of here," he said.

Darby released the brakes and with both engines roaring, lifted the plane into the air after a short run. Just then there was a loud roar as the barrels exploded, sending some of them fifty feet in the air. Jeff turned to look back as dense black smoke rose into the sky.

"Well, they should see that in Palomas," Jeff said. "Somebody will be out there pretty quick as we just cost the hell out of some smugglers."

"You're right about that," laughed Darby. "Keep a sharp eye out, we're coming back to the border fence."

"Yea, that's all we need is for some rancher or BP agent to get a look at the numbers on this baby," Jeff replied.

Just then they flashed over the wire fence that separated the United States from the Republic of Mexico. Darby bored into the low hills just north of the border, just clearing the hills, and then dropping back down in the valleys as they sped north.

When they were twenty miles north, Darby turned northwest toward Deming and started to climb. Ten miles east of the airport he called in and received landing instructions then turned to Jeff.

"Well partner, thanks for the help. Of course we've been out east looking at roads for the last hour."

"You've got that right," said Jeff.

After they landed and taxied to the base operations and Darby had shut down the plane, he said. "The least I can do is buy you lunch."

"That's sounds good to me," replied Jeff as he placed his cased rifle back in his unit.

They both got into the unit and drove into town. After their meal was ordered Darby said, "what worries me now is they will find the empty brass from your weapon."

"I don't believe that'll be a problem," Jeff stated. "It's military surplus and the US Government is giving a lot of it to the Mexican Army. I hope they'll think it was someone they didn't pay off or someone trying to move in on the operation."

"That would be fine with me," Darby stated. "Maybe some smuggler will get his head blown off." After lunch Jeff drove Darby back to the airport and called it a day.

***

The next day some twenty-five miles northeast of Ascension, Chihuahua, Mexico, Felipe Salinas drove into the ranch owned by Cesar Cisneros. He and Cisneros had been driven out of Colombia by the other cartels. After his actions had led to increased actions by the Colombian Government. He had first settled near Agua Prieta, Sonora, Mexico with his smuggling operations. He had smuggled several loads through a tunnel under the International Border. When it was discovered, he had moved to the Mexican State of Chihuahua. He was now using his contacts in Mexico to move aircraft loads using the dry lakebed for fueling.

He was on the patio having his breakfast when Felipe walked in. "We lost almost 2000 gallons of avgas and several planes had to turn back without dropping their loads. I found these where somebody shot the drums," he stated as he handed Cesar several rounds of fired 5.56 rifle brass.

"This is military brass. I thought we had the Mexican Army paid off," Cesar said.

"We have Jefe, I don't believe it was the army who did this," Felipe replied.

"Then who in hell destroyed the gasoline?" Cesar asked.

"I believe it was the Americanos. We found where an aircraft had landed and two sets of footprints by the barrels of gasoline," Felipe stated.

"Find out Felipe. Find out now. I don't want any more surprises and if the gringos are coming into Mexico, I want to know who and when," said Cesar.

"Si mi Jefe," Felipe replied. He left the patio and motioned to one of the men to go with him. Taking a new GMC pickup they drove north and after about an hour pulled into Palomas. Felipe directed the driver to the El Gato Negro (The Black cat) a local cantina just off the main street. Parking the truck they both went inside and sat at a corner table. The owner knew Felipe and hurried over with two bottles of cold cerveza.

Felipe pushed out a chair and said, "Sit down." Paco Rojas set down the beers and seated himself at the table. Sweat suddenly appeared on his face and hands.

"I need a favor," Felipe told him.

"Anything mi Jefe, replied Rojas.

"Do you have any contacts with the police on the other side?" he asked Paco.

"Si, my nephew is a US citizen and works for the police department in Lordsburg. He obtains stolen guns for me," Paco replied.

"We had some gasoline destroyed out southeast of here. See if he can find out who did it. If he can, I'll see that he gets a big reward. I believe it was someone with the Federales from the other side as they came in by aircraft."

"I'll call him at once, mi Jefe," a nervous Rojas stated.

"Fine, call me at the ranch." Felipe got up and dropped a hundred-dollar bill on the table. "Let's go," he told his driver.

After the two men departed, Paco stayed at the table for several minutes regaining his composure. He returned to the bar, picked up the telephone, and called his nephew's home in Lordsburg. When his nephew's wife answered he told her to have Beto come see him in Palomas as soon as possible. Later that night Herberto (Beto) Rojas arrived in answer to his Uncle's summons. Paco told his bartender to take over and motioned Beto into the back office.

"What's happening Tio?" he asked.

"Sit down and shut up," replied Paco. "I have a very dangerous man asking questions about your buddies, the Federales."

"Shit, they ain't my buddies Tio. The son-of-bitches make twice what I make and strut around like they own the country."

"Well, the hombre I'm talking about believes some of them destroyed some gasoline on this side and they may have came in by airplane. Ask around and see what you can come up with, it will be worth a good payday."

"Sure Tio, no problem. I'll see what I can find out and get back to you."

"Okay," Paco replied. "Let's go back to the bar and I'll have some supper sent over."

Beto returned to Lordsburg later that night, but didn't say anything to his wife. The next day he attended an in service training class with police from the surrounding towns. During a break, he pulled one of the Deming Police Officers over to one side.

"Hey Tim, what's going on over in Deming?" he asked.

"Nothing new that I know about," replied Tim Robbins the Deming Police Officer. He didn't know Beto all that well and what he did know, he didn't like.

"Have you heard anything about some of the Customs guys flying into Mexico," he asked Robbins.

"No, why would they be flying down there?" Robbins replied.

"Oh, I just heard they may be flying over the border sometimes," Beto continued.

"Why do you give a shit what they do?" Robbins asked.

"I don't, never mind," Beto said as he walked off. Later Robbins saw him talking to one of the Sheriff's deputies from Deming. When he got a chance he asked the deputy what Beto wanted.

"He was asking me about Customs flying into Mexico," the deputy replied. "I told him, I didn't know and I didn't give a crap." He and Robbins both laughed at that.

A few days later as Jeff drove through Deming he saw one of the Deming Police Officers waving him down. They pulled up with the driver's side facing each other and Jeff rolled down his window.

"What's going on Amigo?" he asked.

The city cop Tim Robbins said, "same old shit, different day."

"I heard that," Jeff laughed.

What I wanted to tell you," Robbins continued. "I was over in Lordsburg last Friday for some training. There's a cop over there asking some peculiar questions. Like if I had heard about any of the feds flying into Mexico lately. He asked me and I know he asked one of the deputies from Luna County."

"Oh, what else was he asking about?" asked Jeff.

"That's about it. It just didn't sound right the way he was asking. Why would he give a crap where you guys are flying?" Robbins continued.

"Who is this guy?" Jeff asked.

"His name is Herberto Rojas. Everybody calls him Beto. I think he has some relatives in Palomas, Mexico. Some of the Lordsburg cops think he's dirty, although nothing's been proven yet. I know I've never liked the bastard, he's just shifty."

"Let's go to the Ramada and I'll buy you some coffee," Jeff said.

"Great, it's slow today," replied Robbins.

When they were seated with their coffee, Jeff asked Tim, "See if you can get Rojas's birth date and SSN number and I'll run a check on him."

"I'll be glad to. I'll have it for you tomorrow," Tim stated.

The next day he called Jeff and gave him the data on Herberto Rojas. Jeff sat down and started entering the information into the Customs computer system.

CHAPTER 17

A month after the gasoline had been destroyed Beto Rojas walked into the El Gato Negro in Palomas. He motioned for his uncle to join him in the back office.

"Que Paso?" asked Paco, as he moved behind his desk.

"Tio, I have a friend in Utah who called me the other day. He wants to know if I can get him some chiva. (Heroin) He said his last contact over in Arizona was killed."

"How well do you know this man? He could be working for the cops," Paco stated.

"I'll vouch for him Tio. He's the guy I've been getting the stolen guns from that I pass on to you. I've know him for years," Beto said.

"Let me think for a minute. Any info on the Federales flying over here?" Paso asked.

"Not a word Tio. I've asked around, but no one is admitting anything. If they did it, they don't want their bosses to know. I did find out that a Customs aircraft fueled in Deming on that day."

"Well, I'll get in touch with Felipe and let him know. He may be able to help your friend with his problem. How much stuff does your friend want?" asked Paco.

"He told me he would like to get a kilo, if possible and if the price is right."

"Okay, I'll call Felipe right now, wait in the bar," Paco told him.

An hour later Felipe walked into the bar along with his bodyguard. After a short conversation with Paco he walked over to the table and sat down with Beto. His driver leaned against a wall where he could watch them and the door.

"Paco tells me that you need some stuff," Felipe stated.

Beto looked at his uncle who nodded his head. "That's right, I've a contact who wants to move about a kilo. He'll want it delivered to the other side."

"We can handle that, cash when we deliver, your uncle here can deliver it," Felipe said.

At that bit of news, Paco turned white. "Wait a minute Jefe. I'm not involved in drugs."

"You are now, he's your nephew. Besides you cross through the Port all the time. They don't search you," Felipe told him. He turned to Beto. "Let me know about a week in advance and the price will be 180,000 US dollars, No Credit, Tu sabes?"

"Si mi Jefe," Beto replied. "I'll call him tonight. I'd better go now, con su permiso. mi Jefe," Beto stated then quickly left the bar and drove back to Lordsburg.

During the last month a lot had happened at the Customs office. Glenn Perry, the Station Supervisor, had been promoted to El Paso and Jeff had been acting in his place. He was in the office catching up on paper work when he received a call from Livingston.

"How about taking another ride with me? I need to check out some info in the Gila National Forest," Darby told him.

"We aren't going in the 337 are we?" Jeff asked.

"No," Darby replied. "This time I've a twin Beechcraft. I'll be at the airport in about an hour."

"Okay I'll see you there," Jeff stated.

He arrived at the Deming airport first and was drinking a cold soda when he saw the twin beech make its approach and land. Darby taxied up to the tie down line and shut down the engines.

"Let me hit the head and I'll be ready," he told Jeff.

While he waited for Darby, he walked around the aircraft looking it over. He was soon joined by Darby who asked, "what do you think of her"

"Another military surplus?" Jeff asked. "When is Customs going to buy some new aircraft?" Jeff wondered.

"Your guess is as good as mine," Darby said. "You ready to go."

EL LOBO VERDE

"Might as well, you can't live forever," said Jeff.

Jeff followed Darby into the aircraft and buckled his seatbelt while the engines were started. They taxied to runway 4, where Darby applied power, then rotated the plane into the air when they reached the correct speed.

When they were northwest of Deming, Darby turned to Jeff. "We hear that the smugglers are using some of the dirt strips in the Gila Forest. I thought you might like to go along for a look. I hear you're the Acting Supervisor in Deming," Darby continued.

"That's right, for now, who knows who we'll get as the boss," Jeff replied.

"Well I hear that you have a damn good shot at it my friend," Darby told him.

After checking out several of the dirt strips, they flew over the Me-Own airstrip. Darby said, "looks like we've had some traffic on this one. I'm going down for a look."

Darby made his approach from the north, landing to the south on the short strip. He turned the plane around on the south end and shut down the engines. "Let's have a look," he said.

The two agents could see where another aircraft had landed, but could not see any sign of a vehicle meeting it. "It looks like a tail dragger by the tracks," said Darby.

"Yea, I can see where he made a pit stop over here," said Jeff. Pointing to some footprints and a wet place in the dirt.

Darby walked over and had a look. "Yep, looks like about two quarts," he laughed. He then looked down the strip. "You know I don't think I've enough room to take off."

"You are kidding right?" asked a worried Jeff. "You're not just pulling my leg."

"No, I'm not. This strip is over 7,000 feet above sea level and it's over 80 degrees. That'll play hell with the density altitude, the air will be too thin to lift off," Darby said.

"Shit, I knew I should have stayed home," Jeff stated.

Darby paced off the runway and looked back behind the airplane. "Come help me, I've a plan," he said. "Let's push this thing as far back into the trees as we can. That'll give us a few more feet of runway."

They pushed the plane backward about forty feet; the tail was almost against a tree. "Let's get aboard," Darby stated. He started the engines and turned in the seat to Jeff. "I want you to get on the brakes and help me hold this thing until I'm ready. Then when I tell you too, get the landing gear up. You ready?" He asked.

"Hell, I guess so," Jeff replied.

Darby increased the power to both engines until they were red lined. The plane was straining and shaking against the brakes with dirt, twigs, leaves flying into the air.

"Ain't this a little hard on the engines?" Jeff asked.

"Hell, It ain't my plane," Darby shouted over the roar. "Let go the brakes." The plane leaped forward and began to pick up speed. Jeff could see the end of the runway coming and the air speed was only about 60 MPH. Darby gave it fifteen degrees of flaps and jerked back on the yoke. The aircraft struggled into the air with the stall warning going off and with Darby hollering, "get the gear up, get the gear up."

Jeff raised the gear just as they cleared the brush at the end of the runway and Darby dove the plane into the canyon picking up airspeed. Jeff was hanging on watching the trees flashing by just off the right wing. He saw a squirrel leap from a tree as the wing almost clipped it. Suddenly the plane started to climb and he looked over at Darby who was grinning.

"Now, that wasn't so bad was it?" Darby asked.

"Oh hell no, Let's go do it again. You just scared the shit out of two squirrels and a crow. Not to mention, I'll have to change my pants," Jeff stated. The rest of the flight back to Deming was uneventful and they landed at the airport.

When Jeff returned to the office after seeing Darby off. The secretary informed him that DEA in Las Cruces wanted him to call. Jeff placed the call to DEA Agent Daniel Dean.

"What's going on over in your country?" Jeff asked.

"Well, it's like this. One of your guys in Nogales, Arizona has been working a smuggling case over there. He's been in contact with a guy in Utah who deals in Heroin. Anyway, to make a long story short, the dealer has agreed to furnish a kilo of Heroin. The kicker is he says his supplier is in Palomas and wants to meet the buyer in Deming this Friday."

"That sounds good, what do you need from me and how can I help," Jeff asked.

"We need three rooms, two connecting and one upstairs where the two can be seen."

"Okay, the Zia Inn is an L shape and I'll make the arrangements. What else do we need," Jeff asked.

"We're going to need an aircraft and I don't know if I can get one of ours or not," Dean said. "Our pilots are like pelicans. All they do is squawk and shit and you have to throw rocks to make them fly."

Jeff started laughing, "don't worry about a plane, I'll get one from Customs. I know just the pilot who'll jump at the chance."

"Okay, I'll be over Thursday and we'll all get together for a meet," Dean continued.

On Thursday the Customs office was full of people as they made their plans. Dean had brought one of his agents and the Customs officer from Nogales, Erin Blackburn. He was a chiseled-faced individual with dark hair and several gold chains around his neck. He told them that he had been in contact with a guy in Utah.

"His name is Rufo Serda. He has a narcotics record and has been supplied by one of the smugglers in Nogales, Sonora, Mexico. Unfortunately for him, his supplier was killed about two weeks ago in a shootout with the Mex Feds," said Blackburn. I was already dealing with Serda when his guy was shot. I've arranged to meet him in the morning in the dining room of the motel. We'll see who he brings with him then," Erin stated.

The rest of the day went by fast as the operation was firmed up. Jeff made arrangement to have a local deputy in the plane with Darby Livingston to act as another set of eyes. Darby had a Cessna 210 just out of seizure parked at the Deming airport.

The next morning Jeff and Dean were in the connecting room with audio equipment in place. They had placed a listening mike under the connecting door and hidden it in the undercover agent's room. Dean's agent was in the room above and toward the front with a clear view of Blackburn's room. He was to act as Blackburn's bodyguard and to show Serda the money when he came to Blackburn's room. He was holding the cash, a briefcase with 180,000 dollars in hundred dollar bills. After he showed the money he was to return upstairs and wait.

It was just before 10 o'clock when Dean and Jeff saw Blackburn approaching his room accompanied by two individuals. One was Serda, who was identified by his mug shot from a previous arrest. The other had a baseball cap pulled low over his eyes and it was not until he entered the room next door that Jeff recognized him. "Shit, he has Beto Rojas with him, he told Dean. "He's a city cop from Lordsburg with ties in Palomas."

The two lawmen listened to the conversation next door. They heard the undercover agent place the call upstairs to bring down the money. Jeff watched through the curtains as the money was carried into the room. They could hear Blackburn unsnap the briefcase and say; "here's the money." A few minutes later Jeff watched as the DEA agent returned upstairs with the briefcase.

"We have thirty ounces," they heard Serda tell Blackburn. "Now that we've seen the money, we'll bring you a sample."

"No, I don't want a sample. You bring the whole thing and I'll take my own sample. That way I'll know if it's all good," Blackburn stated.

While they were talking, Jeff called the airport and told Darby to get in the air. He then called two of his officers who were hidden down the street in a vehicle. "These guys will be leaving soon, see if you can get a description of their vehicle," he told them.

Jeff watched as the two men left Blackburn's room and walked back toward the front of the motel. Dean opened the connecting door was talking to Erin. In a few minutes Jeff received a call on his walkie-talkie, "we can see them standing by a black pickup talking. We're too far away to get the license number."

"That's okay, don't push it," Jeff caution. "Lima four two, Lima four two," called Jeff.

"Lima four two, go ahead," Darby replied. Jeff could hear the roar of the engine as Darby climbed south of the airport grabbing some altitude.

"See if you can spot a black pickup when it leaves the motel," Jeff requested.

"Papa 1401, Papa 1401," called Jeff's agents, who were watching from a nearby service station. "Go ahead," Jeff said.

"One of the guys is walking over to the motel across the street. The black pickup is headed into town. We got the license number when he drove by."

"Okay, drop in behind him, but stay back. We don't want to spook him. Lima four two, do you have him?" Jeff asked.

"We're on him," Darby replied.

Jeff turned to Dean and Blackburn. "I'm going south with the guys. We'll keep you posted by radio or telephone."

"Okay," said Dean. "I'll check out the motel across the street and see if Serda has a room."

With the aircraft holding surveillance on the pickup from the air, Jeff and his two officers could stay a mile to the rear as they headed south on highway 11. They soon passed through Columbus and could see the Customs Port of Entry in the distance.

"Papa 1401, Lima four two, he just crossed into the Republic of Mexico," called Darby.

"That's ten four, orbit north west of Columbus," Jeff requested. "You got it," Darby said.

Jeff and his two officers parked their vehicles at the rear of the port and went inside. The port director came out to meet Jeff as the two officers watched the traffic from the front lobby. Jeff motioned the director back into his office and told him about the information they were working.

After about a half-hour they saw the same black pickup approaching the Customs Port of Entry from Mexico. Jeff told his two officers to take off before the truck pulled up for inspection and contacted the plane. Jeff could see that Beto was driving and had a passenger with him.

"Take a look at the black ford pickup and see if you know the guy riding shotgun," Jeff requested of the Port Director. The pickup stopped briefly at the primary and was then waved through entering highway 11 north bound.

"That's Beto Rojas, a Lordsburg Police Officer and his uncle Paco. The uncle owns the Gato Negro cantina in Palomas," the Director replied.

"Okay, I want you to watch closely the vehicles that follow him. Take down the license plates on any that you don't know and contact me by radio," Jeff stated. He quickly left through the back door and sped north. As soon as he was on highway 11 headed into Columbus, he radioed the aircraft.

"Lima four two, papa 1401, I'm leaving the port now."

"Roger that, we have him just north of Columbus," Darby replied.

Just then Jeff received a call from the Customs Port. "Papa 1401, we had a new dark green GMC pickup, Texas license alpha hotel 3424 about four vehicle behind your suspect. They showed Texas drivers licenses and claimed US Citizenship to the Inspector on primary."

"Roger that, heads up guys, we may have some more players," Jeff stated.

With the aircraft having the eyeball, the two Customs officers sped north into Deming and found a place where they could observe the pickup when it arrived. Jeff was following the black pickup about a mile behind, but keeping a lookout for the GMC in his mirror. When the pickup reached the edge of Deming, Jeff turned east on Dona Ana road and then north on Country Club road and headed back to the motel.

"Papa 1401, Papa 1407," the Customs officers called.

"Go ahead 1407," Jeff replied.

"The suspects have pulled into the little drive-in grocery store just passed the four way stop and the driver has gone inside."

"Roger that, keep a lookout for the green GMC, he may be involved," Jeff said.

Just then Darby came on the radio. "The GMC is a block south of the four way stop."

The two Customs officers were parked east of the store watching with binoculars. A few minutes later one called, "Papa 1401, the GMC has just arrived and parked next to the suspect's vehicle. The driver of the black truck just walked out of the store and is talking to the passenger of the GMC."

"Roger that, I'll park where I can see the motel, where the other crook is staying," Jeff replied. "Dean, you reading this traffic?"

"Papa 1401, we're ready here and Serda is in room 16 across the street," Dean stated.

Jeff parked his vehicle at a service station just south of the motel where he could see Serda's room. In a few minutes Darby came up on the radio.

"They're moving, the GMC is leading and heading your way Papa 1401."

"10-4, I'm ready on this end," Jeff said. In about ten minutes Jeff watched the GMC pull into the parking lot of the motel, neither person got out. He then saw Beto pull up to Serda's room and both occupants exited the truck. Jeff could see that Beto was carrying a paper sack as they entered the room.

Jeff's two officers arrived and took over the surveillance of the two pickups. He then drove over to the Zia Inn and parked his vehicle out of sight. He quickly walked to the room where Dean was waiting and went inside. He was barely inside when he received a call on his walkie-talkie.

"Papa 1401, the guy from Utah is walking across the street to your location and the GMC just pulled out of the parking lot," radioed Papa 1407.

"Roger that, Lima four two can you keep an eyeball on the GMC?" he asked Darby.

"You got it," Darby replied, "We're up here at twelve thousand feet. Just gliding alone, just like a buzzard looking for a meal."

In a few minutes the two lawmen heard a knock on Blackburn's door. There were listening when Serda came into the room and said, "The stuff is here."

"Yea, I don't see it, where is it?" asked Blackburn.

"It's across the street, we can walk over and you can take your sample like you wanted. Then we'll come back over here for the money," Serda told him.

"Okay, wait outside while I tell my money man where I'm going," Jeff and Dean heard the door close and then Erin's whispered voice, "Okay, guys, I'm going over to see what we've got."

Jeff quickly radioed his two officers, "heads up guys, Serda and the UC (undercover) are coming your way. Where's the GMC, Lima four two?" he asked.

"He made a run through town and is headed back toward your location," replied Darby.

"Papa 1401, both hombres just went into Serda's room," 1407 stated.

"Okay, we'll give them ten minutes, if the UC is not out by then, we're going in," Jeff stated. The time seemed to drag with Jeff watching the minutes creep by. In six minutes, which seem like an hour, the radio crackled to life.

"Papa 1401, the UC and the same guy just came out and are headed your way again."

"10-4 guys, thanks," replied Jeff.

The two lawmen listened as Blackburn opened the door in the next room. They heard him say, "I'll call for the money to be delivered. Then you and I'll walk back across the street and get the stuff." They heard Erin called the other room. "Bring the money, it looks like real good stuff."

Both Jeff and Dean grinned at each other. The words "real good stuff" meant that the UC and seen and tested the heroin. Dean whispered in Jeff's ear. "We'll go in behind the money man and take this asshole down."

Jeff watched through the curtains as the DEA agent carrying the briefcase of money approached the room. Two raps followed by a single rap and Blackburn opened the door. "Give me the briefcase," he stated. Turning to Serda he released the snaps and handed him the briefcase. "Here's the dough," he said.

As Serda took the open briefcase of money, Jeff and Dean came through the door, weapons drawn. "On the floor, you cocksucker," Jeff commanded. Serda was quickly handcuffed and left with the two UC's.

Jeff and Dean ran across the road to the Lazy Dog Motel, where Jeff confronted the manager. "Federal officers, I need the key to room 16," said Jeff showing his badge.

"Well, I don't know about that. Do you have a warrant?" he asked, as he peered down his nose at the two lawmen.

Jeff pulled his Colt .45 from his waistband. "Here's my warrant and you've got fifteen seconds before you're under arrest and we take the damn door down," Jeff stated.

"Well, I have never seen such rude behavior," the manager whined.

"You now have five seconds," a hard-eyed Jeff stated.

"All right, all right, here's the key, take it," he stated, as he handed it to Jeff.

Jeff and Dean quickly walked to room 16 as Jeff told his two officers to come in behind them. He and Dean stood on each side, as Jeff softly inserted the key. At a nod from Dean, Jeff turned the key and both went through the door with weapons drawn. Beto and Paco were watching TV, but Beto jumped to his feet. "Don't move," both Jeff and Dean shouted.

They could see a paper sack on the bed. Dean walked over and turned it upside down. Beto had a stricken look on his face as a large tinfoil wrapped package fell on the bed. Jeff's two officers came in and both subjects were handcuffed. A weapon was removed from under Beto's shirt.

Jeff called the aircraft, "Lima four two, where's the GMC?"

"About a half a mile from you coming toward the motel," Darby replied.

Leaving Dean and one Customs officer with the two prisoners, Jeff and Papa 1407 ran outside and jumped into the Customs unit. "Papa 1401, he's just going by the motel," the aircraft stated.

"We've got him," Jeff stated as they sped out of the parking lot. "We're taking him down on the overpass as he crosses the interstate." The Customs unit quickly overtook the GMC and Jeff could see the passenger looking back at them.

"Force him over," Jeff commanded as he placed a portable red light on the roof of the unmarked sedan. With the siren wailing the government sedan forced the GMC to the guardrail on the overpass. Jeff came out with his .45 aimed at the two occupants. Both raised their hands just as Darby came roaring over with the aircraft. The two were quickly removed, handcuffed, and searched. Both were found to be carrying weapons.

The subjects were transported to the Customs office where they were processed and fingerprinted. Beto, at first tried to say he was working undercover on a smuggling ring.

When that didn't fly, he refused to talk. His uncle Paco wouldn't talk at all. Serda on the other hand, knowing he was facing a long prison term wouldn't shut up. He agreed to cooperate and freely gave a statement.

The two persons in the GMC were found to be using false US documents and would not give their names. All five subjects were transported to the Dona Ana County jail and booked in as federal prisoners.

It was the next day before Felipe Salinas and his driver was identified. The DEA office in Washington had a file on the Cartel of Cisneros and Felipe Salinas was identified as one of the main people. His driver was a citizen of Mexico.

Felipe's bond was set at one million dollars.

CHAPTER 18

In the days following the heroin seizure, Jeff and his officers were busy with all of the paperwork and court appearances involved. The newspapers had reporters trying to find out more details and the office's secretary was kept busy screening his calls. One of the El Paso papers had a huge story about the seizure, including a picture of Jeff escorting some of the prisoners into Federal Court. Felipe and the others had several highly paid attorneys from El Paso, Texas representing them, but were still denied bail.

Jeff was in the office when his secretary buzzed him on the intercom. "Jeff, its Inspector Garcia from Columbus on line one."

Jeff punched the button and said hello. "Jeff, this is Juan Garcia from the port. I had a little old man come in this morning asking that I give you a message. I'm going to give it to you in Spanish just like he gave it to me, because it makes no sense." "El hombre con mono, papalote arenas, esta tarde antes puesta de sol." "Do you understand what he means?" Gracia asked.

"Yes, I think so, thanks for the message," Jeff replied and hung up the telephone. Jeff had written down the message in English. "The man with the monkey, arenas windmill, this evening before sunset." The old man who gave me the peach seed carved into a monkey wants to meet me at the arenas windmill, Jeff thought. I wonder what he wants? I'll take a run down there and see later. With that out of the way, Jeff continued working.

At 5 o'clock Jeff drove his unmarked Government pickup to the arenas windmill, which is only a hundred yards north of the wire gap in the International fence known as Arenas gate. He parked the unit and got out slowly with his weapon down beside his leg. He heard a whistle and saw a head appeared just south of his location. The man walked out in the open and Jeff indeed recognized Demetrio Urbano.

He was an illegal alien Jeff had apprehended while working for the Border Patrol.

Demetrio walked up and said, "como está Señor Lobo?"

"I'm fine Demetrio," Jeff replied in Spanish. "What brings you way out here?"

"I have important news for you," Demetrio stated.

"Come, let's sit down by the truck. I've some cold drinks in there," Jeff said.

After they were seated and Jeff had given the old man a soda pop, Demetrio started talking. "I've heard that you no longer work for the Border Patrol, but now work for Customs."

Jeff nodded his head and Demetrio continued. "The people are talking in Palomas about the arrest of Paco Rojas. They say that the person behind the "Chiva" has a place southwest of Palomas called El Rancho Codornoiz." (Quail Ranch)

"Do you know his name and where the ranch is located?" Jeff asked.

"No Señor Lobo, they call him El Patron. (the boss, owner) They also say he is not a Mexican and he is muy malo. No one goes to his ranch and he is protected by some of the Federales. Let me draw you a map of where the ranch is located." With that Demetrio sketched a rough map in the dirt showing the location of the ranch.

"Thanks amigo, you've been very helpful. Is there anything I can do for you?"

"Oh no, you've already done it when you left the Border Patrol. I find it very easy to cross now without you tracking me. I've been working for the last few months and I'm on my way home," Demetrio said.

Jeff laughed and said, "well have a good trip home, can I drop you off closer to town?"

"No, I'll walk south until I come to the road from Juarez and catch the bus."

"Buena suerte amigo," (Good luck) Jeff told Demetrio, as he left in the direction of the border fence. Jeff drove back to Deming and home to Josefina, calling in to sector that he was 10-7 for the night.

***

EL LOBO VERDE

Cesar Cisneros had not said much when he was informed of Felipe's arrest and the loss of the heroin. He made arrangements for some attorneys and then sat on his patio for several days drinking heavily.

He finally called one of his men, "do you know anyone who lives on the other side?"

"Si Patron, my cousin lives there, he has a green card," Mario stated.

"Call him, I want to know where this "cabron" lives," pointing to the picture of Jeff in the newspaper he had been reading.

"At once Patron," Mario said and quickly left.

The next day after Cesar had eaten, Mario came in the room. "Patron, I called my cousin and met him last night. He was able to give me directions and a map. This map is of Luna County with the location where the hombre lives."

"Good, very good. Clean off this table," he shouted at one of the maids. When it was clear, they spread the map out. A red circle was drawn around a house in the east side of the Florida gap.

"My cousin says that he has two pickups. He also told me there aren't any other houses past his place or near it," he said pointing to the map.

"Okay, here's what I want. Get two more men that you can trust. I want men who don't mind shooting and one needs to be able to cross the border. On Monday the man who can cross will drive to Juarez and cross the border there. We'll meet him on the dirt road that goes from El Paso to Columbus. Do you understand?" It's time somebody put this cabron away."

"Si Patron, I'll get on it at once," Mario stated and quickly left.

Monday afternoon Cesar and Mario drove toward Juarez with the other pickup following. When they were still over an hour from Juarez they stopped and pulled to the side of the road. The peak of Mt. Riley could be seen to the north. Cesar walked back to Alfredo who would drive across the border. His passenger walked to the lead pickup and got into the small backseat.

"You know how to find the road?" Cesar asked Alfredo.

"Si Patron, I know it well.

"Okay, we're going to turn north here and will meet you somewhere along the road. Look for two beer cans side by side and pull over just as you pass them. Do not fail me, comprende?" (understand)

"Si mi Patron," Alfredo nervously replied and drove off.

Cesar returned to the pickup and they turned north on a dirt road in bad shape. After an hour of slow driving they could see a wire fence and white monuments, which indicated the International Border. (These resemble small versions of the Washington Monument and are placed in sight of each other marking the line.)

They parked the pickup in a dry gully and Mario covered it with a camouflage net. Using binoculars they studied the area on the north side of the border for an hour. Finally, as the sun was dropping very low in the west, they started walking to the fence staying in a dry wash. When the wash went under the border fence, they walked along one side in the rocks where no footprints would show. Finding a good hiding place beside the road in the brush, Mario quickly placed the two cans they had brought along side the road.

They had been waiting for about forty minutes when Mario said, "there is a pickup coming." Hidden from view, they watched the pickup slow and then stop just passed the beer cans. Alfredo opened the door and stepped out. Carrying their weapons they quickly ran to the extended cab truck. Mario motioned Alfredo and Juan into the backseat and he got behind the wheel with Cesar in the right front seat.

Driving west they encountered highway 11 at Columbus and turned north toward Deming. About five miles south of town using the map Mario's cousin had provided they turned right toward Rockhound State Park. The sun had set and it was getting dark when the pavement turned into a dirt road running between the big and little Florida Mountains. They could see a dust cloud and taillights of a vehicle about a mile in front.

"Stop the truck," Cesar commanded. Using the binoculars he could see the vehicle pull into the yard where Larson lived. "He's home, let's check the weapons."

He directed Mario to pull into the brush on the left side of the road. As they were readying the weapons, Cesar saw vehicle lights come back on and swing around in the yard.

"Get ready, the cabron is coming back out, back the truck across the road," he said.

Mario backed the truck into the road and they squatted down behind it out of sight.

***

Jeff had been busy all day with budget and seizure reports. The sun was setting when he was finally able to leave the office for home. Josefina had called earlier and asked him to pickup a bottle of champagne, but with so much on his mind he had forgotten. He drove into the yard and parked his Government pickup next to his own.

As he opened the door he could see the table was set with candles and their best china. Josefina was in a dark green dress with her hair falling down to her shoulders standing by the table. "Darn, I forgot the champagne, what's the occasion?" he asked. "I'll run back into town and get it."

"It's a surprise, I'll run in and pick up a bottle," she said.

"No, I'm the one who forgot," replied Jeff.

"It's okay Jeffie, it won't take me more than twenty minutes. You rest or take a shower, I'll be right back," she said and picked up her purse and keys.

She ran outside and jumped into Jeff's old green pickup, backed it out and started to town. "I can't wait until Jeff hears the news," she thought as she turned on the truck's radio. She was listening to some Mexican music and softly singing when she topped a small hill and saw a parked pickup. The truck was backed into the dirt road almost completely blocking it and she thought it was a local rancher.

Just as she started to slow down, she saw some men step out from the front of the truck with weapons. She saw the guns come up and start firing. Then the passenger window blew out and she could hear the bullets hammering into the far door and side. Josefina scrunched down in the seat and floored the gas petal. The old truck leaped forward as she rammed the back of the parked vehicle trying desperately to get through. She felt the truck go side ways in a skid and start to roll, as she felt a blow to her back and head. Everything was spinning, her last thought was, I love you Jeff.

The truck turned over twice as it rolled into the ditch, coming to rest on it's top. Cesar walked near it and fired a full magazine into the cab and side. A fire started under the hood and quickly spread.

"Let's get out of here," Cesar shouted. They jumped into their vehicle and fled the area.

Jeff had gotten a beer and looked through the mail, and then taking his beer he walked out on the porch. He was looking at the lights in the Franklin area when he heard a siren in the distance. Stepping down to the yard he walked where he could look toward Deming. He could see an emergency vehicle coming from town in the clear night air. Just then he noticed a fire burning on the road to town that they used. He felt a sudden chill and ran to his Government vehicle.

When he arrived at the fire, a State Police officer was walking back from the burning pickup. The truck was upside down in a small ravine engulfed in flames. Jeff quickly jumped out asking, "Everybody okay?"

"There's no one in the truck but I got the license number," the State Police replied.

Jeff took one look at the number and said, "that's my truck, and my wife is in it." He started down to the truck, but the State Officer grabbed him.

"Stay back the gas tank may blow, there's no one in the cab. The driver's door is open and I could see inside."

Jeff ran back to his vehicle and grabbed a flashlight. He ran over to the far side of the ravine and started looking through the brush as the fire continued to blaze. Sweeping the light back and forth he saw a small crumpled figure nearby and ran to it.

"Here she is, help me," he shouted.

Josefina was lying on her back all bloody as Jeff knelt down beside her. He gently picked up her head and wiped the blood from her face. He could see where she had been thrown from the vehicle when it rolled. Picking her up he started for the road, where the State Police and a Deputy Sheriff met him. An ambulance was just pulling up and she was quickly loaded in with Jeff beside her. At the hospital she was rushed into the emergency room, leaving Jeff to pace the floor outside.

A half-hour later the State Police Officer came in and handed Jeff the keys to his Government truck. "One of the deputies drove it back to your house. We picked up a lot of expended 9mm cartridge cases and some broken glass just before she started the skid. It appears that someone tried to block her on the road. She rammed them as she tried to get by and they shot the living hell out of the truck. How is she?" he asked.

"They are working on her now, I just don't know," Jeff stated.

Just then a doctor came, "we've given her some blood and have her stabilized. But I want to send her to El Paso. We've called for a military helicopter to transport her to Ft. Bliss. They are a lot better equipped to care for her. She was shot in the lower right back and head and she's lost a lot of blood."

"Will she be all right, she will live won't she?" asked Jeff.

"I don't know, only time will tell. The helicopter will be here in twenty minutes," the doctor stated.

The helicopter soon arrived and Josefina with Jeff beside her was loaded on board. When it landed at the hospital, she was quickly rushed inside to the operating room where surgeons were ready. Again Jeff was left to pace the floor. He found a telephone and called the Special Agent in Charge at home. After bringing him up to date, he placed a call to El Rancho Alegre in Mexico and spoke to Cory O'Connor. He told him she had been shot and then thrown from the truck when it had rolled, which saved her from the fire. Jeff gave him the name of the hospital and Cory said they would be there as soon as possible. He talked briefly to Carmen then hung up the telephone.

Jeff was still waiting five hours later, when Cory and Carmen arrived. Jeff hugged Carmen who started crying. "How did you get here so fast?" Jeff asked.

"I called General Huerta, who sent a helicopter to carry us to Ojinaga. The banker there had called for a chartered plane to meet us at the airport in Presidio, Texas. From there, it was only an hour to El Paso. Is there any news on Josefina?" Cory asked.

"No, she been in surgery for over six hours and nobody has told me anything," Jeff said.

Jeff got coffee from a nearby machine and filled them in on all that he knew. An hour later one of the surgeons walked out. "Are you Mr. Larson?" he asked.

"Yes Sir, how is she Doc? This is her mother and grandfather." Jeff told him.

"We had to do some very intense reconstruction surgery," the doctor stated. "She has a bad head wound, and we have relieved the pressure. One bullet went through her stomach and I'm sorry to tell you she has lost the baby." At Jeff's shocked look, he asked, "you didn't know she was pregnant?"

"No, she said she had a surprise, but she never told me what it was," Jeff stated.

"She was about two months along. The bullet went clear through her stomach, killing the baby. Right now she's in a coma. She could come out of it in a day, or it could be a week." The doctor looked at Carmen then dropped his eyes.

"What you are not saying, is that she may never wake up, aren't you?" Carmen asked.

"I just don't know at this time, we'll have to wait and see. She is being moved to intensive care where there are nurses around the clock. I wish I could tell you more. I'm sorry, I can't," the doctor continued.

Jeff stood there looking at the doctor and tears formed in his eyes. "Thanks for everything you've done Doc," he said.

"You're welcome, I'll check in on her every two hours and so will the other doctors. Maybe tomorrow we'll know more," the doctor said and then walked off.

Carmen hugged Jeff saying, "she'll pull through this, I just know it," she whispered.

The next three days passed slowly for Jeff. Cory had rented rooms at a nearby motel, but Jeff stayed at the hospital. He could see into the room where Josefina was hooked up to several machines and was only allowed in for short periods. Customs people would drop in from time to time and flowers arrived to be placed in the hallway. Cory arranged to have a new GMC pickup delivered to Jeff to replace his old ford.

Arturo Mora, Josefina's ranch foreman had called and Jeff had talked to him for a long time. Darby Livingston came by for a visit and had a long conversation with Jeff away from Carmen and Cory.

On the fourth day when Carmen and Cory arrived at the hospital, they saw Jeff in the room kneeling beside Josefina. He appeared to be praying, he then stood up and they watched as he kissed her forehead and walked out into the hall.

"Will you stay with her?" he asked with tears in his eyes.

"Of course, mi hijo," Carmen replied.

"We'll both stay," said Cory.

Jeff looked back into the room once more at Josefina, and then started for the exit.

"What are you going to do Jeff," asked Cory, in a very concerned voice.

Jeff stopped and slowly turned toward them. "Behold a pale horse: and his name that sat on him was death, and hell followed with him." (Revelation 6:8)

Jeff then quickly left, got in the new GMC pickup heading west. When he arrived home he walked inside to a clothes closet. Moving some of the clothes, he removed a small panel in the back. Reaching inside he withdrew a Browning semi-automatic 12-gauge shotgun. He also removed his .45 Colt single action holstered on a belt studded with ammo. He picked up a black bag and loaded the pistol, belt and several boxes of double-aught buck shot in the bag along with a pair of binoculars and a spotting scope.

Taking the shotgun he walked outside to a small shed and clamped it in a vise. Using a hacksaw, he sawed the barrel off just in front of the magazine, and reamed it smooth. He then cut off the stock behind the pistol grip and sanded it down. When he was finished he placed it in the bag and fixed a sandwich.

He had just finished his meal when he heard a helicopter. Taking the bag he walked outside just in time to see it land about fifty yards from the house. He walked over and was greeted by Darby and another Customs pilot.

"You guys sure you want to do this?" he asked the two pilots.

"Hell yes," they both stated. "I want to go with you when we land Jeff," Darby said.

"I really appreciate the offer, but I've some help coming. If you guys can just drop me off, that's all I'll need," Jeff told them.

"Get aboard then," Darby told him. The helicopter engine began to wind up and soon lifted off, headed southeast. Darby turned around and handed Jeff a large envelope and a small green bag. "Here's the aerial photos you wanted and some other goodies."

Staying low the helicopter crossed onto the Republic of Mexico southwest of Mt. Riley. Soon they could see the highway that ran from Ciudad Juarez to Ascension.

"Set me down about a mile north of the road," Jeff requested.

"Okay," Darby replied on the intercom. "We'll be back here in the morning, day after tomorrow."

"I don't want you to do that, you're sticking your necks out as it is," Jeff said.

"We'll still be here," both pilots replied.

Jeff ran into the brush nearby as the helicopter lifted off headed back north. Jeff waited a few minutes until the dust settled and carefully looked around. He then placed the photos in his black bag and taking both bags started walking south. When he came to the highway he found a hiding place under a mesquite bush and settled down to wait. While he waited he studied the photos and chewed on a piece of beef jerky.

When the sun was about to set he saw a pickup slowly approaching from the east pulling a horse trailer. Looking through the binoculars he was able to see that Arturo was driving it and stepped into the road. Arturo saw him and pulled up to him, where Jeff entered the truck and the two shook hands.

"How much further do we need to go," he asked Jeff.

"About twenty kilometers, watch for a large dirt tank on the left side of the road. Just past that we take a dirt road south about fifteen kilometers. There should be a place where we can hide the vehicle," Jeff said consulting the air photos.

They were soon off the main highway traveling south on a narrow dirt two-track road. After traveling south slowly for about an hour they pulled off into some brush. Arturo went back and swept out their tire tracks. Jeff quickly cut some brush and placed it over the truck and trailer. They unloaded two dark colored horses and saddled them. Jeff removed his pistol from the bag and belted it around his waist. He tied the shotgun on behind the saddle and then looked into the green bag.

"Damn, look at this," he told Arturo. "There are some phosphorus grenades in here. I wonder where Darby got them."

He placed them and his ammo in the saddlebags. Mounting the horses, Jeff led the way west. Soon the moon came up and they could ride a little faster. After about two hours, Jeff reined up on a small hill overlooking a valley. They could see the lights of a hacienda about a mile away.

"Let's find a good place to hide where we can watch and stay hidden," he told Arturo.

When the sun came up, Jeff and Arturo were under a large bush studying the ranch. They could see that it had an adobe wall around it, but the house was newly constructed of wood with a tile roof. On the north wall they could see a guard watching the only road in from the north. They took turns sleeping and watching the ranch during the day. Drinking water from a large canteen and eating jerky when they got hungry. The horses were hidden in a dry wash about fifty yards behind them. Just before sunset Jeff observed a guard with a dog on a leash starting to walk around the house. Using the spotting scope he could almost count the fleas on the dog. Arturo joined him and they made their plans.

"We'll turn south from here and approach the place from the south as the guard is watching the road from the north. I've noticed that the man with the dog makes a round about once an hour. This guy must feel very safe here," Jeff told Arturo.

When it was dark they saddled the horses and rode south on the east side of the ridge. They rode slowly through the low brush and mesquite trees until they encountered a dry gully running west. They rode the horses into the bottom, which had a bed of loose sand. As they rode along they could see over the top of the low bushes and stopped when they were south of the ranch. They tied the horses to a nearby mesquite tree and Arturo hobbled them as well.

Jeff had his .45 pistol belted on and removed the shotgun from behind the saddle. He fully loaded it with double-aught buckshot and placed several in his jacket pocket. He removed the two grenades and placed them in another pocket. Arturo had his Colt 38-40 and a short double barrel shotgun. The two men stood for a minute then slipped up the bank of the wash.

They moved quietly through the brush until they came to where it had been cleared. No movement could be seen on the wall that enclosed the hacienda. They ran quickly to the wall and stopped to listen. Arturo lifted Jeff up until he could grab the top of the eight-foot adobe wall, careful not to cut himself on the broken bottles that had been imbedded on top. He rolled over and dropped inside.

Jeff opened the small wooden gate that was dead bolted from the inside. As Arturo came inside Jeff whispered, "watch for the dog."

Walking softly they crossed the yard to the house. While Arturo stayed hidden by a small tree, Jeff walked to the outside patio. He eased up on the patio and was standing by one of the supports when the patio door slid open and Cesar stepped out.

Jeff recognized him from a picture in the DEA file. This was the man who had shot Josefina or ordered it done. Cesar removed a cigar from his shirt and lit it with a match.

Blowing the smoke into the air.

"Hope you enjoy it. It'll be your last one," Jeff said, stepping into the light.

"Quien es?" (Who is it?) Asked Cesar, as he turned and saw Jeff standing there.

"You shot the wrong person this time, you dope dealing son-of-a-bitch," Jeff said.

Cesar removed the cigar from his mouth, "I heard that I shot your puta by mistake."

He then flipped the burning cigar at Jeff's face and went for the pistol in his belt. Jeff didn't move as the cigar hit his cheek, other than to raise the semi-auto shotgun and start shooting. The buckshot knocked Cesar back against the wall and held him there until Jeff fired it empty. Then Cesar slowly slid down the bloody wall. Just then he heard Arturo's shotgun go off and saw that he had shot the guard and his dog as they came running around the corner.

Jeff pulled his pistol and walked over to where Cesar lay. "That's for Josefina," he said. Just then Mario came running into the room and toward the patio. He skidded to a stop when he saw Jeff and fired his pistol. Jeff felt a burning on his left leg and dropped the hammer twice on his old Colt. Both slugs hit Mario in the chest and he fell to the floor dead.

Jeff limped through the house and found it empty. He heard Arturo's shotgun firing again from outside. He ran back to the patio door and pulled Cesar's dead body into the house. He pulled the pins on the two grenades and tossed them into the hall. When he got outside he found Arturo waiting.

"There's two more that won't sell any more dope," he told Jeff.

"Let's get the hell out of here," Jeff said as he grabbed Arturo's arm. Both ran for the small gate and were quickly through. As they ran south they heard several shots fired but none came close.

"They don't have the guts for this with their boss dead," Jeff said.

They soon reached the horses, untied them and rode east toward the truck. As they rode they could see the glow of the fire as the ranch house burned. When they arrived at the truck a few hours later, the horses were unsaddled and turned loose. They pitched the two saddles in the trailer and removed the brush from it and the truck.

"The horses are unbranded and somebody will keep them," Arturo told Jeff.

Jeff dropped his pants and placed a small bandage on his leg where Mario's bullet had glazed it. Arturo backed the truck and trailer out of the brush and they were soon headed back toward the highway. They reached the Juarez highway just as the sun came up and turned east. When they were close to where Arturo had picked up Jeff they both saw a low flying helicopter coming south. Jeff opened his door and started waving. The aircraft circled them one time and then dropped to the ground.

Jeff shook Arturo's hand. "Will you be okay going back?" he asked.

"Sure, I've a letter from the General if I'm stopped," he replied.

Jeff ran to the waiting helicopter, which lifted off as soon as he was inside headed north. They soon crossed the border fence and were in the low hills east of Columbus, NM. They stayed low until they were east of Deming then turned toward the gap between the Floridas Mountains.

They dropped Jeff off at his house where he took a hot shower and fell into bed. It was dark when he finally arrived at the hospital and found Josefina had been moved from intensive care to a private room. Her Mother and Grandfather were sitting with her when Jeff walked in. Still very weak, she was able to smile at Jeff.

"She came out of the coma yesterday," Carmen told him.

Jeff picked up her hand and felt her squeeze his. He saw her lips move and leaned down.

"I lost our baby Jeff," she whispered as tears ran down her cheeks.

"Don't worry honey, we'll have more," Jeff said. "As soon as we can move you, I'm taking you to El Rancho Alegre and then Rancho Las Palmas. You rest now, I'm here. I'll always be here," he said. He then leaned over and kissed her forehead.

The End Lobo Verde

EPILOGUE

It was over two months before Josefina could be discharged from the hospital. Cory made arrangements for a helicopter to fly her and Jeff to his ranch, where Jeff stayed as long as he could and then returned to Deming. Several months later he was promoted to the Resident Agent in Charge of the Deming office.

He made monthly trips into Mexico to check on Josefina. Four months after being discharged she went to her ranch for another two months of rest. In the meantime Jeff had purchased a house southwest of Deming and had it furnished with new furniture.

***

Five years later they are en route to Oklahoma to attend Jeff's older brother's funeral. Jeff was driving with Josefina in the front seat with him. She had regained her weight and the only visible sign of her ordeal was a streak of white hair on the right side of her head. She turns to look into the back seat of the extended cab pickup.

For there strapped into his car seat is three-year-old Robert Napoleon Larson. She smiles at the baby and is rewarded with a smile in return from the black haired brown-eyed boy as he plays with his plastic gun.

ABOUT THE AUTHOR

Donnie Daniels was born in Oklahoma but was raised in Texas on a cattle ranch. He applied for the US Border Patrol and was accepted in 1967. He was stationed at Rio Grande City, Texas, Miami, Ok and Deming, NM In 1977 he transferred to US Customs Patrol in Deming,NM. He was later promoted to Supervisory Customs Patrol then to Customs Special Agent and finally as the Resident Agent in Charge,Office of Investigations, Deming, NM.

After retiring from Customs he was employed as a Deputy Sheriff, Narcotics Investigator and Captain of the Luna County Sheriff's Department. In 2001 he and his wife moved to Wyoming where he was briefly a Town Marshal. In 2002 he returned to New Mexico to train the Federal Air Marshals for five months. In 2004 he again returned to NM as a firearms instructor for the commercial airline pilots. He is now retired and living in Wyoming.